Twin Cities

K.D. Thomas

Edited by: J. Ellington Ashton Press Staff
Cover Art by: David McGlumphy

http://jellingtonashton.com/
Copyright.
KD Thomas
©2014, KD Thomas

This book is dedicated to my Mum Pat Rylett and brother-in-law Mel London. Mum would have loved to have this book to read, Mel would have waited for the film! Miss you both very much.

I have been waiting years to be able to write one of these! Thanks to J. Ellington Ashton Press for the break; David McGlumphy for the cover art, Kate Crowther for all her encouragement since the year dot, Tom Keating and Maddie Dale for their patience and support, and everyone who buys this book.

Chapter One

The petting was getting hotter and heavier by the second. She could hear him panting and felt a throb deep inside her; it made her breath hitch in her throat and she blushed in the dark still night. It felt so good, she didn't want him to stop. The warm air outside had barely penetrated the inside of the dark, gloomy space and Tommy felt goose bumps ripple across her arms.

"Tommy..." Her voice was low, breathless and full of desire. "Oh God! Tommy, wait. I..." Tommy concentrated on his efforts to push up her shapeless pale pink sweater, finally revealing disappointingly small breasts encased in a baggy, white, utilitarian bra.

"Tommy... Tommy! Hold on... Please. Stop, I can't..." Tommy pulled his lips reluctantly from her nipple, now peaking out over the top of the pushed-up bra. He peered at her, saw her eyes half closed with longing.

His voice was a whisper, full of promise. "Come on honey, it won't hurt, I promise."

"Oh, Tommy, I don't know..."

She tried to sit up and her head banged into Tommy's chin. "I shouldn't..."

"Ow!" Tommy sat up, pulling his arm from around her roughly to rub his head.

The solid stone floor they lay on was cold and unyielding and not the most romantic of places. Some men may have been put off by the huge black and gold crucifix too, but not Tommy.

She giggled, missing the fleeting black look that crossed his face in the dark.

"What the fuck...?" he said, sitting up. "Look, you said..."

"Tommy, it's just... the first time. You know? I'm worried my dad..."

He shifted his weight and moved away from her. She reached her arms out and hooked them around his neck.

"Oh, Tommy, come on! You know I want to. I love you. It's just that..."

"Just what? Oh come on! You keep doing this; there are plenty of other girls who I could go with, you know?"

"Don't say that! I want to. I do. You know I do! I just need time. It's a big deal for me."

"It's only sex for fuck sake!" he snapped, "I didn't realise you were such a fucking prick tease!" Tommy took a deep breath, trying to shift his hips; his erection was painfully pressed against his tight jeans.

The young woman tried to smile. She looked up at him adoringly. "Don't be cross." She reached up and stroked his face. "You do you love me, don't you?"

Tommy sighed and rolled his eyes in the gloom of the empty chapel. She missed this too, busy nuzzling at his neck. "For fucks sake! Look, you know I do. I said so, didn't I?" He reigned in his thinning patience. "Come on baby," he crooned, "You're so beautiful. I want you so bad."

He pushed her shoulder to get her to lie back down, his hand grasping roughly at her breast again. He nuzzled into her neck and for a moment or so they lost themselves in their longing. She so wanted this. *Fuck, he loved virgins.*

Tommy squeezed her breast again and she tried not to cry out. He was just a little excited, that's all. He didn't mean to be rough. As if he'd read her thoughts his hand moved from her breast and she smiled into his kiss. Instead he pulled his face back and his hand groped for hers. He pulled it roughly to his crotch, rubbing hard down the length of his cock, straining at the zip.

For a moment her desire overcame her conscience and she gasped at the hardness she traced beneath the supple, worn denim. He moved her hand away and she felt him reach back down to tug his fly open and shove her hand in. A second later she felt the rock-hardness of his cock beneath the velvety softness of his skin and she groaned. His pubic hairs tickled her wrist. Her breath caught in her throat and she moaned slightly. Tommy took this for acquiescence and deftly, firmly, he manoeuvred her fully onto her back, pushing up her floral skirt and pulling at her white knickers.

As her body felt the uneven, bumpy floor beneath the rough woollen blanket, she felt a prickle of anxiety.

She tried to shift beneath him, "No, Tommy wait... Hang on! I..." Tommy did not appear to hear her and he knelt up, his eyes greedily taking in the sight before him. Clumsily, he tugged down his jeans and underpants, finally freeing his erection.

"Just a minute! Tommy, I..." she said.

He pushed his trousers and underpants down to his knees in one fluid movement before lying back down, one hand flat on the pristine floor of the chapel beneath them, the other stabbing at her wetness, his middle finger tracing the length of her slit. He breathed in the smell of her, "Oh, yeah! You know you want this!"

'Ohh, oh Tommy! Tommy, no, wait! I'm not ready! Hang on! Oh God, Tommy!" He stilled her bucking legs with his own and pushed his finger into her cleft, feeling her vaginal walls clench around it. She gave a little shriek, "Tommy *stop*! Oh, please..." He looked into her eyes as she tried bucking her hips to dislodge him. He looked away, back to her wetness, just as plump tears spilled from her thick, dark lashes, plopping onto his shoulder.

"No, no, wait, just a minute," she said. "*Stop*!"

"Uhh... keep still!" Withdrawing his finger Tommy sniffed it. He flicked it with his tongue and grunted, shifting his weight. He grabbed her hand as it flailed at his chest and pushed it up, above her head. With his right hand he pushed his huge stiff erection in hard, feeling her hymen tear, forcing himself into his hot, tight, deliciously coy virgin.

Chapter Two

Tom sped through the soft summer rain. He was oblivious to his wife Ashleigh's increasing screams and the breathless sobs of Meghan, their seven year old daughter, wailing in the back of the car. He felt like he was flying. The sedate Vauxhall Zafira was more, at this moment, like an Aston Martin, a Corvette, a Jag. All around him, the car felt huge and powerful. *Get Away. He had to get away before...*

"For God's sake, *Tom*!" Ashleigh screamed and at last her panicked tone pierced the fog in his brain. Tom suddenly realised the car carrying his beloved family was racing just south of the High Street in the centre of Stratford at a speed of 101 miles an hour, *in the outside lane*.

Suddenly he could hear the sounds of other cars honking furiously and the hiss of their tyres as they raced past them on the sopping wet road, swerving on the wet road to avoid him. Ashleigh's ragged breaths and his own laboured panting punctuated the sobs of their daughter, terrified in the back seat. His heart felt as if it would beat out of his chest and he was breathless, as if he has been running instead of driving. Sweat beaded his brow and his hands were damp.

"Tom, please!" Ashleigh's voice was plaintive and he felt a tide of shame overwhelm him. The car slowed, almost without his help. He indicated with exaggerated care and shaking hands, gliding to the left side of the road, hands clenched tight around the steering wheel, breaking hard. As the car shuddered to a halt, the sounds of the ticking engine were muffled by the stuttered, hiccoughing sobs of his daughter, her winning junior judo certificate scrunched and ruined in her hands. Tom wiped his hands on the knees of his jeans.

Tom's wife sat leaning forward in the front passenger seat, her hands on her knees. She looked behind her once, unable to smile at Meghan, but allowing her to see her face before she tugged open the passenger door of the Zafira. Wrestling with her seat belt to free herself before she made it out of the car, she vomited on to the grass verge as cars streaked past.

Drivers were still shaking their heads and mouthing obscenities as they flashed by. She ignored them, head down, one hand protectively across her pregnant bump, the other swiping at the tears blurring her eyes and the spit dripping from her chin.

Tom sat in silence, sweat cooling on his face. He couldn't speak. After a few moments he reached across to Ashleigh, but she pulled her arm from his, turning her back to the car, her legs still outside the vehicle.

"Daddy?" Meghan's voice was soft and wobbly, her tears subsiding as she watched her parents for signs of how to react. Tom didn't answer.

"Daddy?" She tried again.

"What? What love?" he replied, not turning around.

"Is mummy poorly? Is it the baby?"

"No, I... I don't think so." This time he turned to look at her. Her face was red and wet with tears and snot and Tom's breath caught in his chest. "She's fine, honey!" he said, turning back to face forwards, banging his fists on the steering wheel and shaking his head. He lowered his face to his hands and sat like that until he felt his wife clamber shakily back into the car. He felt her pause to compose herself before she reached back to their daughter, stroking her cheek and smoothing down her hair, loving her with her touch.

As Meg calmed, Ashleigh turned back to the front in stony silence. Headlights swept past them and rain hissed on the road. She sat for a moment or so and then reached down to pick up the bottle of Evian, taking a big slug and grimacing at the residual taste of puke in her mouth. She pushed her hair back from her sweating forehead.

Eventually she looked at him. He lifted his head from the steering wheel.

"What the..." She looked back at the child in the backseat trying to straighten out her ruined certificate. She lowered her voice dramatically. "What the *fuck* was that?"

Tom blanched to hear her swear, she hardly ever swore and never before in front of children. "I... I don't know."

Behind them, Meghan gave a nervous giggle. "Awww! Mummy, you said a naughty word!" Both ignored her.

"You don't know?" Ashleigh's face was flushed and livid and her fringe stuck to her forehead. "Are you fu...? *Are you kidding me?* You were driving like a flaming lunatic. *I* was screaming at you, Meg was screaming.

You nearly killed us all never mind all the other fu... the other drivers! 100 miles an hour you were going, at one point! Through a sodding town, for Christ's sake!"

"Ash, I'm so sorry. I don't..."

"*No Thomas! No!* Not again! I do not want to hear that you were 'seeing things'!" She made angry quotation marks in the air, "That you 'spaced out again' or something else completely bollocks! You could have killed us! For God's sake, Tom, go see the GP. I mean it! Enough is enough. Please!" She reached out her hand towards him and Tom looked at it hopefully for a moment. "Keys!" she said icily, "I'm driving!"

Chapter Three

The party was in full swing. Given it was being thrown by his mother this meant only that everyone was sitting around uncomfortably, praying for the time to pass. Distant relatives, neighbours and a collection of assorted strangers sat with soggy paper plates rested with exaggerated care on their knees, juggling warm, sour red wine trying to control bored, restless children and make conversation with bored, restless relatives.

Tom moved to the food table set up in the over-bright dining room and once again picked at the remains of the buffet. Lights twinkled on the Christmas tree in the far corner but the tree too, showed its age. Tinsel drooped and a carpet of green needles blanketed the ground around its base. Half its lights were out and the tree itself listed to the right precariously.

Conversation drifted around him and he picked up a turkey leg, dry and tasteless now, some five days after Christmas. As an afterthought, he plopped some congealing homemade mayonnaise onto his plate to help it slide down. The beetroot he piled on bled its juice onto the grey meat, turning it an artificial blushing pink. Behind him he heard Ashleigh whisper severely to Meghan and he sighed inwardly. Meghan was amongst the most placid and obliging of children; if she was playing up it was officially time to slope off. Maybe they could use his wife's early pregnancy as a suitable excuse?

He turned and caught Ashleigh's eye. She seemed to be staring at him and self consciously, he looked down at his sweatshirt, his trousers. He was wearing clothes his wife had bought him for Christmas, a pair of faded black jeans and a striped black and grey hoodie, both from Next. His hair, dark blond and thick, was neat, and he was clean-shaven and freshly scented, again courtesy of another Christmas present from Ashleigh. *Diesel* for Men. It was rank, but she liked it.

At last she smiled and, much relived, he smiled back. Although still cool with him following the 'speeding incident' as it was referred to, she clearly shared his desire to escape from the annual seasonal party his mother threw.

To be fair, when his dad had been alive, these parties had been one of the highlights of Christmas. Of course this was before the bastard vascular dementia which saw his father institutionalised at the age of 55 and dead from a massive stroke at 61.

Tom looked around the room as Ashley once again excused herself to use the bathroom. He looked over at his mother. Rose was dressed in an old-fashioned, high-necked, green velvet thing which fell to just below her knees. Her shoes were a low-heeled black court pump from the Gods of Design at Marks and Spencer's; her deity, praise be. Her golden-brown hair looked immaculate with not a grey lock in sight, not even at the roots, a bronze-coloured, green studded diamante comb pinning it up at the sides. Only her eyes were dull, but all credit to her, she was trying hard to be jolly. Tom sighed. She looked more like she was in her early 80's than her early 60's.

Uncle Rob, Rose's brother-in-law, was on all fours' with various children chasing him in and out of all the furniture. Rob was braying like a donkey with the kids taking turns riding on his back, weaving in and out of the furniture. Tom smiled. Rob was such a character. Pauline, Tom's aunt, was another matter. Shit, fuck, bugger; speak of the devil. There she was, swaying towards him in some sort of snake-striped caftan affair, chunky jewellery clinking and bouncing off of her skinny bosom as she made her way towards him with the studied care of the very, very drunk. He stifled a groan.

Tom looked as Ashleigh backed deftly out of the room, grinning at him. He pulled a face back, shaking his head. Bugger, he'd been hoping for an ally. Still, at least the thaw had definitely begun by the looks of it. Thank God. He turned as Pauline's hand patted his wrist, oblivious to the glass of red she was spilling on his sleeve as she greeted him.

"Thomas!" she crooned. "How are you, sweetheart?" She leaned in to kiss him and he blanched as a waft of stale alcohol and cigarette smoke enveloped him. Across the room, Tom saw Rob stand and try to leave the kids to their games. He heard the children whine that they wanted to keep playing, but Rob shook his head ruefully, rubbing his back and pretending to wince and hobble with pain. The kids laughed and he escaped, walking purposefully towards Tom and Pauline. He put his arm protectively around his wife as he reached them, twiddling his wedding ring with his thumb as usual.

"Tom mate, good Christmas?" Tom smiled and nodded, reaching out his right hand to shake Rob's, but Pauline grabbed it, swaying slightly as Rob released her. Rob steadied her with his arm and she turned and frowned at him.

"Robert, don't cling, sweetie!" She looked from her husband to Tom, waving slightly as if standing in a breeze, comically trying to get her eyes to focus. "So, another baby on the way then, eh? Lucky you. How exciting!" Tom's mother joined them. Rob leaned over to give her a tender kiss and put his arm around his unsteady wife.

"Great party again, Rosie!" he said, turning to Pauline to get her agreement.

"Um..." Pauline took a slug of her wine, spilling some down the front of her dress. "Yes, darling," she slurred, "Malcolm would have been thrilled!"

Rose's smile dropped momentarily and Tom looked at her sympathetically. He opened his mouth to reply, but Pauline spoke again, cutting him off. "I was just congratulating Tom on the new baby," she said, looking around to see where the nearest full bottle was. She looked back at Tom, still struggling to focus. Tom saw Rob and his mum exchange glances. He sighed inwardly.

"Yeah, it's great news!" He looked at his still full plate. "Right, well, I'll just..."

"So what is it?" Pauline peered at him intently, trying to stop her eyes from crossing.

"The baby? Oh," replied Tom, "so far we've opted not to know, let it be a surprise! As long as he or she is healthy!"

"Let's just hope it isn't twins, eh?" Pauline interrupted, giving a high tinkling laugh. Rob and Rose once again exchanged worried glances.

Inwardly, Tom rolled his eyes. "No reason to think that!"

"Besides," said Ashleigh, arriving at his side and putting her hand on her husband's arm, "none of the scans show...".

"Well, they don't always show up this early!" Pauline lectured. She liked to think she was an authority on all things pregnancy and over her head Rob, Rose and Tom all shared a complicit, indulgent smile. Ashleigh looked at Pauline.

"God, twins would be a bit of a shock though, wouldn't it Tom?" She gave a nervous laugh.

"Still, at least you're past the danger point for miscarriage I suppose?" Pauline took a hearty swig of her wine, spilling tiny drops that looked like beads of blood before they were absorbed into the fabric of her tent-like dress.

Tom felt his mother's hand on his arm "Pauline, we would rather not..."

She leaned forward drunkenly, "Well, twins do run in some families, like miscarriages run in ours..." For a moment, Pauline looked bereft and she exhaled through pursed lips and looked with surprise at her drink, as if wondering where all the wine had gone.

Ashleigh was getting a little flustered. "Well, yes, but... oh goodness, we hope we..."

"Good, good!" said Rob heartily, as if they had cleverly averted any potential dangers, tried to steer his wife away.

Rose looked at Pauline and pursed her lips. "How about you help me put some coffee on, love?" she said, taking Pauline's arm. For a moment it looked as if Pauline was amenable to being distracted but she cocked her head and turned back to Tom.

"Anyway," Ashleigh was trying to be fair. She smiled at Pauline, "There are no twins on either side of either of our families, thank goodness!"

"A-ha!" Pauline said, "but what about you..."

"Pauline!" Rob's voice was loud and clipped and she blanched. She looked up at him, trying to meet his eyes. "Coffee, love?" he hissed, pushing his ring back onto his finger and pulling her away. "Now, Pauline! Let's go!"

Rob steered his still protesting wife towards the door, out of the dining room, and through to the lounge. Tom turned to his mum. *"What's she on about now?* he asked. Rose's hand reached up to fiddle with her necklace, a golden crucifix on a thin, delicate chain.

Rose sighed. "Oh come on, Tom, I love the woman, but she does talk a load of old nonsense when she's had a few! You know how she gets!" She looked away. Her neighbours Mike and Marjorie were sliding towards the hall. "Excuse me!" she said with a high, twinkly laugh, patting her hair, "I need to go spice up the party! Can't have anyone sneaking out early!"

Chapter Four

Tom was in the Crown Public House at Hallow, a long-time favourite hang-out with mates Russ, Mark, and Joe. All four of them sat at a table close to the door so Mark and Russ could nip for out the odd cig or ten. The table between them was full of empty pint glasses, a rare night out in celebration of Russ's recent 40th birthday.

Around them the pub was rammed, two deep at the bar and every table occupied, the delicious smell of char-grilled steak thick in the air. Muted chatter swelled around them, competing with Adel, crooning softly on the house stereo.

Tom had been dropped off by Ashleigh and was planning on getting a cab home although, unusually for Joe, he wasn't drinking so Tom may get a lift. Joe had only had the one, Russ and Mark were now quite drunk, and Tom wasn't far behind them.

"What's with the abstinence, mate? Not like you!" Tom peered at Joe over the top of the glass. Joe shrugged.

"Just not in the mood!" he said, playing with a beer mat. "What was up with the lovely Ash earlier?"

Tom looked away. The door opened and a blast of chilly air flowed around them. Tom shivered. "I don't know!" he said. "Bloody women!"

Joe laughed, "Cut the crap, Yogi!" he said. "You and her are like, joined at the frigging hip usually. Is it pregnancy hormones or something?"

Tom grinned at the nickname. He was quiet for a moment. "Nah," he replied. "Not really. We had a bit of a..."

"A row?" Joe grinned. "*You and wonder-girl*?

Tom smiled sheepishly. All his mates took the piss out of him, knowing that he and Ashleigh were generally inseparable. They always had though, the nickname 'Yogi' for instance; a reference to his surname Bearing. He'd been Yogi all through his school, thanks to Joe here. He shook his head, draining his fourth pint. Joe stood.

"My round!" He went to join the queue at the bar as Russ and Mark, mates from work, came back in, rubbing their hands to warm them.

"I frigging *hate* January!" declared Russ. He smelt of cold and cigarettes.

"Nah, mate, it's just 'cos you're getting old!" Mark laughed at his own joke and picked up his pint. Joe waved Tom's glass at him from the bar. Mark shook his head. "We're off to go get a curry! You two coming?"

Tom shook his head. "No. Thanks mate," he said, "I'd better not!"

Mark and Russ spent a moment or so debating where to go for their curry and Joe came back with a pint for Tom and another coke for himself.

"Russ and me are off for a curry, but lover boy here just wants to get home to the old ball and chain!" Mark was grinning at Tom.

Russ laughed. "We want to be togever!" he said, parodying an old TV advert.

"Piss off!" said Tom good naturedly. "She's pregnant again! I don't like to leave her on her own for too long."

"Well," Russ and Mark stood and pulled on their jackets. "If you're sure. Joe, you don't fancy a nice hot vindaloo?"

"Nah, thanks. I fancy a nice hot babe, not a crap hot curry!" Russ and Mark grinned, said a noisy goodbye and left.

Tom looked at his pint sweating on the table. "Everything ok?" asked Joe.

Tom shrugged. "I... fuck, I dunno. It sounds mad, but I'm..."

"What?"

"I've been having these... oh shit; I don't know what they are. Visions or something! It is beginning to fucking freak me out!"

Joe looked at him. "*Visions*? he said dubiously. Tom sighed and took a slug of his pint. He slammed it down on the table with more force than he realised.

"Steady, mate!" Joe leaned forward. "What is it?"

"Just before Christmas - we'd been to Stratford to take Meg to a Judo comp..." Tom paused, glass in hand. Joe waited. "Coming back, it was like, I could see..."

"For fuck sake, Tom! See what? You going all fucking hippy-dippy on us?

"No, you pratt! It was like I could see myself sort of pressuring this bird to have sex. She was crying and kept saying 'no, Tommy wait' but I was like, I dunno, I couldn't stop."

Joe exhaled. "Well... shit! But you know it wasn't real man. It was just a dream! Anyway, with a gorgeous bird like Ashleigh at home, what else would it be?

"Joe, I was driving! I was racing down the fucking high street in Stratford with my pregnant wife yelling at me and my daughter screeching like a banshee in the back of the car. I couldn't even hear them. It was like... I had to get away. Shit." His head dropped. They were silent for a moment or so.

"I don't know what to say, mate!" said Joe. "Had you been drinking?"

"No! Of course not! I had Ash and Meg in the car. One minute I was fine, the next I was driving like a bat out of hell to escape after raping some bloody kid!"

"A kid? Whoa! Fucking hell man! You never said..."

"Not a little kid. Like 16 or 17 I think. Young though. I don't know her. It wasn't like, some bird off the telly or anything. It just... it seemed so real. Then Ash is screaming at me, cars are swerving to avoid us and Meg is in bits in the back."

Joe exhaled loudly and picked up his coke. "Sounds bloody heavy, man!" Both were quiet for a moment or so. The noise of the pub swelled around them. They both watched as a pretty waitress carrying a heavily laden tray glided past them. She was wearing a tight black skirt and low heels, a fitted white shirt and a grey apron with the pub's name stitched on the front. They both stared at her arse as she walked away. Joe turned back to Tom and raised his eyebrows. Tom grinned. "Sod off," said Joe, still staring after the waitress, "You've got one like that at home!"

"It's happened before, too."

"What has?" Joe was still looking at the waitress as she served up the food to a table of two couples. He smirked as he clocked both the men watch her as she walked back to the kitchen.

"These... *visions*. I've been having them for a few months now."

"Tom, mate. I don't know what to say. What does Ash think?"

Tom shrugged. "She's pissed off at me still, about the one when I was driving. I think..."

"What? said Joe. "What do you think? Was it like, I dunno, like a fantasy or something?"

"No!" snapped Tom. "I think..." he looked up at Joe and swallowed. "I think maybe I'm more like my old man than anyone

17

thought." Joe looked confused. Tom gulped a swig of his lager. "I think...
fuck! What if it's the early signs of dementia? Like my dad?"

Chapter Five

Rob opened the door and smiled broadly. "Hi Tom, on your own?" Tom nodded. "Come in, come in!" Rob turned and walked back across the substantial hall, heading into the large, modern, open plan kitchen, Tom following behind. "Everything ok?" Rob stopped at the counter and flipped on the switch for the gleaming new kettle. He gestured to Tom to sit at one of the tall, high gloss stools tucked under the bench and turned away, busying himself making tea for them both. He placed the steaming cup in front of his nephew. "Sugar?" he asked. Tom shook his head.

"Is Aunty Pauline here?" His voice was quiet. Subdued. Rob shook his head.

"What is it?" Rob's tone was resigned; he was used to his wife's Gatling gob, he'd had to make amends for her more than once when she'd had a bit too much to drink.

"At the party at Mum's..." Tom was hesitant.

"Yes?" said Rob patiently.

"It's something she said..." Rob looked away, staring at the barren garden. A robin was sitting on a branch just outside the window. It cocked its head, looking at him. He waited.

"She told Ash that she thought the baby may be still-born."

"She what?" Rob looked at him aghast. "Why would she say that? Was that when I was there? I didn't hear that!"

"No, it was after, Ash said. Just before we left. They were talking in the kitchen and Pauline told her again that it was something that did run in the family. What with you and her losing..."

"Losing four babies?" Rob looked pained. "Well, yes, I know it's hard for her, but she shouldn't have said that..." He paused as his wife entered the room, almost sober for once.

Her tone was brittle. "'She' shouldn't have said *what* exactly?" She walked towards the huge American fridge, pausing. After a brief hesitation, she purposely ripped the door open and grabbed a bottle of

19

white wine from inside the door. She ignored the look her husband gave her and stepped to a high cupboard, selecting an elegant long-stemmed wine glass, filling it to the brim. She took a long sip, smacking her lips dramatically. She looked at Tom. The half full bottle sat sweating on the side.

"*In vino veritas,* Thomas!" she told him.

"What? What the hell does that mean? Why did you say that, at the party? You really scared Ash."

"What did I say? Oh, and it means 'in wine, there's truth, sweetie!"

"Oh come *on,* Pauline! You know damn well!"

Rob moved around the kitchen counter towards his wife.

"It's alright, love!" He looked back at Tom.

"Maybe you should just leave it eh, son?" he said.

"No, Rob, I'm sorry, but she was out of order!"

"In wine there's truth! It may be a twin! Although you probably would know by now, I suppose! Anyway, that was weeks ago. Why are you getting aerated about it now?"

Tom was confused. "Because she only just told me! And what about twins? Now what are you on about? I'm talking about you telling Ash the baby could be still..."

Rob stepped forward, his left arm outstretched towards Tom and his right appearing to be trying to hold back his wife.

"Well, it could! Still-births do run in our family, maybe they run in yours too?"

"Pauline, not now, please!" Rob's tone was pleading.

"No, Robert. It's gone on for long enough. Malcolm never wanted this and you know it. It's down to her. To Rose. Tom should know!"

Tom was getting agitated. "Know what? So still-births run in our family? Well, there was still no reason to..."

"In *our family,* Tom. Not necessarily in yours." Her eyes were bright. She sipped her wine delicately.

"Pauline, no!"

"Robert, yes!" she mimicked him, turning to Tom.

"Your dad..." she paused, taking a deep breath.

"What about my dad?"

"Pauline!"

"I've started so..."

20

Rob slammed his hand down on the kitchen counter, making the neatly stacked plates from the dish-washer rattle.

"Pauline!" She looked away; Tom noticed that the hand holding the glass was shaking.

"Tom, leave it for…"

"No! Somebody just tell me what the fuck you're going on about!"

Pauline looked briefly at her husband then at Tom. The only sound in the room was the humming of the fridge and the ticking of a clock above it. "Go talk to your mum, Tom. Ask her."

"Jesus Christ! Ask her what?" Tom's frustration was evident.

Rob cleared his throat. "Pauline's right, son. Ask Rose. Go talk to your mum." Tom stared at him, confused.

"Right," said Rob brightly, "shall I make more tea?"

Tom was on his way around to his mothers, 20 minutes away when his mobile rang. He glanced at the screen. Ashleigh. Carefully checking the traffic for any sign of the police, he pulled the phone towards him and read the text message. 'I'm spotting blood. Can you come home?' He turned the car around and headed home. His bloody mother could wait.

Chapter Six

The following day, Tom sat in his chair at home. The TV was on in the background with Meghan glued to Hannah Montana. In the kitchen he could hear the sound of his wife singing softly along to the radio as she made their dinner. He smiled.

A late March snowfall had turned the outside world white, but drizzly rain ensured it was useless for playing in, so even the kids were crabby. Slush piles of dirty ice lined the roads and getting home on the motorway had taken three times as long. Tom had tried several times during the day to get hold of Rose, but no joy. Either she was out – 'keeping herself busy' as she had since Malcolm's death – or, more likely, she was call-screening.

Ashleigh waddled in, her pregnant belly seeming to enter the room half an hour before the rest of her. At only five months gone, she was far bigger this time than with Meg.

"What are you smiling about?" she asked, scratching the stretch marks on her stomach. She winced.

"You ok?" Tom sat forward.

"Baby's kicking!" she smiled. "So, come on, what are you smiling for? You weren't smiling yesterday when you got back from Pauline's and Rob's."

Tom ignored the not-so-subtle ploy to get the story of what had happened at their place. So far, he'd played it down, telling her he'd been worried about her spotting blood at this point in the pregnancy. He decided not to relay the whole conversation as he did not want to worry her, and besides, he didn't have a bloody clue what it was about.

"I was smiling because I'm glad to be home. Because I'm glad it's Friday. And... I'm glad because you are talking to me again."

Her eyes clouded. "I do think you still need to see the GP, Tom." She patted his cheek to take any sting out of her words and then turned back towards the kitchen.

Their small but perfect house on the far edge of Warnhill Villages in Worcester was warm and welcoming. Their three bedrooms were all decorated in mostly subdued, tasteful colours. Meghan's room was painted orange with fluffy purple cushions; nothing pink, she hated anything pink. Even the small spare room was newly decorated as a nursery, complete with teddies, a shed-load of disposable nappies and a state of the art baby monitor. Having given away Meg's cot, as they didn't plan any more kids, the only remaining job was for Tom to erect the new crib which was still in its box.

Ashleigh waddled off, saying over her shoulder, "Dinner will be about half an hour. Spaghetti bolognaise."

Tom smiled and sat back in his chair. Outside the noise of passing cars' subsided and he felt sleepy and relaxed.

Through his doze, Tom felt the chair beneath him shift and tilt, his feet no longer resting on the pale blue carpet of his lounge. He found himself upright in a dark, dingy bar, a smoky haze clouding the air. He coughed and waved a hand in front of his face, trying to clear the fog. He looked around for Ashleigh and Meg. The place was full of strangers.

Faintly, he heard Ashleigh call to him, "Did you say something, love?" she asked.

"Sweetheart?" he replied, looking around again to see where she was. A man to his left looked down on him and sneered. Tom turned back and picked up a glass of amber liquid on the scratched bar in front of him. He threw some down his throat, wincing at the unfamiliar, strong, sharp taste.

He heard a sweet, high voice say something to him, and he turned towards the sound, thinking it was Meghan. The man standing to his left was very tall, over six feet, and thin, a dirty greying beard rough on his lean face. Tom, at five feet ten inches, was aware of the relative disadvantage of his height-but then he wasn't planning to fight. Something about the man's stance, however, told him it was not a mutual preference.

Tom ignored him and turned back to his drink. He nodded at the bartender, who silently placed another glass in front of him. He was vaguely aware of Hannah Montana singing in the background and he smiled into his drink. The man beside said him spoke again.

"Daddy!"

Tom turned to the man. "Daddy?" he said, confused.

"Fucking faggot!" The man spat his reply and turned back to the bar.

Tom went to respond, but he felt something touch his foot and looked down. There was nothing there. He looked back at the man, who sneered at him again.

"Let it go, mister!" Tom said quietly. He saw himself slam the glass down on the bar and frowned; the action entirely contrary to his words. The man turned away and Tom heard himself say, "Careful out there mate!" The man turned back and smiled.

"Bring it on, you poof!" he said. Tom almost gasped as he saw himself turning to reach to his right, to grab the bar stool next to him, clearly planning to use it as a weapon.

"Not in here!" said the bar-man sharply and the belligerent stranger chuckled and left, heading towards the toilets. "See you around, faggot!" he said over his shoulder.

Tom threw some money from his pocket onto the table, picked up his drink and drained it. "Thanks!" he said and left. His eyes stung from the smoke and the alcohol. He coughed again. Some moments later, he headed out to the car park, looking for his Zafira.

The car park was wide, dark and empty; dirt and mud on the floor instead of the smooth, grey-black tarmac with painted spaces at his local pub. Tom looked up, trying to see the name of the pub, but the lights over the sign were out. A moment later the man he had argued with came out of the pub, fastening his fly. He saw Tom.

"Dad? Daddy?" he said, again in Tom's daughter's voice. Tom looked at him, puzzled.

"Daddy?" the man repeated.

Tom stood with his head cocked, wondering how his daughter's voice came out of the man before him.

"Daddy? You fucking fairy!"

"What?" said Tom, stupidly.

"I'm not your fucking daddy! Whadda you want? Fuck off, queer! Don't want your kind 'round here." This time the man's voice was deep and gravelly.

Tom leaned in towards the man. He looked up into his face. "*I am not a faggot!*" he said with studied menace.

The man finished fiddling with his fly and waggled his hands over his groin at Tom. "Want some of this, eh?" he asked, "Fairy!"

"I told you," Tom saw a glob of his spittle land on the man's cheek, "I'm not a faggot!" He leaned in towards the man, smelling his rank scent of sweat and unwashed clothes. His tone was oddly placid, belying the build-up of anger behind the words. He felt dizzy and looked away.

The man shoved Tom roughly from behind on the shoulder and turned away snickering. Tom felt himself twist around at the speed of light and lean forward, effortlessly. A small, very sharp knife appeared from nowhere in the palm of his hand, fitting neatly, as though he had been carrying it forever. He saw it glinting in the darkness, felt its smooth, ebony handle and long, brutal serrated blade.

He blinked in surprise. He saw a mirrored look of shock in the man's eyes and then saw them cloud in the instant before he dropped like a sack of coal to the floor.

Tom watched in abstract fascination as a bright froth of red appeared at the corners of the man's mouth and a brilliant red flower blossomed in the centre of his chest. His lips parted and he blew out bright red bubbles which popped in the air. He moaned and more bubbles appeared. Tom could see his knife sticking out of the man's chest, just over his heart.

"Fuck!" the man groaned. He shifted his legs and the bloody flower bloomed further across his chest. Bubbles popped at his lips.

Tom laughed aloud. "Meghan loves bubbles!" he told him. The man lay on the dirty, dusty floor and Tom, someone watching the scene unfold before him, saw himself lean down. "I didn't want to do that!" He wiped his knife on the man's blue jeans and put the knife back in his boot. "I told you I am not a faggot! You made me do that." He looked sorrowfully at the man on the ground. "Sorry, mate, but you asked for it." Turning on his heel, he walked out of the car park towards the distant blinking lights of town.

"Daddy? Daddy? Daddy?" Meghan's voice penetrated the fog and the lights of the town faded, once again he could smell his own home. He found himself back in his chair in his modern blue lounge, with Meghan crying and tugging on his foot, trying to get him to wake up.

"Mommy what's wrong with him?" Meg's voice was tremulous. Tom blinked. He was sat forward in his chair, his breathing shallow and rapid, back in their front room. Meg was cowering before him, staring at a pen in his hand which he brandished like a knife. In the background, Ashleigh stood in between the kitchen and the lounge, leaning against the door frame, one hand across her mouth, staring at him in horror. He stood, mortified, reaching out to her.

Chapter Seven

Staring off into space, the woman was rocking slightly, perched on the edge of the bed. Questions were ignored. All attempts to engage her proved fruitless. Shit, he had better things to do than this. He tried again. Zilch. It was only when he tutted, sighed and brought her chin round, roughly, to make her face him that she reacted.

"Cut the crap, Goldie!" The sudden viciousness of his tone made her flinch. "You listening now?" She tried to pull her face away but his fingers pinched her tightly. He glanced towards the door. It was half shut, against Trust policy but really, who gave a shit?

"Funny, isn't it, how you can turn it off and on? When it suits? Eh?" His hand left her chin, smacking lightly against her cheek, her head snapped backwards, smacking slightly against the dull, institutional grey/green of the wall behind the small, sparse, single bed. "You listening now, eh?" She looked at him, keeping her head down. He chuckled. "Thought so!"

She whimpered. "Well, say something then!" She looked away and put her head down onto her knees. Shaking his head he stood, meaning to leave. *Pathetic cow.* She cowered on the bed, knees up, arms tight around them, rocking again. Slowly, he turned back. Sensing the movement, she stopped rocking, her breathing suddenly shallow, almost imperceptibly leaning backwards, seeking safety from the wall, but going nowhere.

With deliberate menace, he stepped back towards her, smiling as she held her breath, her fear visible. He reached out, grabbing one of the wrists that were clasped around her knees. He turned it over. Criss-crossed scars were etched into her pale skin, leaving marks like cold air vapour from airplanes narrates its passage in clear skies. *Her story, her sorry, stupid story, just another loser. Just another waster. Taking up precious NHS resources.* He threw the wrist back at her. She remained as still as a sculpture. Almost gently, reverently, he reached over and caressed the cheek he had just slapped. She turned her head away and, angered, he drew his hand back to slap her, harder this time.

A keening sound emanated from her throat, deep and guttural, feral almost, full of fear and confusion. He paused. The sound was quite soft. He glanced once more at the door before allowing his hand to wander down her cheek, down her neck, to her breast. He moved aside her jumper, tatty, washed-out and, at one time, yellow, pinching roughly at her exposed nipple. She exhaled sharply, then resumed the keening noise, the shallow breathing. He smirked. "Like that, *do you*? he asked.

"Dr Blue. Dr Blue!" Her voice was high with fear and pain as he continued to pinch her breast.

"Yes, yes, I'm Dr Blue!" he told her, spittle dripping from his lips onto her face. She flinched and pulled back, banging her head against the wall behind her.

Some primal self-preservation instinct made him jump away from her just as the door was pushed open and the large, shapeless form of the ward matron bustled in. By the time her gaze had snapped to the squalling, distressed patient hunched on the bed, he was standing with obsequious professional concern at the end of the bed, drug chart in hand.

The nurse took a look at him and rushed across to the bed. "Jennifer? Jenny? It's ok. You're ok! What is it? What's happened now?" She looked up, but he shook his head and shrugged, a look of concern furrowing his brow.

"Dr Blue!" said the patient, "Dr Blue!"

Glenys turned to the man who had stepped forward and held out her hand. Wordlessly, he handed over the drug chart.

"Oh dear!" said Matron Glenys, "and she's been doing so much better for the last couple of days. Time for more erm... 'rest' I think, don't you?"

He nodded; his expression artificial and sad. "Poor thing!" he said. He turned to go, reaching out to pat the patient gently on the arm. Still wailing, she began to pant.

"I'll go get the doctor!" said Glenys, turning to leave. He stepped around the bed to follow her out.

"Get some rest, sweetheart," he told the patient tenderly, "I'll come back to see you later, when you feel better." Matron smiled at him and together, they left the room.

Chapter Eight

Tom knocked on the door, persisting even though his mother seemed unwilling to answer it. He knew she was there; the TV had been on when he'd arrived, he had seen the glow through the curtains. Finally, when it was clear he wasn't going to go away, she opened it. For a moment, the small, forlorn figure dressed in her late husband's thick, faded grey towelling dressing gown, wore a look so bereft on her face that it made him hesitate.

"Mum," said Tom. "I've been trying to get hold of you! Why didn't you answer the door? My key won't work!"

"Oh, hullo love!" she said, "I'm not feeling too good actually, do you mind coming back later?"

Tom hesitated. "Erm... not really," he said. "Why did you double-lock the door?" He waited, but his mum looked down at her slippered feet. "Were you in the shower?" he asked. She shook her head. At 11:30am on a Saturday it was unusual to find her still in her night clothes. He waited. After a moment or so of uncomfortable silence, Tom cleared his throat. "Mum... please can I come in? I really need to talk to you." Still she looked at the ground. "Are you ok?" he asked, tenderly.

Eyes closed, she took a deep breath and nodded, stepped back and opened the door wide. Tom entered the hall and wordlessly removed his coat and scarf. He handed them to her and she took them, and, as she always did, hung them carefully on the wall hooks beside the stairs, smoothing them out before she turned away.

They walked together into the kitchen, still no words exchanged. She walked to the kettle and flicked the switch. The light inside the kettle glowed a dull red, making an ostentatiously loud noise as the element heated up.

She carefully selected teabags and added them to the cups, opening the drawer and selecting a tea-spoon with elaborate care. She walked slowly to the fridge, as if in pain, retrieved a plastic bottle of blue-topped milk and waited in awkward silence for the kettle to boil.

Finally, tea made, bags discarded and milk bottle returned to the fridge, she brought the tea to the table. She blew on it before placing the cup in front of her son. He smiled. The gesture was a familiar one, born of a primitive mothering instinct to protect her young from danger, even the relative harm of a hot drink.

He cupped his hands around the drink. Damn it was cold outside and the heat of the cup felt blissful.

The silence lengthened and Tom looked around the room. Photographs of himself, Ashleigh and Meg were dotted around, along with others of his brother and sister, her late husband and a dog long since dead. The kitchen was a modest one, decorated by him and his father some years ago, decor now showing its age. Dust dulled the surfaces of the top of the fridge and the counters had crumbs on them, residue of an earlier breakfast.

"What's going on, Mum?" he asked at last, breaking the stillness. "Pauline said..."

"Pauline!" his mother spat. Tom looked at her in surprise. She and Pauline had always appeared close. Rose was even tolerant of Pauline's drinking habit, understanding her latent grief and sad, childless world. As his late father's only sibling, Pauline had always been a regular feature in their lives as had Rob since he and Pauline had begun dating after Zach, her first husband died.

Tom, his younger sister Helen, and their younger brother Peter had spent many happy hours with Pauline and Rob, especially since their fruitless efforts to start a family had brought them closer. Days and days at the seaside, on the dunes, at funfairs and the like, sometimes even for weeks at a time, in caravan's and bigger camping sites. In recent years Pauline's drinking had become far more of an issue but, God, four times they had lost babies about five or six months in. It must have been hell. And Rob, he was great. Always babysitting, always there.

His dad and Rob had been mates before Rob and Pauline got together, so the two couples spent a lot of time together:-holiday'd together even. To hear the vitriol in his mother's voice was a big shock.

"Did you know she told Ash at the party that the baby may be stillborn?" he asked, watching her face carefully. She looked down, twisting the handle of her cup.

"I'm sure the baby will be fine!" she replied, picking up and taking a tentative sip of her tea. "Have you got any names yet?"

"Tom!" he said. She smiled.

"Or Rose?" she asked with an attempt to lighten the atmosphere. "Although *I* think it's a boy!"

"It is! We've decided to get the scan results after all." Tom smiled and lifted his steaming tea to his lips. He sipped, feeling the scalding liquid scorch its way down his gullet. Silence descended once again, interrupted only by the humming of the fridge and the chirping of a few birds in the cool early spring garden.

"Mum?" Tom put his cup down and looked at her across the familiar, scarred table of his youth.

Again, she took a deep breath. "Do you want a biscuit, love?" she asked.

"Mum!" Tom's tone was exasperated.

Don't blame your father!" she said. Tom looked at her, puzzled.

"He always said we should tell you. Oh, love!" she dropped her head to her hands, almost onto the table, spilling a little of her tea.

"What mum? Is it about his illness?"

"His illness?" she looked up.

It was Tom's turn to take a deep breath. "I think... I'm worried I've started to get the same symptoms."

"What?" Her surprised laugh hurt him and he shook his head.

"His dementia," Tom took another deep, shaky breath. "I've been getting... well... confused I suppose!"

"Oh, love!" she said, "Oh, Tom!" She reached across the table and placed a pale, slight hand over his large masculine one. Tears pooled in her eyes.

"You aren't getting his dementia, love," she said. "Your dad... Oh, Tom, my love, you were adopted."

Tom made his way home in a daze. As he parked the car and locked it by reflex, his phone rang. Expecting it to be his mother, he looked at it, slight distain on his face. It was Ashleigh. Hurriedly he let himself into the house, flung the keys onto the console table in the hall and walked quickly through to the lounge.

Ashleigh was pacing the floor while their next-door-but-one neighbour, Pam, was sitting on the sofa with Ashleigh's mobile in her hand.

"Oh, Tom, love," the neighbour was breathless and flustered. "I was just about to call you!"

Ash looked up as he entered, bringing a flood of cold air. Pam shivered, but Ash was flushed and sweating. She looked over and smiled, but resumed her pacing, her breathing increasingly laboured and as he watched her, a rush of fluid like water from a basket intended to stop forest fires dropped from between her legs.

"Oh, my goodness!" exclaimed Pam, moving her feet out of the deluge.

"My waters broke!" said Ash, somewhat redundantly. Tom smiled. "It's too early!" Her tone was anxious.

"It's ok, sweetheart!" He turned to their neighbour, "Pam, can you..."

"He's not due for another month though!" Rob pulled her to him and hugged her. "It'll be fine!" he whispered.

"I'll stay with Meggie!" Pam held a hand to her chest. "Ooohh!" she said, "how exciting!"

Chapter Nine

The birth was never really going to be a happy one, given recent circumstances. Nevertheless, hope, as they say, springs eternal.

She pushed and pushed, for hours it felt like, and finally, eventually, she pushed again and felt a rush of heat between her legs. Momentarily it seemed over and yet the tightening ramped up again.

"Ohhhhh Goooood," she groaned before a scream ripped from her. "Arrggghhh! Tommy!"

"It's fine, honey! You are doing juuust great!" The calm, laid-back voice of the midwife washed over her as she once again braced herself to push. 'It's sure not called labour for nothing', the nurse told her, just before her voice was drowned out as the labouring mother moaned again, bearing down with all her strength, screaming aloud and praying silently for it to end.

Tom watched as the woman on the narrow bed, legs impossibly far apart, began straining, muttering a low, profoundly mournful cry from deep inside her. She strained and pushed, sweat pouring off her. 'Come on, love, you're doing great!' he told her, reaching up to take her hand and recoiling as he suddenly realised it wasn't Ashleigh. The girl looked at him blankly before she moaned and sat forward, panting. The contractions increased in frequency in what seemed like only minutes, until at last the midwife said, "She's crowning!" and with a monumental push and in a rush of tarry-shit and vernix, delivered a small, squalling, pink son.

Yet only moments later the sweaty, exhausted girl moaned again. Tom watched in amazement as, huffing and panting, he saw her straining with all her might. He watched, anticipating the delivery of the afterbirth, ah, the modern man. He stared in confusion as she screamed and another baby was pushed, squeaking and mewing into the world. He stepped forward.

The girl on the bed, feet in stirrups and legs akimbo turned to him, sweat and tears streaked on her face, still breathing heavily from her labours. "Who are you?" she asked sleepily, before she fell into an exhausted sleep.

Chapter Ten

Dr Sunhil Ashkarahn, known to the patients as Dr Blue on account of the literal translation of his first name, was chairing the weekly 'care' meeting. Around the small table before him, which bore the scars of many such boring assemblies, sat Matthew, an African male nurse with an almost comically butch disposition; Anna, a pathologically shy, skinny and morose nurse of Polish extraction; and Tulip, a Nigerian mental health nurse with the loudest laugh Dr Blue had ever heard, she was however, his favourite; stoic, discrete and very hard to upset.

Dr Stringer and the ward clerk were also present, but distracted; Dr Stringer on his BlackBerry and ward clerk Pam whispering to the only other person present, one whom Dr Blue despised, Stewart. Thick as thieves they were, though for the life of him he could not understand why. Pam seemed to have too much sense, as far as Dr Blue was concerned, to consort with the likes of him. He challenged every decision, every request. He was constantly poking his nose into things which were none of his business, as if he was the doctor and not just a nurse's aide. A busy-body, that's what his mother would have called him.

Dr Blue glared at Stewart and cleared his throat for the second time, trying in vain to get the attention of his staff.

He tapped the table, but was still unable to get their attention. "Umm... hello? Hello?" Ostensibly the get-together was a regular, bi-weekly affair designed to review the care and treatment of the twenty four residents of the two units which comprised Windermere Ward. In reality, however, it tended more towards a social gathering unless there was some other terribly pressing business.

The door opened and Dr Blue looked up in frustration- this damn meeting would still be going at dinner time. His demeanour brightened suddenly as Susann Halligan entered, nodded to him and took a seat. He smiled at her, relieved to see her, waiting whilst she settled in her seat. He tapped the table again, more forcefully this time.

"Hullo colleagues." Still conversation ebbed around him. "Erm... Colleagues...?"

Susann looked around her work-mates thoughtfully.

"*Hello?* Her tone was brisk and conversation stopped gradually, albeit reluctantly.

"Dr Ashkarahn?" Susann turned to the short, somewhat untidy Indian medic, "Shall we begin?" Not for the first time he thought she would have been a much better choice for the newly appointed Matron's post, but he swallowed, took a deep breath and turned to the staff waiting to hear him commence the agenda.

"We have the usual standing items," He dove straight into to policy amendments, urgent memos and clinical SOPs – standard operating guidelines - that made up their daily grind.

The main part of the meeting involved a review of the current patient cohort; a sharing of concerns, medicines review and any pending investigations, discharges or expected admissions.

When they reached the cases of Jennifer, a paranoid schizophrenic, and Bella, a manic depressive, Susann coughed and sat up in her seat.

"I would like to again raise the issue of sexual allegations in relation to these two patients," she said, her voice clear and confident.

Matthew groaned. "Bella? Hell, she come on to me all the time. Man, she jus' horny!" He grinned around the table, but no one smiled back. His smile faded.

"Oh, come on!" He sat back with a jolt. "She in for sleeping wid everyone. She tole me she had an addiction to sex."

"So?" Susann looked at him across the table. "Does that mean we should discount any allegations of assault that she may make?"

Tulip sat up. "No is no at the end of the day. But Matthew... he got a point." Her accent was heavy and thick and her delivery, as ever, slow and measured. Everything she said, however grave, always sounded lyrical with her lilting native accent. She had clearly, as he would have expected of her, considered the issue and formed her own conclusion. She continued, "We have reported eleven incidents of sexual assault to the police in the past five month. I tink we should..."

"If I may?" Pam, the longest serving member of ward staff, was a serious, conscientious and popular member of staff. She was also married to a hospital doctor and consequently, was taken very seriously, all of which made her friendship with the overly camp Stewart, very odd. All faces turned towards her.

"May I just point out that I personally caught her having sex in her room with a male visitor last month? From what I saw, she was certainly consenting. Fully... erm.. *participating,* shall I say."

"Again," said Susann, "So? No still means no, even in here."

"My point," replied Pam, "is that the following day she then insisted on the police being called, saying she had been raped. I think it's very difficult to determine, but..."

"Yes. *It is.*" Susann's tone was cutting. "In fact, it's a clinical decision - or at the very least - a professional one, whatever you believe you saw."

"Even if she later recanted?" Pam was not offended by the comments, her tone was measured and calm. She stood her ground.

"What about Jennifer, though?" Tulip interjected. "She was doing so well! I don't think she done that before. Now, she just, you know, like a little shadow these days."

"I know!" Matthew nodded in agreement. "She played a game of chess with me a few weeks ago, now she won't even talk to me!"

Glenys tittered, "Who won?" she said.

"Me!" he replied. Susann looked at Dr Blue. He sighed and sat up straighter.

"Granted, it's not the first time Jennifer has made allegation of this type," he replied, "I have to say, she wasn't terribly convincing!"

"Who did she say it was this time?" Stewart asked.

"She wouldn't say. She just kept calling for me. She was distressed though. Still, I don't know if she even gave anyone's name in particular."

"Well," said Stewart, "given that there have been no strangers around here for ages, that's not very likely."

"No," Matthew added, "she know ever' body here!"

"Even so!" Susann was quietly emphatic. "The policy clearly states that we are required to call the police if a client requests it. So it can be properly investigated."

Stewart laughed and scribbled something on the pad in front of him. "Then we would need our own police force!" he said.

Matthew nodded.

"Whilst I agree that it appears... something of a pattern, Susann is right, it is not within our gift to determine when to apply a given policy or not." Dr Blue looked around the table. "I must confess, I have some concerns about these allegations..." he paused, "certainly in Jennifer's case. However, I think we must undertake more internal investigations, before, we... umm... call in outside help." He turned to Susann. "May I ask you, would you be willing to conduct the investigation? If that's ok with you, Matron?"

Glenys shrugged; it was less work for her. The agenda moved on to the next patient and the more pressing issue of her determination on examining her own shit, searching for proof of alien possession.

Chapter Eleven

Pauline was uncommonly subdued when she came to visit the new baby. *Even*, Tom thought to himself, *sober*! Ashleigh lay supine on the corner sofa, her legs stretched out in front of her, Meghan at her side, cooing over her beloved new brother. Baby Elliott lay flat on his mum's chest, his tiny head moving slightly with her every breath.

"What a little treasure!" said Pauline softly, gently stroking his down-covered dome.

Rob looked uncomfortable but then Tom thought that was to be expected. They had barely spoken since Tom's visit to their house and the subsequent shock announcement of his adoption. He had yet to respond to Helen and Peter's concerned calls. Ashleigh's response had been the only momentary relief in a fraught and frantic weekend.

"Well, love," she had said, when she could speak, "there is no rule book for parenting. And, if not your father, he was definitely your dad, and she is still your mum." She had paused, in between contractions; "Though Tom..." she gasped as a contraction peaked.

"What?" he'd answered.

"What?"

"I guess there is one silver lining..."

"Oh yeah? What's that then?"

"You defiantly haven't inherited his dementia!" She gasped and looked at the baby monitor stationed beside her trolley and tethered to her massive, shifting, bulging belly.

As the contraction subsided, she shifted again, sweat blooming on her face. "Hummm..." she said.

"What?"

"There must be other reason!" She wiped her face with the towel, smiling at his confusion. "Another reason you are going mad!" She laughed then winced as another contraction tightened her belly.

He had looked at her and at her pulsing abdomen. "But that's just the problem," he replied. She cocked her head; stomach tensing as he next contraction began to peak.

"What? It's good news, love." She grunted, "Of a sort anyway!" She was panting; Tom tightened his grip on her sweaty hand.

"Yeah? You think? Just what the hell *have* I inherited then?" he asked.

Still, she heard. "Oh, love, you shouldn't... oooohhh! Ohhh!" Her voice rose and the conversation ended as she rode the pain with Tom squeezing her hand whilst she puffed and rocked through the worst of it. He had just watched, and waited, praying for the imminent arrival of his perfect, healthy son, praying it was just the one.

Chapter Twelve

Tom sat and watched his wife feeding their five week old son.
They had decided on the name Elliott. He was indeed perfect. His
scrunched up little face had lost its birth-trauma strain and the wrinkles
made by his arduous journey down the birth canal had disappeared; his
cheeks were now deliciously smooth and plump. Meghan doted on him.
She was playing upstairs with her Sylvanian Family dolls, but every ten
minutes or so she popped down just to give him a gentle kiss or to stroke
his head.

Tom was relieved; no sign of jealousy at all. Ashleigh had smiled at
him as he pointed this out. She had never expected any in the first place.

Meghan's parents had spent hours cuddling him and both had
brought presents for Meghan too. Only Tom's mother had been dry-eyed
when presented with her new grandson for the first time. Her response
had been curiously and uncharacteristically lack-lustre. Certainly she'd
made a fuss of him and solicitously asked after Ashleigh's health,
sympathising with tales of sutures, haemorrhoids and cracked nipples.
She'd brought gifts for mother, child and sibling, but Tom felt she was
holding something of herself back.

Ash said he was imagining it, but Tom was certain. His mother
wouldn't meet his eyes, was monosyllabic, was ever-so-slightly brusque
with him. After the revelations at her home recently, he felt like he was
being wrong-footed. Surely it should be him that had the right to
indignation? It felt to Tom that his mother resented him for forcing her to
tell him the truth.

He was, it transpired, the only adoptee. Both Helen and Peter
were really his parent's offspring. It was the age old story, having been
told they couldn't conceive naturally and having turned to adoption,
seven months after Tom's adoption discovered that Rose was expecting a
baby of their own. To be fair – and Tom always tried to be – not once,
growing up, had he ever suspected there was a difference between him

and his siblings. They were all treated the same. And undeniably, it was a happy, happy childhood. He sighed and caught Ashleigh's eye.

"Make us a cuppa, love? she asked. He smiled and nodded.

He headed into in the kitchen, opened the small fridge beside the patio doors for the milk, and said an automatic 'Hi Harry!' to Meg's new hamster, who lived in his cage on the top it, a present from her new brother.

"Sugar, babe?" Tom peered around the door into the lounge. The baby was asleep, making little snuffling noises and flexing his tiny fingers as if dreaming. Ash leaned down to kiss his head. She nodded.

"Ah," she said, "bliss!"

The days passed slowly. In spite of Elliott's somewhat premature appearance into their lives, all adjusted within moments of his arrival at home, and they were, to everyone who knew them, the perfect family.

The only cloud on the horizon for Tom was the issue of his adoption, he knew it was inevitable that he would at some point, want more information.

Otherwise, the ongoing – albeit infrequent – dreams or visions or whatever the fuck they were still worried him. There seemed no pattern to them. He couldn't blame tiredness or drink, since he hardly drank and he never took drugs other than a paracetamol for the occasional headache. Most of the time he was doing something mundane, shopping, driving or something routine at work and something would drift across his mind, like smoke.

Some months after his last episode, when pressed by Ashleigh about their frequency, he left Ash and the kids with Pam and went for his scheduled appointment with his GP. He was reassured that nothing immediately obvious was wrong, the neurological exam the was normal. Eye pressure normal. Reflexes all normal. There was a slight prickly patch when the GP had said he understood Tom's concerns about his late father's condition, and Tom felt it better to be honest and say he had recently learned he had been adopted. The GP had looked at him over stereotypical half-moon glasses and pursed his lips.

"Humm..." Dr Fowler fiddled with his pen for a moment. "Well of course, that is good news from the point of view of developing vascular dementia, or any form of vascular complications, come to that." He exhaled. "And I take it you had no knowledge of this previously?" Tom shook his head. "Do you intend to try to find your birth parents?" Tom shrugged and cleared his throat.

"I guess, maybe... at some point. Anyway, for now at least, I guess I can't immediately blame that on my... erm... symptoms."

The GP took a full, detailed history from Tom, being careful to determine that the beginnings of the 'visions' preceded the announcement of his birth. After examining him, he told Tom to try to keep a diary of the events, where he was, what he was doing at the time they happened, what he had been eating, drinking or erm... taking."

"I'm not taking any drugs if that's what you mean!" he replied.

"I've known you a long time, Thomas!" Dr Fowler was unruffled, "and I'm sure you are not. However, it is something I must ask as part of the history. Now, the other thing to record is your mood, happy, sad, cross etc. OK? So..."

"My mood?"

"Umm... Yes. It could be that this has a psychological cause. In fact, that's probably the most likely explanation."

"Like... mental illness?"

The doctor nodded and shrugged. "Not as rare as you think!" Tom rolled his eyes. "Having a new baby. It's a stressful time."

Tom's laugh was brief and nervous. "Bloody hell!" he said, "what else could it be?"

"Well... aside from a mental health problem, epilepsy is something I would like to exclude as a matter of urgency. The presence of tumours..." He paused and smiled at Tom, "now, now, it's purely precautionary. There is absolutely no need at this stage to suspect anything so drastic. It is often the case that some form of temporary chemical or electrical imbalance in the brain can manifest such occurrences. Do you, for instance, experience an 'aura' around the time of the visions?"

"What's an aura?"

"Many patients with epilepsy have a sort of unique warning sign before they have a fit or indeed an experience of this nature. A certain smell, a strange taste. Try to see if this is something you can determine. I'll contact the hospital and set up some tests. But Tom, take it easy. Try not to worry and I assure you, if there were any real nasties lurking around; there would almost certainly be some clinical signs, given the reported frequency of your dreams. I mean, they have been going on for ages now and there isn't any sign of any... umm... serious pathology. As for the mental illness issue," He stood and came around from the desk to shake Tom's hand, "I'm sure we will find a rational explanation.

"Congratulations on the baby by the way!" Tom smiled, shook his hand and left. He sat in the car in the car park for an hour, trying to compose himself before he went home to his family.

Chapter Thirteen

Tom looked around him; yet another bar. How the fuck had he got here? This one, like the others, was dark, dingy, and smoky. He'd never been in so many bars in his life. Oh God, he thought, not again. This one was almost identical to the last one, except the decor. Otherwise, he had no idea where he was. He struggled to think. The last thing he could remember was driving to an Easter fair with Ashleigh and the children in Ledbury somewhere.

He looked around. There were people all over the place. At the bar, on the dance floor, huddling in corners. Music was being played live by a four piece band dressed in grungy clothes and singing covers of U2 by the sound of it. Fair enough. Cool group. Raucous laughing. The noise of people shouting, competing with the music. He listened for a moment or so until he heard a voice talking to him.

"What'll it be?" the voice was immature; high and sweet and when he looked he saw a woman, young, wearing all black, with black-highlighted eye-brows with a piercing through one and multiple piercings through both ears. A black stud glittered in her nose. Her hair added the only real slash of colour to her outfit; wildly styled with red, pink, purple and blue highlights. The following thoughts scuttled though his brain without conscious thought; she was sexy; she wasn't Ashleigh, he was horny.

"A pint of lager, please!" he said and watched, bewildered, as she placed a neat glass of Jack Daniels, before him. She smiled and picked a bank note up off the counter and though he went to call her back, she turned and bounced off to the other end of the bar, leaning across it and taking the cigarette off a young man the other side between her blood-red lips to inhale deeply. She leaned back, retaining the smoke for a moment, then blowing it out with a deep sigh of satisfaction, aiming it at the ceiling in a series of perfect smoke rings.

Tom sat on a stool and picked up his drink. He sniffed it suspiciously and took a sip. It burned its way down and he coughed. The girl behind the bar looked at him and whispered something to her friend with the cigarette. He looked at Tom and laughed. Tom glowered. He turned away.

The band moved on to a song Tom didn't know, didn't recognise, but he felt the words of the song echo in his head. Odd. He sat for some time, leaning against the bar and watching the girl. Fuck, she was sexy. So totally different from Ashleigh. Ashleigh; feminine and shy. Where was she?

He hunted in his pockets for his mobile, but couldn't find it. His clothes were unfamiliar, rough and unclean. He could smell something dark and dry, some sort of aftershave he thought. Maybe it was someone in the bar close to him. He touched his chin and felt a couple of days' worth of beard growth. He could have sworn he had shaved that morning.

The girl spoke to him again, nodding at his glass. To his astonishment, it was empty. He nodded once and she refilled it, giving him a cheeky wink as she placed a full glass in front of him. He glanced over at the youth in the corner, but he'd disappeared. The girl leaned on the counter, playing with one of her purple locks.

"Not seen you before!" she said.

"Where am I?" Tom asked. She nodded and smiled.

"Where are you travelling to?" she replied, as if this is what he had asked.

"Worcester." He heard himself say. He frowned. Worcester was home. Why would he be away from home in a bar without Ash?

"Worcester's nice!" she said, "Better than Glastonbury. This place is a shithole!" She turned away as she was called from down the bar to a customer. Tom shook his head. Why on earth would he be in Glastonbury? Never been there before, somewhere in Essex wasn't it? Anyway, it was a rustic and run-down place, certainly didn't look like any part of Glastonbury he'd heard of.

He found himself watching the girl flit around behind the bar and was pissed off when he saw her friend reappear and sit once more at the far end. He felt Tom staring at him, looked up, grinned and went back to rolling his cigarettes.

Again the girl brought him a refill, asking in a flirtatious voice if he wanted anything else.

"No!" he said.

"Oh, hey, behave!" she laughed. Tom shook his head, smiling. Maybe she was drunk? Hell, maybe he was.

"It's Jo," said the girl.

"I didn't ask your name!" he said.

"Well, hi, Tommy!" she answered. Tom frowned.

"What time do you finish?" He heard himself ask the question and re-coiled. He had never cheated on Ash. Had never even thought about it.

"No, no!" he said, "I'm married! My wife is called Ashleigh."

"Persistent bugger, aren't you Tommy?" She cocked her head as if considering. "About two-ish!" Turning, she blew him a kiss and walked away, busying herself behind the bar, tidying and washing glasses.

Tom watched as a man walked behind the bar, completely ignored by Jo, who was wiping the bar with a dirty looking cloth, opened the till and walking away, a wad of notes clutched in his hand. Time passed, she kept him supplied with more JD, smiling at him before flitting off to serve other customers.

The youth at the end appeared not to notice and Tom found himself wondering what their relationship was. It seemed odd to Tom, to ignore the boss like that.

The band played on and Tom realised that he was enjoying the evening. He tapped his toe in time to the music, even tunes he did not recognise. He nodded to people in the bar, as if he knew them. They nodded back. The smoke curled around him, and he sang along to words he did not know he knew.

Jo visited the youth at the end of the bar again several times, each time taking a hit of the youth's fag. Tom watched them through narrowed eyes, feeling an unreasonable jealousy. By now the heavy spirits had inhibited any conscience and he watched Jo as she worked the bar, smiling at all the men, grinning at the woman. She was professional and cool, both at the same time, not stopping but making it all seem effortless, like there was nowhere else she wanted to be.

Punk hair aside, she was very pretty, around twenty or so, slim with small, high breasts. She was wearing an open checked shirt over a black cropped vest top with a faded image of *The Who* on it with a pair of faded black, very tight, drain-pipe-type trousers and the obligatory patent black boots which he thought may be Doc Martens.

When she turned and bent to retrieve a coin from the floor, he saw her that arse was high and tight and he shifted in his seat, feeling the beginnings of an erection. He rubbed his crotch and she saw him. She smirked and turned away, serving another punter.

Tom saw her leer at the kid at the end of the bar and he turned away, struggling to focus, but the drink and the smoke were clouding his judgement. Hell, just cos he was horny and she was clearly available, didn't mean he was going to do anything about it, did it? He was too drunk to realise he was rationalising his behaviour and she bent over again, smiling at him as she did so. He blinked.

A screeching sound made him look around. Sharp feedback from a microphone made him flinch. The band were packing up and somehow the packed bar was now almost empty.

Lights came on, making him blink, and he fell forward off his bar stool, feeling very drunk. Jo came over to him and whispered something to him, but he didn't catch what she said. He just smiled drunkenly at her, struggling to keep his eyes open by now. The lights came on, blinding him for a moment, and Tom could see properly what a dump the bar was. Dirty and uncared for, full ashtrays, trash piled in corners and broken bottles and empty glasses littering battered tables.

Jo whispered across the bar to him again and Tom, managing to keep his eyes on the prize before him, reached across and patted her bottom as she turned to lock the till. She looked at the man who had appeared behind the bar and Tom realised it must be the manager, as it was the same man who had taken the money from the till some time ago. Jo nodded at the exit. Tom stumbled out and felt, more than saw, her following him.

Outside, the air was thick and warm, the faint smell of smoke outside, like someone had been having a barbeque. Weird, in early March. Tom took a deep breath, looking around for Ashleigh. Meg and the baby must be asleep. Shit. Ash was going to be pissed off when he got back. When Jo appeared at his side though, Ashleigh and his children disappeared from his mind. She nuzzled at his ear and all he caught was the word 'park...' He must have responded because she smiled and led the way to the rear of the car park and up a small incline.

Beyond the car park, the ground beneath his feet became springy; grass. The air smelled slightly fetid and Tom sensed there was water nearby. In spite of the warmth of the night, he shivered. There was no sound except his breathing, fast and ragged. He looked around for Jo.

From around 20 feet to his far left he heard a whisper and staggered drunkenly towards the noise. Was she talking to herself? He could hear voices. He jumped when someone touched his arm and he spun around. Jo was standing before him, still dressed in her bar clothes. He reached out to pull her to him, but she moved backwards. By the light of the stars he could see a smile on her face and he followed her, stumbling to her as she continued to walk backwards.

"Come on, baby," she crooned, "I'm over here!"

At last she stopped. He reached her; she had backed against a tree. He reached out blindly and felt her breasts. They felt small and mean. He snickered in the night. Mean breasts! Ashleigh's weren't mean... Jo backed off again, sneaking behind the tree.

"Keep still!" he told her.

"Round here, Tommy," she whispered back, "where no-one can see us! Come and get me, baby!"

Grinning, he went around the wide tree and bumped up against her. She looked to her right and then back at Tom. She reached up and put her arms around his neck. He sighed and leaned into her embrace. She pulled his mouth down to hers and he kissed her deeply. It wasn't like kissing Ash. He lips felt cold and hard. She didn't taste nice. She tasted of cigarettes.

He gagged and pulled back, releasing her, but she pressed forward, thrusting her hips against his groin and grinding. He felt his cock jump and throb and his erection decided what his conscience could not, filling and pressing against her. She moaned softly and pushed him back, gently at the shoulders, reaching down, pulling aside her shirt and pushing up her vest top, exposing her breasts.

"No!" he said, and bent his head, pulling the flimsy material away and taking her nipple in his mouth.

"Now!" she said and Tom paused, *'now' what*? He felt footsteps behind him and was knocked off his feet as a blow to the side of his head sent him flying to the ground. Blood trickled feebly from his temple. Jo laughed and Tom heard a voice behind him say, "Move then, I can't reach him from here."

Swiftly, he rolled to the side, shocked but nimble, surprising himself. He swore as a bat of some description thunked hard in the space where he had just been. He blinked in the gloom, feeling the whisky rise, sour and foul in his mouth. He turned, trying to see who had hit him, expecting to see Jo's young boyfriend.

"Fucker!" said the voice and Tom realised it was the manager of the bar. He swallowed down the vomit in his mouth.

"Get him, dad!" said Jo.

"Go back to the bar, JoJo," the man replied. "You don't wanna see this."

"Hit 'im!" she answered, her voice cruel and mean. Tom felt fear prickle down his spine as the man before him altered his stance, preparing to beat him with his paddle. Before Tom knew what was happening, he was on his feet with a knife glinting in his hand. Where the fuck had that come from? He slashed through the air in the direction of his assailant, who yelped as the knife sliced his hand. He dropped the bat. The man stumbled backwards, cursing.

"Watch it, Dad!" screamed Jo as Tom lashed out once again with the knife, catching the right flank of the man, slicing a wide gash through fabric and flesh. He grunted and fell sideways. Jo screamed again and fell to the ground beside her father. She kicked out, narrowly missing kicking Tom's groin.

"Bitch!" he said.

"You bastard!" she cried jumping up; "We were after your wallet."

"Fucking wanker!" The man's voice came out hoarse and wheezy and he struggled, trying to stand.

"Come on, Dad, get him!" said Jo.

"You asked for this!" Tom heard the ice in his voice and, like watching a horror movie in slow motion, he saw himself reach down and stick the knife, with careful deliberation, into the belly of the man moaning on the ground. "It's your fault," Tom told him, "You made me do it. It's self defence." The man moaned and Tom leaned forward, the knife glinting again in the blackness.

Crying, Jo scrabbled backwards like a crab, intent on fleeing. Tom watched in abstract fascination as she stopped, picked up a rock and threw it at him. He laughed as it missed and she turned on her side to pick up another.

"Now, now! You owe me, lady," he told her in a voice he no longer recognised as his own, reaching down and grabbing her hair. She scrambled to her feet, wrenching out of his grasp, leaving him with a handful of hair. He sighed. When she stumbled, a short distance from the prone figure of her father, Tom reached out, grabbing her again easily, knocking her roughly back to the ground. He bent down, ripping her shirt and vest top, slashing both at the seams with his knife. She was screaming and flailing and Tom found himself looking around to see if anyone could hear them. She tried grabbing at his hands to stop him.

There was no sign of anyone else in the area except the man groaning at his feet and the frantic girl, scrabbling, once again upright, trying to flee from his touch. He slapped her across the face and knocked her back, finally to the ground for one last assault. With horror he saw himself pull at her jeans.

"Fuck!" he screamed.

"Please, no!" Tom saw tears glinting off her face in the murkiness, and he heard Jo's father, still moaning and panting on the grass beside him.

"Please, *yes*, bitch!" Tom heard himself reply, mockingly. He looked around to see where the voice had come from and when he looked back to the girl again he saw that her jeans were off and her knickers were around her ankles.

"Please, Tommy. Oh God, please!" She was still trying to wriggle backwards and Tom saw his hand reach out and grip her neck, holding her in place. She choked and tried twisting her head to free herself of his hands. One hand flailed at his chest, hitting him feebly. He saw himself as a figure on the ground, leaning back and freeing his erection from his jeans. Roughly he pushed his jeans down, forced her legs astride and pushed himself hard into her.

She screamed again and hit him with both hands, but he was grunting and thrusting into her, feeling his climax build and build. Fuck! He was wild. He could hear the moans of the man lying some 10 feet or so away, could smell the blood which dripped from his gaping belly and still Tom pushed himself harder and harder into the girl, both wanting to hurt her and wanting to run, to get far away from this nightmare, as fast as he could.

"Ashleigh! Ashleigh!" Tom cried, hearing only his deepened, callous voice saying it was her fault, she had asked for it; she had made him do it, it was her fault.

"Tommy, stop!" Suddenly she stopped hitting him and her arms fell away, "Oh, God!" she cried, "No!" Tom pushed into her once again and she grunted. Tom shouted out as her arm pulled back and she struck in on his arm with a sharp stick or stone or something, he knocked it away. Then he felt her pull to the side slightly, but was too close to coming to stop. She reached across and grabbed at another rock, a sharp one which she slashed at his already bloody arm causing him to issue a bellow of rage.

Tom felt dizzy. He leaned forward and spewed the contents of his stomach to the side. He gagged again, drool leaking from the side of his mouth at the smell of the vomit. He wiped his mouth on his sleeve and stood. He saw himself as if he was watching a movie, saw himself twist so his cock was still deep in the girl; saw himself lean to the side and snatch the rock from her hand. He saw and felt the spasm rock through him as he climaxed, still deep in the moaning woman on the ground, watching in abstract horror as he watched himself hit her on the temple, hard, side on. The rock pierced her skin and shattered the thin bone. Blood pooled up and out with such swiftness that he pulled out of her, dribbling semen onto her thigh, frantic to get away, feeling like he has once again entered his own body. He hit her again and again until she shuddered and lay dying before him.

The man beside them was still trying to make his way over to the girl and Tom watched as he shuffled on his bottom over to her shuddering body, one hand holding his split belly, the other reaching out to touch his dying daughter's face, oblivious to the blood which soon covered his hand. She shivered once, her eyes opening and searching for Tom's in the dimness.

When he next looked back he was almost a quarter of a mile away, the hills hiding his shame in the distance, running as fast as he could, pausing only to retch every few steps, vomit occasionally and swipe away the tears blinding his eyes.

He struggled to open his eyes. He could feel hands pulling at his arm, tearing at his shirt and stabbing pains in his hands. His arm felt sore. He grunted and thrashed about, trying to free himself. As he remember fucking the girl, he felt vomit fill his mouth again, he leaned quickly to the side, spewing onto hard, cold, orange coloured tiles. Dimly he heard Ashleigh's voice, full of anguish and tears and he tried to open his eyes.

"Ashleigh!" he moaned, "I didn't mean to hurt..." He fell back, dizzy and queasy again. He struggled not too throw up anymore.

All around him the noise of crying and exclamations of shock filtered into his weary brain and finally he tore his eyes open, stinging tears still blinding his vision.

"Tom!" He felt his heart jump in his chest at another plaintive wail from his wife. Shit, did he really just screw someone else? Rape someone? His gorge rose and he leaned over and puked again, feeling it splash against his hand and all over the floor. He moaned in fright and confusion.

"Sarah, can you get another vomit bowl please!" The voice was deep and calm and still Tom struggled, trying to free himself, groaning as he felt a band tighten painfully around his upper arm.

"Tom? Tom, can you hear me? My name is Matthew. I'm a paramedic. Tom, can you squeeze my hand, mate?"

"Tom?" He felt Ashleigh's hand on his leg and tried to look in her direction, but the movement of his head made him throw up again and his eyes closed, feeling very faint.

"Sit up, Tom. Can you open your eyes for me?" Matthew's voice was solid and reassuring and Tom felt that even if Ashleigh knew about the rape, she was not talking about it. Had he been caught and arrested? "Steady mate!" the paramedic said.

"Water!" he whispered and moments later felt a plastic cup appear in his hand. Supporting him, the paramedic helped him raise the glass to his lips and he sipped gratefully, grimacing at the sting of the fluid as it travelled down his throat. Must be all that Jack Daniels, he thought.

"Do you know where you are, Tom?" Another voice spoke to him, a woman and he turned his head to look at her, gasping in horror. She had dark brown hair and was slim and pretty. He squinted and half closed his eyes again. She looked like Jo. His head spun and he felt darkness closing in once more. "Is he drunk?" he heard the female paramedic ask his wife.

"No," she replied indignantly.

She turned to him, "Tom?" His wife's pleading tone made him open his eyes again and the dark-haired woman repeated her question. He tried to lean away from her, thinking she was Jo.

"*No!*" he cried, "No, no."

"Tom, its' ok, she's a paramedic!"

The female paramedic stepped closer and squatted down to him, "I'm Sarah. Can you tell me where you are?"

"Erm... dunno... Glastonbury?" he said.

Ashleigh sounded bemused, "*Glastonbury?*"

"Ok, hon, you're doing ok." Tom tried to stand, but the paramedic put her hand firmly on his shoulder. "Stay there a while, Tom," she said. She stood up and conferred in a whisper to her colleague.

"What's wrong with him?" Ashleigh's voice was high and anxious. "I don't think he's ever even *been* to Glastonbury!"

"Not sure at this point, Mrs Bearing. We should take him to A&E, get him checked out."

Tom shifted, feeling a numbness in his buttocks which suggested he had been sitting for some time. "No hospital!" he muttered, rolling, trying again to stand.

"Tom, it's ok. Stay there! I'll take the kids to mum and..."

"No. Not going to hospital!" He looked at his arm as he felt a tightening begin again and realised it was an inflating blood-pressure cuff. He ripped it off.

"Tom!" Ashleigh was still crying, but Tom thrust the cuff at the paramedic called Mathew, who shrugged and took it.

"You were really out of it for a moment there, mate," he told Tom, "it could be a fit of some description. I'm sure they wouldn't keep you in..."

"No, really. I'm fine. I..."

"You're not fine at all!" Ashleigh shouted. Tom flinched. "Tom, you disappeared on me for an hour!" Tom was aware of people peering in, he felt acutely embarrassed and woozy, but made himself sit up. He looked at his wife. She continued, "I got everyone looking for you. When we found you, you were in a store cupboard thrashing around and screaming. You've cut your arm and you were practically unconscious for five minutes, at least! You are certainly not fine!"

Tom stood, shakily. "I just... umm... fainted! I got too hot! I want to go home. Please? You'd better drive!" He turned and left, weaving his way through the small crowd who had gathered to watch the drama. The paramedics stood watching him leave. Ashleigh went to follow him.

"Can you get him to sign a form saying we tried to...?" said Matthew.

Ashleigh looked at him, interrupting- "I don't think I can get him to do anything right now, do you?" She said and left, grabbed her children from the centre manager and followed her husband.

Chapter Fourteen

Rob and Tom sat in the bar at the Hotel Diglis, near the swanky canal basin in Worcester. The bar, one of those suffering constant refurbishment, was still dated and dull. Tom was nervous. He kept thinking of the rape and murder of the girl from the last pub he could recall and, although Ashleigh had told him he had only been gone for an hour and that the car hadn't moved in that time, it had felt so real. He could feel the heat of Jo's skin as he'd fucked her. He could smell the coppery scent of blood from the abdominal wound he had inflicted on her father, hear their cries of fear and pain.

Every time he thought about it, it made him feel sick again. He had lost seven pounds in the past two weeks since it happened, he just couldn't face eating.

The wound on his arm was real, although he was told he had scratched it during his 'collapse'. His climax had felt real too. And good, very good. And the hatred, the bitterness. That had felt awful. His breathing quickened as he recalled the feel of Jo's skull shattering with each blow of the rock. Shit. His breathing quickened and he thought he may puke again.

"Are you sure you're ok?" Rob asked.

Tom nodded weakly. What was going on? Was he going mad? Ashleigh had suggested he was- more than once. He closed his eyes against a wave of depression.

"You look like crap, Tom!" Rob told him.

"Cheers, mate!" he replied, "Erm... I've just got a bit of a headache."

"Have you taken anything for it?"

"Nah." Tom paused. "I'll be alright in a bit." They sat quietly for a while, sipping at their drinks. After a few moments Rob coughed to clear his throat. Tom looked at him.

"Come on, out with it!" Rob looked at him. Tom continued, "You've obviously got something on your mind, Rob!"

Rob looked out at the darkened garden. Down the slope, the River Severn raced along its path, swollen and treacherous. Its banks had flooded and all around water glistened where it ought not to be. Even the basement of the hotel they sat in had fallen victim, although those parts were off limits.

The bar was still busy enough, given its location alongside the river, overlooking the Worcester Cricket Ground and within spitting distance of the cathedral, it would always be a popular venue.

Sedate looking patrons sat in dignified silence, dotted around the bar and the large conservatory to the side of the hotel. Waitresses, discrete and professional – nothing like Jo - were trundling around, smiling at one customer, nodding at another, moving glasses, fetching more drinks, loading tables, clearing tables.

Rob's keys sat on the table in front of him, along with his mobile and Tom's. The GP, hearing about the 'faint', had advised Tom not to drive until epilepsy had been ruled out and the EEC, the tracing of his brain which would show this, was still two weeks away. Rob was his chauffeur tonight.

Rob looked back at Tom. "I spoke to your mother yesterday. She said you were still not talking to her." He took a pull at his pint. "She's in bits, mate!" Tom said nothing, draining the last of his own pint and placing it carefully on the table.

"Get you another?" Rob stood turned to go as Tom nodded. "Actually..." Tom called out, "can you make mine a JD, please? Straight." Rob looked surprised, but he nodded and in just moments, came back with another pint for himself and a Jack Daniels for his nephew.

"I need to talk to you about something, Tom." Tom said nothing, just picked up and took a sip of the smooth, smoky, amber liquid.

"The thing is... Look, mate, I know you're pissed off that we didn't tell you. It's just... your dad always thought you should be told. As time went on though, it was like it never happened. You were as much theirs as Helen and Peter and then Malcolm fell ill and your mum... well, she just couldn't cope with anything else on top."

Still Tom said nothing; he just looked at his uncle over the top of his glass.

Rob coughed again. "Right, son," he said. "Full disclosure!" He gave a small laugh. "For what it's worth!"

"What?" said Tom, placing his half empty glass down. "What are you on about?"

"I mean..." Rob swallowed. "I'll tell you anything you want to know."

"Huh!" said Tom. "Guess I kinda thought I knew it all by now!" Rob looked down and Tom shook his head, exhaling. "I guess not!"

"Sorry, mate!" Rob looked him in the eye, then looked away as if the contact was too much.

"Come on then!"

Rob took a deep breath. "Well?" Tom's tone was harsh. "Shit man, come on! I'm not about to start playing twenty frigging questions!"

"Christ, Tom! I just don't know where to begin. It was all such a long time ago."

"Yeah," replied Tom, "which means you all had over thirty five years to tell me. Do you know I've spent the last few months thinking how to tell my wife I may have inherited my dad's dementia? Hell, that was bad enough, but now... now I don't know what the fuck I may have inherited!"

"Keep your voice down. I..."

"Fuck that! So no one knows what a monumental pratt I am? At the tender age of 36, I find out all of a sudden that nothing was what I thought it was. Nothing was real!" He looked away, breathing hard.

"No!" Tom looked back at Rob. "It was real, Tom. All of it. We didn't keep it from you for a laugh, to hide the truth or anything. It was just... it was... Oh shit!" He hung his head. "Man, this is so hard!" he said.

"*You think so*? Tom's tone was still unforgiving. He picked up his JD and took a deep sip, blanching at the taste.

"When did you start drinking JD?" asked Rob.

Tom looked up. "That's what you brought me here to talk about is it? My drinking habits?" His tone was sarcastic and Rob looked surprised.

"Don't be an arse. Listen, your mum, she was..."

"Wait... Rose?"

"No," Rob replied. "Look, I don't know what to say, Tom, so I'll just start... You know I used to work at Bell Hall?" Bell Hall was an infamous psychiatric hospital in the nearby town of Ross on Wye, long since closed. Rob still worked as a psychiatric nurse, currently employed by the commissioning arm of the local NHS as a Psychiatric Nurse

Consultant although Tom wasn't sure what that meant. Something to do with improving care pathways.

"Yeah. So?" said Tom.

"It was in 1971. Your mother – your birth mother - was a patient in the unit. She was kind of a 'revolving door' patient. She'd come in for a few weeks, then get released. Then she came back again. We all knew her. She was only young..." He looked pained, turning his wedding ring around and around nervously.

"She was a manic depressive. Para-suicide, that means she tried to kill herself several times." He sighed. "I'm sorry Tom; I know this must be hard." Tom shook his head wryly, taking a drink. Rob didn't touch his.

Taking a deep breath, Rob continued, "One day, she'd been in, oh, about four weeks I suppose. Anyway, she disappeared and we didn't find her for three hours. She was eventually found wandering in the gardens, blood everywhere, clothes torn, no shoes. She was a mess." He picked up his pint and took a small sip. "She didn't say anything and we just thought... we thought maybe she'd fallen, hurt herself, you know? Anyway, she was in for the long haul this time. Months. The only known relative was an elderly mother and by then, well, she'd stopped visiting. We didn't know if she'd died or what..."

"And?" Tom was terse, sitting on the edge of her seat.

"And... about three months later, we... Oh fuck!"

"What?"

"A male nurse, he'd been there about five months or so I guess... Anyway, he was caught in her room..."

"They were having sex?"

"Not exactly."

"For fuck sake Rob, just tell me!"

"He was a lot older than her. In his late thirties by then. He was raping her. Apparently, she was covered in blood and just about unconscious." Tom groaned.

"They pulled him off her and called in a doctor. He came and examined her, by this time she was conscious again. It was around this time that I arrived. I talked to the doctor. He said she had been raped in both... well anyway... she was cut and battered. Bleeding a lot. And the doctor said..."

"The doctor said what?"

"The doctor said... Christ, she was pregnant mate. With you."

Ashleigh remained silent as Tom told her about his evening. She was sitting on their dark blue sofa, sat back comfortably amid scatter cushions decorated with varying amounts of crayon, felt tip pen and, unfortunately, new baby drool. The children were quiet upstairs. She gave Tom a coffee and sat holding his hand as he told her how the police had been called, but that the male nurse had disappeared by the time they arrived and it transpired that he had committed similar abuses at previous hospitals. Nothing that he was ever charged with apparently. Since then, he had disappeared.

There wasn't a lot of fuss, given her mental state. Everyone agreed that it was sad, sure, but maybe she'd wanted it. Anyway, that's what the unit administrators had suggested. Ashleigh shook her head. His mom had stayed on the psych unit, it was kind of planned to transfer her once she was due to give birth, but... Rob was unclear about the arrangements in any event and Tom got the distinct impression that no one was especially worried.

In the end, she had delivered, screaming and delirious, in her shitty little shared room at the psych hospital, with Rob arriving half-way through, a useless pair of junior psych nurses and a bitch of a hospital administrator acting as midwives. She had lost so much blood that she was never going to survive it, Rob had told him. He couldn't answer the question about why they hadn't called for help. Even after it was clear she was dying. The administrator's decision, he'd said. Wait and see, that's what she'd said. They called the psych doctor on call, but he said he couldn't get it. Flat tyre or something.

"But I don't understand," said Ashleigh with tears in her eyes, "how could they just stand there and watch her die?"

Tom shrugged.

"It's unbelievable!" Ashleigh wiped her face with her sleeve, leaving mascara streaks on her cheeks. "I mean, it's not as if it was even that long ago!"

He leaned forward to kiss her. "I know," he replied. "The poor thing..."

For a moment they sat in silence, considering the awfulness of the situation as Rob had explained it. Rob had gone as far as telling Tom that maybe it was for the best, after all, what kind of mother would she have made? A real one, Tom had replied.

Rob had looked dreadful, Tom told her. He'd said she was just about gone as her babies came into the world. One, healthy, squalling and pink, the other quieter, but still beautiful.

Anyway there had been some minimal debate about what to do, and how best to handle it. Still, no one thought to call the authorities. So, after much debate, Rob had been persuaded to intervene. He took the healthy one to his sister and brother in law, and they took him in as their own. Their desperate need for a child finally satisfied, they asked no questions about the circumstances and Rob told them only that the birth mother had died during labour.

Rob, his own wife pregnant at that time, six months gone - safe, you'd have thought – wanted his in-laws to have the chance of a child. The other baby was weaker. When the child turned blue, panting for breath, the administrator took him away to a treatment room. After a few moments, Rob had gone after her, leaving Tom, who was initially named Paul with the two junior mental health nurses.

Within an hour, the flustered mental health nurses were just told that the second baby had died at the same time as his mother and that the administrator would see to all necessary arrangements.

Tom sat with tears rolling down his face in the public bar of a classy hotel, heedless of the curious stares of fellow customers.

The sad irony was that a month after the illegal adoption of the sole surviving twin, Rob and his wife lost their son to a late miscarriage. And all their following four pregnancies too. Meanwhile, Tom was cherished. Loved. Part of a growing, happy family.

"So," Ashleigh's eyes were luminous with tears, "your real mother is dead, but..."

His eyes searched her face. "But...?"

"But who is your father, and where is your brother buried, and your mom, come to that? They must be buried somewhere, mustn't they?" Her voice was soft and contemplative. The only sounds were those of the humming fridge and the hamster on his wheel.

Tom shook his head. "I don't know. I didn't think to ask." Silently they sat, grieving for a woman they had not even known had existed, for a brother who died at birth and all the secrets which helped make Tom into the man he was, without knowing it.

They sat together, still holding hands until, a couple of hours later, they heard Elliott crying. Tom kissed his wife and went upstairs to collect him.

Tom was asleep. He was dreaming. He was in his bed, he was sure of it, yet the dream felt as real as the belly of his wife, pressing up against his backside.

In the dream his movements were furtive, sneaky. He was dirty and dishevelled and he could clearly taste the bitter tang of JD and cigarettes, and smell his own rank unwashed smell.

He journeyed miles, crossing rivers, impossibly travelling miles and miles, hopping on and off trucks, hitching his way around. Places he passed and stopped at were all familiar; Oxford, Manchester, Norwich though he saw no familiar landmarks. In each one he felt invisible, like a ghost. He watched, almost like a fast-forwarded movie, as he stole beer and cigarettes. He cringed as he saw himself in an isolated petrol station, beating some kid about the head, knocking out his teeth before stealing the contents of the till, several packs of fags and two bottles of Jack Daniels. He found himself finally in Marlborough, another place he had never been, but which seemed so familiar in the dream.

As he tossed and turned Ashleigh awoke, once to feed their son and the second time to watch in silent, helpless fear as her husband cried out in his sleep, moaning about blood and rage and loss and death.

Chapter Fifteen

The snake-like EEG leads were placed strategically on his head. Tom sat still and endured the ordeal in silence. Ashleigh was outside with Elliott in case he cried and disturbed the test. Once the leads were all in place, the technician, an extremely camp, but capable young man who bustled around the room, patting Tom's arm repeatedly. After a few moments, another man arrived and the technician seemed to defer to him. Both were silent whilst the test was conducted. Tom tried to read something in their mirrored pursed lips and furrowed brows as they stared at the computer screen in front of them.

"All done, Mr. Bearing!" said the technician cheerfully. The result will go back to your doctor and to your consultant."

"What consultant? Does it show anything?" asked Tom.

"Well... the tests are usually interpreted by a senior, then onto whichever consultant you are due to see. Did your GP not tell you who that was? Humm... I see...!"

The two exchanged a look and the second, more sombre of the two sat in the chair opposite Tom. He felt nervous.

"Well... er... Actually, really, there's nothing on the test to indicate any problems."

"Oh!" said Tom, "well that's good. *Isn't it?*"

"Umm..." said the first technician.

"What?" said Tom.

"Well, this certainly doesn't explain your symptoms. I think it's likely the GP will request further tests and get a consultant to see you after that."

"What sort of tests?" Tom was tense.

"Oh... well... there could be any number." He stood, "We'll send this on as a matter of urgency shall we? Get your GP to make up his mind what he's going to do next?"

Tom sat whilst the pair freed him of the electrodes and then stood, wiping off the conduction gel. It was all in his hair making it stand up at bizarre angles. He ran a hand through it. *Sod it, messy hair was the least of his problems. They clearly thought he was cracking up. Good job he hadn't told them what he had seen whilst they were taking the test. They would have had him committed.*

Inside the small, dark, old-fashioned room, the air was fetid and rank. A smell of decay and stale body odour permeated the room and a visible depression coloured everyone and everything grey, not just the shrunken, dying figure on the bed. A young woman sat beside her.

"Mom?"

The woman didn't answer although her eyes were open and focussed on a large wooden crucifix hanging on an otherwise bare white wall behind the girl's head.

"Let her be!" The girl sitting beside the bed jumped and turned. She hadn't heard her father enter the room. She nodded and hung her head, her hands lying listlessly in her lap.

Her father stood behind her and she could feel him smiling adoringly down at his wife. The woman shifted her gaze although her head didn't move. Her look softened as she caught the eyes of her husband over the head of their seated daughter as if she wasn't there.

"Move, girl," he said in a gruff, choked voice, moving closer to the bed. The girl shifted and rose to her feet, reaching out tenderly to touch her mother's hand. Imperceptibly, impossibly, her mother draw back from her touch and tears filled the girl's eyes.

"Momma!" she whispered. "I'm so sorry!"

"Best you just go, child!" said her father, not unkindly. She smiled at him through tear-filled eyes, then realised his tenderness was not for her; it was for his dying wife. She stood silently by the door, watching as her father leaned forward, taking the hand of his beloved spouse, gently stroking and patting it, bending his head to kiss it. Finally the dying woman closed her eyes, soft moans of pain from the putrid, open wound of her breast cancer emanating from her until she eventually she died. For a long time the man sat beside her, holding the hand of his dead wife.

At last, roused by the distant sound of crying infants, he turned to look at his only child. She flinched at the naked hatred on his face, and ran, bursting from the room as he glowered, cowed and frightened by his luminous anger. She fled to the relative safety of the nursery, closing and locking the door behind her, trying in vain to keep in the noise of her bastard children.

Chapter Sixteen

He was lost. Signs on the unfamiliar road rang bells, but he could not find one which directed him to the M5. If he could just find the motorway, Tom thought, he could orientate himself, and get home to Worcester. Ashleigh must be wondering where he was.

He drove on aware of nothing more than the roar of the tyres on the isolated streets. He passed several houses, large and expensive looking, but he saw no pedestrians, no one he could ask for directions.

Without warning, the car abruptly turned right and Tom sighed in relief. Up ahead was a sign for Manchester. He was shite at geography but even he knew Glastonbury was in Somerset and Manchester was like, several hundred miles in the opposite direction. Clearly it was another dream. He swallowed hard at the memory of his previous vision. He felt distant, cold, like he was driving through fog. There were no identifiable landmarks, people or anything remotely familiar. In fact, he could see nothing. Still, the car continued its involuntary journey. Tom laughed aloud in the silence of the cab. *Maybe it was a 'Chitty Chitty Bang Bang' dream? He had watched it just last week with Meg, perhaps that's all it was.*

Up ahead, Tom could see a turning to the left and a small, forested driveway. Without conscious effort, the car shifted down a gear and turned, sand and gravel flying into the air when he turned too fast. Tom took his hands from the wheel and grimaced out into the gloomy evening sky. The car skidded to a halt. Tom felt himself propelled forward and flung back in his seat, the seat belt tightening against his chest.

For several moments he sat; the engine still running, peering out into the darkness, waiting for something to happen. To the far right, down the side of the huge white house with black-stained timbers, emerged a figure. Tom waited. The figure, oblivious to the car, it seemed, peered out down the drive and crept around, glancing back nervously. Tom frowned.

He felt himself walking suddenly and glanced back towards the car, unsure of how he had gotten out and walked several paces away from it without realising. *Ah, dreams*, he thought. The door of the car was open and he reflexively turned back to close it, but instead found himself thrust forwards, towards the cowering figure.

His footsteps crunched on the hard, stony path. The building before him seemed familiar somehow. *Possibly a familiar style perhaps?* Approaching the figure, he recognised the girl, but was still trying to place her when she spoke.

"Oh, Tommy!" she whispered.

"Mary!" Her name popped into his head and he looked around, unsure if someone had spoken it aloud. She seemed hesitant, but stepped forward and he reached for her, grasping her to him and burying his face in her neck. She smelled unfamiliar, of soap and laundry powder. A memory surfaced like bubbles in the bath. He had seen the girl before. He tried again to recall where and then realised they were walking down the side of the house.

Up ahead of them was a practical square building, like a large white box squatting in the darkness, its windows frames arched and ornate against its blank utilitarian walls. Tom could see stars reflected in the glass, glinting, even in the dark.

A noise to his left startled him and he turned in fright. Mary laughed and he felt, rather than saw, some of her apprehension dissipate.

"Oh, Tommy!" she laughed, "It's just the cat!" He felt her take his hand and together they sneaked around the back of the building, twigs breaking underfoot. The cat sneaked around his feet and he pushed it to the side gently. It purred and arched its back against his legs.

"Bug off, kitty!" he pushed it away again.

"Oh, Tommy! Don't hurt him! Come here, Archie!" she whispered, picking up the cat.

They reached the front of the building and she let go of his hand, turning the handle and pushing hard at the huge door. It creaked and opened inwards. She turned to him, finger at her lips. "Shush!" she whispered, "Wait here!" Briefly, she disappeared inside. Seconds later, she reappeared and gestured him in, minus the cat. He walked inside, his guts tightening at the smell and feel of the place. When she turned, suddenly he could see, she was the girl from one of his visions or dreams, from months ago. The girl who had said no.

He gasped and she turned in alarm. "What?" He said nothing. She stepped back, a hand to her chest. "Tommy?" Her voice was low and anxious. Tom was finding it hard to breathe. "Tommy?" she said again, "What is it?"

Tom turned and sat heavily on what turned out to be a pew of some sort. Behind her, the room spread out and in the far end of the building, as white inside as out, was an enormous crucifix. To the sides of it Tom could see two tall, slim lecterns with delicate angled lights suspended above each. He shifted in his seat, to the left he could see an image of Jesus suspended from a cross and to the right a portrait of the Virgin Mary, head bowed in chaste repose.

Mary stepped tentatively forward, reaching out and touching his arm. He recoiled. A noise to the back of the chapel made them both jump and she laughed again, a small, delicate sound reverberating around the huge, cavernous room. "Its Archie," she whispered, "It's just my cat!" Tom turned back towards her.

"Tommy!" she repeated, an element of wonder in her voice. "Why did you come back?"

"For you!" He heard himself speak the words and felt panic billowing up in his chest. No, no. Fuck, no.

"Oh!" she breathed. She stepped forward and sat beside him. He turned to her and she took his hand.

"How can you feel so cold?" she asked him, "its summer!" Her face, her voice, this room, it all seemed so familiar and yet so foreign. He realised she was wearing a nightgown, a flimsy, flowery affair, high at the neck, prim at the breast and down to her ankles. Her feet were bare. He shivered. "Darling," she said, "are you cold?" She leaned forward and offered her lips to him. He could see her nipples through the thin material. Tom stood up hurriedly, making her jump backwards.

"Oh!" she said.

He walked quickly away from her, heading deeper into the small chapel, towards the cross.

"Tommy wait!" she rose to follow him and, at the same time, the door to the chapel opened with a painful creak as lights blinked on brightly above them, blinding them. Mary gave a moan of fright. Tom turned towards the door.

In the entrance stood a man, tall and hunched, silver white hair sparse on his head, a pale pink scalp showing through, patchy with liver spots.

"Daddy!" Mary swiped at tears sweeping down her face, "Daddy, oh no, please..."

"You whore!" he hissed, his eyes burning in his face, coals of anger visible in the artificial whiteness of the room. He walked towards them.

"You!" he spat, slowly turning to Tom. "You animal!"

"Daddy?" she said. Tom turned to her.

"Meghan?"

"Do not dare to speak that name!" The fury in the eyes of the man standing before him seemed to ignite more and Mary shrank back, sitting back on the pew she had just vacated, looking like a child. Tom could hear her moaning softly.

Tom turned towards the man, glancing at Mary in confusion. "What?" he said.

"My wife, my Meg, died. Because of you. As surely as if you had taken a gun and killed her. You killed my wife!"

"Daddy, oh God, please! Daddy!" Mary stood, her nightdress billowing at her feet from the open door behind them.

Tom snorted with laughter, "What the fuck...? I never even saw your wife. I was talking about my daughter!"

"Your daughter? Just how many bastards have you sired? We have had to have two of your bastard children here already. It killed my wife. My only love. Do you care? Did you even visit? Of course not. You took my daughter, my only child, and turned her into a whore! The shame of it. The shock, it killed my Meg. It caused the cancer that ate her up from the inside."

"Daddy!" By now Mary was wailing.

"What are you talking about? What children? Mary, what is he talking about?"

Mary sobbed louder and flopped to the floor, her nightdress riding up to expose her knees.

"Get off the floor! Get up! You harlot!" her father roared, "why do you prostrate yourself before this, this animal? Mary, you killed your own mother! She died of shame!"

"No, Daddy, no! I'm sorry! I'm so sorry!" Still on the floor she crawled towards her father, putting her hand out, pleadingly. Angrily he knocked it away, swatting her as though she was a fly, a wasp, a parasite seeking to suck on his flesh. She cringed at his feet and, reaching down, he swatted her again, across the side of her head.

"You... you animal. You raped my daughter. You turned her into a harlot. I wish I had a gun, I would have shot you then!"

"Daddy, no!" Mary was pulling at him; again he swatted her away like a fly.

"Don't you fucking hit her!" Tom heard the fury in his voice and as he turned and moved towards the man, Mary's father whirled around and reached across to the alter, which lay three feet from him. He grabbed an immense brass candle stick, sending the thick, white candle clattering to the floor. Turning back, he brandished it like a sword, almost comically trying to lift it despite its heft.

Tom advanced slowly, sneering as he watched him try to raise the candlestick to use as a weapon.

He curled his lips, a cruel grin stretched across his face. "Wish you had that gun *now*, eh?" he said, bending down and effortlessly taking the instrument from the man.

"No, Tommy! *No!*" Mary scrambled backwards as Tom raised the candlestick high above his head.

He shoved and the man fell backwards, stumbling against the alter table. Tom saw himself as he raised the weapon and Mary fell back too, knocking items off of the top, which clattered and fell.

The first blow made Tom dizzy, but he saw himself raise the instrument again.

Mary stood and rushed forward, "Daddy!" she cried. Tom half turned and put his hand up to stop her.

From the side, a punch landed on his temple and Tom yelled out. Mary cringed and her father crowed, "You will rot in hell for what you have done!" he cried. Mary grabbed at his arm as he reached again, fingers clenched in a clumsy fist thrust once more at Tom. But Tom, with the grace of a cat, swung around, dropped the candlestick, and launched his own fist, straight at the man's nose. He connected and watched in fascinated horror as blood spurted out, a fountain of glistening red spilled on to the floor of the rustic chapel.

Tom could hear manic laughter and realised it came from him. Mary screamed. Her father rallied, steadied himself, and reached again to the altar, grappling for balance and pulling another of the religious icons towards him, a knife of some description, heavy, ornate, sharp.

"Ha!" he yelled, "I've already called the police, you bastard! You won't get away with it *this* time!"

He swung the knife around towards Tom, catching his denim shirt. Blood beaded up though a rip in the fabric. The man laughed, oblivious to tears coursing down his face. And Tom, watching as though seeing it all on a movie screen, saw himself launch at the man and knock him to the ground. His movements fluid with fury, he grabed up the candlestick and knocked the knife out of his opponent's hands. It dropped to floor with a tremendous clatter which reverberated around the chapel. Tom heaved his weapon aloft and brought it down, with tremendous force and precise aim, onto the skull of the man, laid prostrate on the hallowed ground before him.

Mary screamed and ran to her father's side. "Daddy! Daddy! Oh God, he was right! You are the devil! Oh God, I'll see you burn in hell for this!"

Ignoring her cries and attempts to reach her father again and Tom, all reason lost, bashed the man who had obstructed him in his desire, obliterating his flesh and surrendering him to the heaven he had longed for since the death of his wife.

Chapter Seventeen

Daylight streamed in, uncensored. Tom woke, sniffed, stretched and yawned. He cleared his throat and scratched his balls before rubbing sleep from his eyes. Man, what a freaking weird dream. He swung his legs over to the side and encountered a hard, cold stone floor. Opening his eyes wide, shielding his face from the morning glare, trying to orientate himself. Shadows flitted across the windows and he struggled to see through the blur of sleep-filled eyes.

Intellectually he knew that the events he recalled had been a dream and had fully expected to wake up in his bed – God willing – or, at worst, with paramedics surrounding him and watching him drool like an idiot.

A noise from the corner, a dark and shadowy spot where the rough white corners of the chapel met, caught his attention and he stood and turned his body in the direction of the sound. In spite of the brilliance of the day, the gloominess in the corner caused him to struggle to see the outline clearly. Slowly, his eyes adjusted. When he did fully understand what he was looking at, he gasped in horror and stepped back involuntarily, stumbling and falling down heavily onto the hard pew behind him.

The unlikely tableau before him actually led him to pinch himself several times, trying to make himself wake up. On the floor, the bloodied, still figure of a man dressed in pyjamas lay prostate, a halo of blood glistening around his head. He could not help but glance up at the image which framed his death bed, that of Jesus on the cross with beseeching peasants prostrate at his feet.

At his side lay Mary, the girl Tom now recognised from the earlier vision, when she'd begged and pleaded but still he had fucked her.

Tom felt panic rising in his throat. He swallowed bile which filled his mouth. *Was she dead too? Why was this dream taking so long? It must be a dream. It must be.* Tentatively he walked towards her, but a sound from the rear of the building made his head snap around.

He stood again, unsteady and frightened. The girl looked up as a figure walked steadily towards them, a policeman of some sort; utility hardware hanging heavily from his hip. Tom did not recognise the uniform, not the standard UK police issue, as far as he was aware.

From the point of view of a casual spectator, Tom watched as the girl, dripping with her father's blood, half rose, beseeching the police officer to help her. She pointed at Tom and he could see her lips move, knew she was blaming him, but he could not hear the words. The cop glanced around, seeing Tom, but not acknowledging him. Shifting the weight of his armoury at his hip, he lent forward, reached out and placed two fingers at the precise aspect of the carotid artery of the prone figure. Tom could see his head bow as he registered the lack of a pulse, the lack of life.

Mary realised this from the policeman's stance and once more began wailing and screaming. She was rocking on her haunches and, for a moment or so, the policeman seemed unsure of what to do, but, roughly, he reached down, tugging her away from the body.

Tom glanced towards the door, fully expecting to see his wife, but there was only one policemen standing in the glare of the sun, confusion on his face as he tried to make sense of the scene before him.

The cooling body of the man lay on the ground. Sunlight shimmered and danced around the bleached white walls, bounced off the immense black crucifix lit by the Christmas like blue and white of the lights from the police car outside.

Ten minutes later, by the time the police man too, laid dead, a single wound to his heart drip, drip, dripping to the hard stone floor, the girl once more lay prostrate beside the body of her dead father. Tom noticed that darkness had once again fallen. It filled the desolate space of the chapel with the stench of death and despair. He felt sick, dizzy; the room seemed to spin like an unscheduled ride on a nightmare fair-ground ride.

The arrival of more police cars outside, sirens wailing and lights made disco patterns on the walls, breaking up the inky darkness. Armed police by the dozen, all with weapons now trained on him, visible through coloured, arched windows, served only to confirm what he now knew, the darkness came not from the sky, it came from himself.

Chapter Eighteen

The visions seemed to have just stopped. Months passed. The last one, the chapel thing or the 'big one', as it was known, made Tom request every test known to man his GP was willing to pursue. All clear. By the end of the tests, the visions had disappeared, although it took a while for Tom to really believe it.

Two years passed in a blur, yet Tom had seen himself commit crimes so horrific he still woke sweating from his dreams. A year after the last one Rob and Tom were still cool with each other; lots had been said and there was the issue of the secrets Rob had kept, Tom found it hard to let that go. Pauline continued to drink, Rose continued to avoid the issue of his adoption, he and Ash were as happy as ever and the children grew and thrived.

A few months after a birthday party for two-year-old Elliott, Rob called Tom at work.

"Can you talk, son?" he asked.

"I guess. Everything ok?" His tone was cautious.

"Yeah, um... I wondered if you and I could meet. For a drink?"

Tom paused. "Any particular reason?"

It was Rob's turn to pause, "Well, to catch up... you know..." He paused, "Sorry we missed the party. It would be good to see you."

Tom sighed. "Yeah, I dunno... It's pretty busy at the moment!"

"Please? Come on! I'm buying!" Rob was clearly trying to restore their previous relationship and Tom felt small for denying him. Clearly Rob had had his reasons for not telling him, and at the end of the day, it was really up to Rose, in his father's absence, to be the one to spill the beans. So, she had chosen to keep the secret. It was all a long time ago.

Tom gave a brief, decisive laugh, "Sure, ok," he said, "Why not! What are you thinking?"

Rob laughed too, "Well," he said, "Maybe we should avoid the Diglis! Think maybe we outstayed our welcome there!"

Tom thought for a moment to consider the options. Rob beat him to it. "Hummm..." he mused, "how about the Cov Arms, on the Stratford Road?" A somewhat unusual choice; a quiet, out of the way pub they had rarely visited.

"OK," said Tom dubiously. "When are you free?"

"Tomorrow any good?" Rob's tone was light and the disquiet Tom had been feeling was gradually dispelled.

"Yeah, ok," he replied. "I'll just check..."

"With Ashleigh!" Rob finished the sentence for him.

"Well... you know, it's just cos the kids..."

"I know! I'm just teasing! No problem. Lunch time or evening? Won't be a late one though. I'm working Sunday."

"Working on a weekend? How come?"

Rob exhaled in mock exasperation, "Don't ask! Bloody job is driving me mad! I'll be on the other side of the desk soon, just wait! It'll be me that needs committing! Anyway, see you there then or do you want me to drive?"

"Nah, I'll see you there. About 7:30?"

They agreed, signed off, and Tom went to talk to Ash. For some time it seemed she had been pushing for him to make things up with Rob, but she was uncharacteristically silent when he told her the arrangements.

"Come on, babe," Tom sighed and leaned against the kitchen counter, nearby, Ash was ironing.

"'Come on, babe', what?" she asked, folding an impossibly small T-shirt with a faded transfer of Thomas the Tank Engine on the front, belonging to their son.

Tom watched her, waiting while Meg wandered into the kitchen, opened the fridge, withdrew a bottle of milk, swigged from it and replaced it before wandering back out, totally oblivious to her parents standing watching her. Both laughed as she went back into the lounge. They heard her flop back onto the sofa and the sound of The Simpsons waft through before she kicked the door shut with a bang.

Upstairs, the sounds of Elliott stirring floated down, but he settled again and Tom turned back to Ashleigh. He waited.

"What?" she repeated.

"If you don't want me to go out, just say, love."

She concentrated on her ironing, saying nothing.

"Ash", Tom suppressed a sigh, "what is it?"

She picked up an ancient, flowered Ikea quilt-cover from the basket behind her and spent a moment or so folding it in preparation for ironing. She cleared her throat, standing the iron up carefully so it wouldn't scorch the fabric.

"I don't know... I'm not sure I trust him now. He's up to something!"

Tom raised his eyebrows, "Who? Rob? What do you mean?" he asked, "What makes you think that?"

Ash shook her head, smoothing the creases out with her hand before picking up the iron.

"It's just... I don't know babe. I've got a... a bad feeling about him." Tom leaned back against the kitchen counter, a half smile on his face.

"Since when?" he asked. "Bloody hell! Last month you were moaning at me to invite them to the party, now you have a 'bad feeling'?" He made quotation marks in the air. She rolled her eyes. "Oh God," said Tom, pretending to hold his head in despair, "don't say it's your turn now! We'll both end up as patients of Rob's in that case!"

"Don't even joke about it!" she said as she flipped the quilt over. "I know it sounds ridiculous, it's just... oh, sorry! Just ignore me!" She used the iron to squirt water on the quilt to help with the heavier creases. Eventually she looked up. "Can you honestly tell me..."

"Tell you what?"

She sighed and laid the finished, folded quilt on the growing pile behind her. She picked up a white school blouse of Meghan's and shook it.

"I just don't know... I don't know if we ever had the full story... Do you?"

"No," said Tom, standing up, "maybe not. Come on though baby; tell me what you're thinking, I mean, what else could there be?"

Ashleigh took a deep breath and put the iron down on the holding tray again. She stood upright. "Ever since your mom told you..." Tom waited. "Since then, Rob has seemed a bit... odd. Cagey."

"When? We've hardly seen them for months." She shrugged. "So you think there is more to tell? That he knows more about it?"

He shook his head, "I dunno Ash, he knows we've been pissed off about the whole secrecy thing, but it's not just down to Rob, is it? Mom

75

really should have said something, but I can sort of see why she didn't. Can't you?"

She shrugged. "I don't know!" She re-started her ironing. "I mean, what more could there be? More about your real mom? Your dad?" Tom said nothing. "Seriously love," she said, "you know the circumstances of your poor mum's pregnancy, the birth, the weird adoption. I'm just letting my imagination run away with me, aren't I? What else could there be?" She laughed and added Meg's shirt to the pile.

"What things?" Tom's face was serious and Ash was puzzled. "Well, you said your imagination was running away with you. What sort of things are you imagining?"

She gave a mock shudder, "Oh God, I don't know! Maybe your father is still around here somewhere? Maybe your mom is still alive, in the hospital and they stole you! Oh God, maybe you were one of triplets or something?"

"Well, it's clearly what bloody Pauline was on about at the party that time." He paused, looking thoughtful.

"What?" she said.

"Humm..." he said slowly, "I don't think my father, my *real* father could still be around, why would they lie about that? And I really don't believe – well - I guess I don't want to believe my Mom's alive and still in some nut-house somewhere, wondering what the hell happened to her babies. I guess we do at least know that twins do run in my family - on my mother's side anyway. We don't know anything really about my dad- my natural father's side do we?"

"No, but then if he is a rapist, do we really want to? Do you think Rob knows more about that then? Maybe that's why he wants to talk to you?" Tom moved away and switched on the kettle.

"Who knows!" he said, spooning coffee into two cups. "I can't be doing with all that crap again!" Drink love? U-ho," he turned at the sound of wails coming from upstairs, "Sounds like young master Elliott's awake. I'll go get him!"

He turned to go. "Tom?" He stopped at the tone of her voice and turned around.

"Maybe we should find out more?" He said nothing for a moment, considering.

"Maybe," she continued, "where are they buried? I would like to know that at least." He nodded, but before he could reply, Elliott, upstairs, wailed even louder and Tom grinned at her. "Well, I'll find out later from Rob, won't I?" He left and went to fetch his son.

In the pub, no longer able to stand the taste of Jack Daniels, Tom was back to drinking a pint of Carling.

The Coventry Arms was something of an odd pub; forever changing hands and one day packed to the rafters, the next, as deserted as a ghost town. It was about a fifteen minute drive out from Tom's house and they passed the time talking about work and anything else neutral they could think of.

Once in the almost empty pub, they took a seat near a picture window which framed the open countryside at the rear of the pub. The odd farm building was dotted here and there breaking up the scenery. The pleasant sound of grazing sheep wafted in through the partially open windows, interspersed by the sound of an occasional passing car.

Behind the bar, a tall, thin, dark-haired barmaid was serving someone who must be a local; tatty Barbour-style faded green jacket with corduroy collar, torn pockets and a pair of ripped green, muddy wellies. At his side was a shaggy, muddy collie dog, sitting patiently at her master's side, totally oblivious to anything except him.

"Given up on the hard stuff, eh?" said Rob as they settled down at their table. Tom smiled.

"So... how have you been?" Rob's tone was jovial, but Tom could detect an undercurrent of tension behind it.

"Oh, fine. Yeah, good thanks. How's Pauline?"

"Oh... you know. The same." Tom acknowledged the unspoken truth. They sat in silence for a moment.

"How about your visions?" Rob's tone was direct, a reflection of his professional confidence. Tom smiled.

"Not had any episodes for ages!" Rob smiled. The both took sips of their beer.

"Rob..?" Tom's hesitant tone made Rob look up. Tom continued. "You and Pauline..." he paused again, but the look on Rob's face seemed to give him permission to continue. "Did you ever get tested? To see what the problem was? With having babies I mean?" At the bar, the owner of the dog was handing over coins for another pint. His dog lay on the floor beneath the small round table to the side, her eyes never leaving her owner.

Rob sighed. "It was different then." He took a sip of his pint, then replaced it carefully back on the table. "It just wasn't meant to happen for us." Tom nodded and picked up his own drink. "I mean," Rob said, conspiratorially, "who wants to get poked and pulled about in that department, only to be told it's not working properly!" He gave a wry laugh. "Anyhow, Pauline refused point blank to even talk to the docs about it. Said it was bloody karma or something!" He gazed out of the window towards the river. "That's when she started drinking."

Tom nodded. "She didn't drink at all when Colin was alive." In fact her first husband had been the heavy drinker at that point, but neither of them saw the need to bring that up.

"She and Colin never got around to trying. She said Colin was too busy building up his company and making money to get bogged down with kids. Maybe that was the problem. Maybe then- we just left it too late."

Tom could think of nothing to say for a moment, so he remained silent. Rob seemed to shake himself and he gave a sad little laugh, picking up his pint and taking another sip. "Ash ok? And the kids?" he asked again.

"You asked me that already!" he said, but he pulled out his mobile phone to show Rob some recent baby pictures anyway.

"Oh, wow. He's lost that chunky baby look totally, hasn't he? He's a proper little man now!" Rob cleared his throat, "I hear it's going to be nice weather next weekend."

"Is it?"

Rob nodded. "Maybe we could all take the kids to the Safari Park near Kiddy or something? We haven't seen them for ages."

Tom shrugged. "Yeah, I'll check with Ash. Meg's got a lot of fights booked at the moment. Not sure where she is next weekend."

They spent a few minutes discussing Meghan's blossoming career in Judo, rated very highly for one her age. In fact, there was only one other girl in her class better than her around at the moment. "Funny thing," said Tom, "she lives in Worcester too! Little blond girl. Tough little thing! Sian something I think."

"Yeah," said Rob, "I've seen her picture in the Worcester News. They reckon she's headed for the Olympics in a few years."

"Yeah? Not sure Meg's *that* committed!"

Uncomfortable silence descended again for a moment or so. Rob cleared his throat. "Got something on your mind, Rob?"

"I never could keep things from..." He realised what he had been about to say and the sentence tailed off.

"I don't know about that!" Tom said, evenly. "But if you've something you want to say...?" Rob sighed. "I was talking to Pauline. It wasn't her idea or anything, don't get me wrong..."

"What?" Tom was careful to avoid any negative tone to creep into his voice.

"After what happened, we were saying that... Well, Pauline and Rose, they thought... Oh hell. They thought that maybe you would want to know more about your father. Even though he..." His voice tailed off.

"Umm..." Tom scratched his ear. "I think it may be a good idea. Ash and I were talking about it earlier as it happens."

"So..." Rob's tone was gentle. "Are you going to, you know, do some research or anything?"

He hesitated, "Yeah!"

"You are?" Rob's face showed his surprise.

"I am!" Even Tom was surprised how definite he felt.

Rob took a long sip of his drink. "Good for you!" he said. "Well... I can help, if you'd like?"

"Oh no, don't bother," said Tom, "I'm sure you've got..."

"It's no bother," replied Rob. "Anything I can do to help. You know that son!" He drained his glass and stood, "get you another?" he asked.

Chapter Eighteen

"Tom!" He awoke to find Ashleigh pulling on his arm, shaking him, fear and irritation in her voice in equal parts. "Tom!"

"What?" he sat up hurriedly, blinking furiously and pushing a hand up through his hair, making it stick up comically, like the skinny one from Laurel and Hardy.

"What? What?" He looked wildly around the room, but could see no signs of anything amiss. He turned to look at her. She was sat up in bed staring at him.

"Come on Ashleigh! What? Did you hear a noise? Is it the kids? What?"

"Don't you know? You were shouting in your sleep! Really loud," she paused as they heard Elliott wailing in his room down the hall, piercing the stillness of the night. "See, I told you, you were bloody noisy!" Tom pulled back the quilt to climb out of bed. "I'll go!" Ashleigh said.

Their door squeaked open and Meg's tousled head peeked around. Behind her the wails of the baby masked the squeaking of the hamster wheel.

"Why is Daddy shouting?" she asked in a deliciously sleepy voice. "Is his head all funny again?"

Ashleigh threw Tom a look and climbed out of bed, reaching for her dressing gown. She addressed her daughter whilst looking at her husband, "Go back to sleep, Meggie! It's three o'clock in the morning!"

Glaring comically at Tom she turned to go.

"I'm sorry!" he said, "It's not my fault! I don't know what I was dreaming about!"

Ash tutted, shook her head in mock disgust, and disappeared from the room. "Men!" she said. Tom lay back listening to her pad down the hall, hand in hand with Meg, then her soft whispering to their son as she tried to coax him back to sleep.

He was dead to the world when she came back to bed and all they had time to discuss that morning, between the rush of getting Meghan ready for her judo comp and Elliott's terrible-two's tantrums was to tell her he really couldn't recall what the dream had been about. She rolled her eyes, but kissed him and bundled Elliott into a new outfit as he'd just wet himself all over the last one. Again.

The journey itself was uneventful, unless you can count being cut up by a geriatric in a dark purple Volvo, twice. Tom had been to Bristol many times and almost knew his way around, bypassing the chaotic city centre to get to the competition ground in the south of the town. They were slightly rushed as Elliott had decided to throw Meghan's obi – the belt for her judo uniform – out of the window. Cue Meg screaming, Ashleigh yelling and Tom turning the car around and sifting through crap and foliage to find the sodding thing. At least, being orange, it was relatively easy to spot.

For everyone but Meg, the whole thing – preparation, having to weigh in hours before the fighting started, was tedious and dull, but since Meg had been placed in the regional finals, it had got far more exciting.

Sitting on the hard competition seats nearly five hours later, he sat watching as Meg warmed up on the mat. Her arch judo enemy, petite blond Sian, warming-up by her side. He smiled as he saw them laughing and whispering together, heard their giggles from where he sat; fierce rivals or not, they were still just kids.

Meg was confident and hyper. He smiled and settled down to watch the numerous games which compiled the competition. It always amazed him how often and how hard his young daughter could fight - well, all the kids in the competition really. Hour after hour they battled; most of them with a smile on their faces as they pushed and pulled at each other, seeking the edge they needed to win.

Several sets of parents were dotted around the place. Most of them he recognised. Tom could see Sian's mom sitting over on the far side, next to their coach, both of whom were clearly excited and hollering encouragement at a red-faced, sweaty Sian.

It was only when Sian had Meg on the floor, Ash screaming again, this time in support of her daring little girl – she always got very overexcited at these things - and Elliott racing around behind them, that Tom sat suddenly very still. Ashleigh was oblivious. Tom felt the world tilt as he clearly heard the referee say, Meghan on her back with Sian locking her there, 'you have been charged with murdering...' Tom looked at the ref puzzled, *why would he say that?* He shook his head to dispel the image. Neither of the two corner care judges reacted.

What the...? Nah! He was tired. The Shawshank Redemption had been on TV a few days ago. It was only when he heard the referee tell the squirming girls that *'[he] had been found guilty of the killing of Lay Minister Walter Arthur Passlet and Police Officer Joseph Allen Kielty'* that Tom remembered his dream. Shivers raced down his spine and he felt sweat beads pop out on his forehead. He shook slightly, as he remembered.

It had been a graphic re-enactment of the murders in the chapel and the shouts that had woken his entire family, had been him trying to escape the legions of armed police who had him surrounded. So, he thought, his heart sinking, *it was starting again.* His head slumped and Ash turned to him, hitting him lightly on the arm.

"Ash..." he muttered.

"Oh, Tom! Don't be so dramatic! She did brilliantly! And she'll still be placed." She shook her head, "God, that Sian's good though, isn't she? Elliott, stop it. Do *not* pour your coke into Mrs Hardy's handbag! Elliott, stop! Oh, Tom *do* something! I'm so sorry, Mrs Hardy!"

Chapter Nineteen

The Christmas decorations were already driving Ashleigh mad. The kids were a nightmare, constantly on about Father-sodding-Christmas. In between, she was holding the fort down at work – bloody Wendy, off sick again - coping with an increasingly emotional Rose, stressed about Tom and Rob's joint efforts to find more about the man who had fathered Tom, and worried to death about Tom now his 'visions' seemed to have started again.

Privately, she thought it was due to Rob and Tom chasing information about the bastard rapist who left such a mess behind him, then disappeared like a puff of smoke in the wind. She refused to consider that her husband might be in the throes of a mental breakdown. Tom was simply trying to find out where his brother and mother had been buried, although Rob was the one looking into this; they both thought he would have more access to anyone who may know. It would stress anyone.

Just then, Elliott came barrelling into the lounge, arms and legs pumping like a piston as he ran around shouting at inanimate objects and shooting them before he fell into the Christmas tree, knocking it over for the third time in four days.

"Elliott!" Ashleigh exclaimed, exasperated. The child stood, stopped jumping around in the fallen contents of the tree and stood, stock still, staring at his mother with an intensity in his eyes that shocked her. Glass crunched and tinkled under his feet. "Come on, little man!" she said, holding her hand out, "come and help me pick the tree up, again!" With careful deliberation, Elliott leaned down and picked up a fragile, crystal bauble, one handed down to her from her grandmother. She smiled at him and reached out to take it, instead he crushed it to him, pulling it against the tin buckle of his cowboy belt.

"Careful, sweetie," she said, reaching out to take it. Elliott stood and stared, ignoring the proffered hand. His thick blond hair stuck up from his head and his little cowboy outfit, ripped and worn out though it was, was still too big for his two and a half year old frame, but he rarely consented to wear anything else. He clapped his hands in tighter and she heard the fragile glass shatter. He dropped the pieces like confetti into the debris of the Christmas tree. Ashleigh gasped and pulled her hand back.

Elliott had a weird little smirk on his face and refused to move, even as she struggled to get past him to collect all the baubles and other hand-made ornaments, trying frantically to pick up razor sharp shards.

"Elliott!" she was on her knees, collecting items and putting them onto the sofa behind her for safe keeping. "That was naughty!" She sat up. "Did you cut your hand?" She took his hand and he let her, but there were no cuts or blood that she could see.

"You could have hurt yourself!" she told him, taking his arm and trying to manoeuvre him back so he didn't step on anything else. "Nanny Gold gave me that and I'm sad that you broke it. You should apologise, ok?"

Elliott continued to stare at her, his head on the side, until, discomforted, she concentrated on clearing up.

She sighed and reached around him, putting the tree back together haphazardly, past caring how ornate it looked. After all this was the fifth time she had decorated the bloody thing this year so far. "There!" she said, standing and turning to her son, leaning forward to pick up the last delicate glass snow flake off the sofa where it had landed. Elliott stood and watched her dress it, using her hands to scrape up some loose twigs, casualties from where it had fallen.

"Let's try to keep it up this time, shall we?" She was aware of the tenor of her voice and smiled to take the sting out of the words.

Elliott smiled back at her; he was so cute, she was unable to stay cross with him for any length of time... She carefully placed the delicate snow flake back on the tree and lent over to drop the twigs into the rubbish bin. She felt Elliott lean past her and groan as he shoved the tree with all his infant might, pushing it back over, where it smacked into the window and knocked bits and pieces off of the sill, some of which shattered on the floor. She jumped back.

"Elliott?" she gasped, "*Why did you do that?*" As she watched, he stepped forward and ground his foot into the crystal snow-flake, shattering it into the carpet. She stared at him, aghast. He just smiled at her once more and resumed his racing and indiscriminate shooting.

"I'm gonna kill you, Sam!" he yelled, "bang, bang, you dead!" Slowly Ashleigh sank onto the edge of the dark blue sofa, watching her son play, her hand at her throat.

"I'm telling you, Tom, you didn't see him!" Tom was sat at the kitchen table trying to read the *Sun Newspaper*.

"Oh come on, love, it's just high spirits!" His eyes widened at the model on page three and he quickly turned the page. Ashleigh didn't respond to their usual joke, she was washing up with obvious fury, slamming plates and cups down on the draining board.

"Ashleigh?" She ignored him. He stood and went over to the sink, "Ash? Come on, what is it?"

She turned around to face him and he saw tears glistening in her eyes. "Bloody hell!" he said, "what did he do?"

"It wasn't so much that he wrecked the tree..." she shivered and shook her head, "Tom, it was the look on his face. He was like a different child. He broke those things deliberately, to be nasty. Not like Elliott. He was... hateful."

"Maybe he was just getting carried away? Tinsel-itis? It *is* nearly Christmas. And little boys are very boisterous!" He grinned, "That's where the word 'boy' comes from I reckon!" Still she didn't smile.

She shivered again. "Yeah, right. And... you know, he was running around, pretending to be killing people, shooting everything in sight and yelling that he was a murderer." She mimicked him 'I'll bash your head in!' and "I'll shoot you dead! I'm just like my dad!" She shook her head and turned back to her washing up, more temperate this time, "oh yeah, and he said he was going to kill his brother, he called him Sam! It was so weird!" She didn't notice Tom stood behind her, and this time, he was the one shivering.

She turned on her heel, headed into the kitchen, snatching her coat from the back of a chair.

"I'm going for a walk," she said "I... need some fresh air". The stiffness in her body and the thinness of her lips told him to let her go without saying another word.

Chapter Twenty

Ashleigh raced down the Droitwich Road. She was heading towards Brewstairs, where Tom had worked for seven years; she knew the way by rote. She was aware that she was driving erratically, but thought that if she was stopped for speeding, she may just be able to get a police escort, given the circumstances.

She arrived at reception and Lynn, the office manager, met her.

"How is he?" Ashleigh was racing through the office suite, knowing her way to the canteen, where she had been told Tom was. Lynn was racing to keep up, her three inch spike-heeled shoes clattering on the lino floor.

They reached the canteen and Ash raced over to Tom's side. "Sweetheart!" she cried, throwing her handbag onto the battered, scratched table, throwing herself to the floor to sit beside her husband.

Without waiting for him to answer, she turned to Max, Tom's manager. "Why is the ambulance not here yet?" she asked.

"No ambulance!" Tom whispered.

"He wouldn't let us call one!" Max was sheepish, "By the time we got around to it, he came to and got really agitated when we tried to convince him!"

"Oh, Tom!" Ashleigh leaned in to hug him, "why? You need to get checked out, love!"

"We did try, honestly!" said Lynn, wringing her hands.

Tom leaned against his wife, resting his head on her shoulder momentarily. Though a little pale, she thought he looked ok. He was a bit sweaty, but she thought perhaps this was inevitable, given the fact that about eight or nine people were all staring at him like a specimen in a jar.

He said something but Ashleigh didn't hear it. "What love?" she said, stroking his cheek.

"...home!" said Tom quietly.

"Don't you think we should take you to see Dr..."

"I want to go home!" His voice was getting stronger and he leaned forward, forcing her to sit back on her haunches. Max and Lynn stood back to the side, looking uncomfortable.

"Umm... we'll bring his car back, Ash!" said Max.

"Yeah," said Lynn, glancing at Max, "I'll drive it round and Max can bring me back to work!" Max nodded.

"Right, right!" he said brightly. Something about the way Lynn and Alex eyed each other made Ash take a second glance, but she ignored it, she was trying to help a very shaken Tom to his feet. For a moment or so, he wobbled and then steadied himself.

"Sorry, Max!" he said, "racing around too much, not eaten properly today!" Ash looked baffled. It wasn't quite lunch time and she knew he had eaten a big breakfast, like he always did. She didn't contradict him though.

Together they made their way through the small industrial complex and out the back towards her car, hastily parked in the loading bay.

She unlocked the car and they climbed in. She watched carefully as he did up his seat belt. He looked straight ahead, studiously ignoring her obvious anxiety.

"Tom," She cleared her throat, clearing intending on trying to persuade him.

"Just drive!" His tone was snappy and she shot him a look. "Sorry!" he said, adding "Please!"

"I really think you should see the GP, babe." She said.

"No!" he replied shortly.

"Tom!" The hurt she was feeling was evident in her tone.

"Please, Ashleigh!" he said, "just... let's go home!"

Her hand was shaky as she put the key in the ignition and turned it. The car spluttered and turned over but didn't start. She tried again, this time the engine fired up. She fastened her own seat belt and put the car into gear. They drove in silence for a moment or so until she tried again. "Sweetheart?" He ignored her, looking resolutely out of the windscreen. "Tom?"

"Oh shit, Ash, please!" He said, dropping his head into his hands. "Please, just let's get home. I'll explain then."

"For goodness sake!" she cried, "you had a fit!" Her teeth were gritted and she was red-faced and close to tears. "*Why are you being such a flaming arse*? You need to see the doctor!"

She pulled the car over, into the car park of a large pub in between Droitwich and Worcester. Tom sighed. "Ashleigh," he said, "it wasn't a fit!" Turning in his seat he looked at her, reaching over to take her hand clenched tightly on the steering wheel. "Ash?"

"Lynn said... she said you'd collapsed... she said it was a fit!" She shook her head. "What the hell was it then?" Tom closed his eyes. "Oh, Tom, oh God, come on! You're killing me here!" Tears spilled from her eyes.

His tone was gentle. "Ashleigh? Love? Let's just go home, eh? We can talk there!" She wiped the tears from her eyes took a deep breath and nodded.

"OK!" she said, putting the car into gear and driving away.

They walked into the house. It was cold, given the time of day, the heating had not yet come on and Ash kept her coat on when she sat at the kitchen table. Tom busied himself for a moment, putting the kettle on, turning the heating boiler switch to constant and returning to the kitchen, made tea for the two of them. Ashleigh sat still and dignified, silent and cool.

Tom sat at the table and gave her the tea. Still she sat not speaking. He sighed.

"It wasn't a fit."

Ashleigh picked up her tea. She blew on it to cool it and took a tentative sip, wincing when it burnt her tongue. Tom smiled at her and she gave him a watery smile back.

"Come on then," she said, "Out with it!"

He took a deep breath. "Fuck!" he said. Ashleigh raised her eyebrows, waiting.

He sipped his tea. "This is gonna sound really nuts!"

"Yeah? So what's new!" she saw his look and smiled. "OK!" she said, "What's going on Tom?" She reached across the table and took his hand. "Whatever it is, we can sort it out, together!"

Tom rubbed his eyes. Ashleigh let go of his hand and sat back.

"The kids are with Tanya. She can give them their tea. There's no rush."

Tom shook his head again. "I don't know where to start" he said. "You had another... vision?" He nodded.

"Oh God!" Her head drooped. "Can you tell me about it?"

"I was in a small, square room. It was really dark. It stank. There was just a single bed and a sink. Like a really shite youth hostel, you know?" She nodded. "This voice... dunno who it was, he sounded really odd... He said, your mum is here. Turn around."

"Turn around?"

"Yeah," He took a sip of his tea. "Next thing, I was in another room, like a shitty canteen, like at work but sort of, dirtier. Colourless. Lots of tables. It was really busy, there were kids crying. Not ours though."

"Was it Rose? It wasn't Rose, was it?"

"No. I don't know who she was. She was cold, really... oh I don't know, distant. She didn't really say anything much... Oh wait, yes, she said I have always been a disappointment to them."

"Cheeky cow!" said Ash, "go on."

"I could see myself before her, growing, like from a kid to a man. I looked the same, but different, somehow. I had tattoos, one of Yogi Bear! Then... I don't know, I felt really odd."

Ashleigh smiled and cupped her hands around her tea though it was almost cold now. "You're always odd!" Tom gave her a wry grin. The room was silent for a moment, there wasn't even any traffic sounds from outside.

"Sorry! I'm just kidding! What happened then?"

He shrugged. "I felt all hot and cold. Like I had a fever. I remember lying down, trying to stop shivering. I must have fallen asleep. When I woke up..." He rubbed his hand across his eyes.

"What?"

"When I woke up, I was on the floor in the canteen, at work. They said I was out of it but it wasn't a fit. It wasn't a vision either. Ash..."

"What love?"

"What if... I think I saw my real mother."

Rob waited until the lights changed and turned into the monstrous, grey prison-like building. He drove forward, anxious and edgy. The car was filled with documents. It's usually pristine interior was strewn with folders and papers, some with sticky post-it notes adhered to their sides.

His briefcase was on the front seat, unlocked but not open. In it, his mobile phone pinged with another text, since he had and Tom had started this, he was getting hundreds of contacts a day. It was turning out to be an interesting process actually; he seemed to have an aptitude for it.

He reached the end of the long, sweeping drive and switched the engine off. His car was his pride and joy, his baby (although he did not say that in front of Pauline). A Range Rover, only four years old, dark blue with spoilers and a grille on the front. He consoled himself, it was his only real indulgence these days. He took a deep breath and mentally shook himself, remembering why he was here.

Climbing out of the car, he grabbed his mobile phone out of the case and stuffed it into the pocket of his trousers. The air was fresh and cool and there was a fragrant grass smell from a newly mown lawn. There was no one around outside the building which was good as he had parked in a spot marked 'Doctor'.

He snapped the briefcase latches shut and closed the door, locking the car remotely with the key fob, hearing a satisfying clunk as the locks engaged. He stared up at the imposing entrance and made his way cautiously into the foyer. The smell, one he was all too used to, hit him; a stale, fusty mixture of over-cooked food, ineffective anti-bacterial sanitizers, overheated dust and a general, all pervading air of isolation.

Once inside he passed through another set of double doors, waiting as a buzzer hummed inside, confirming the release mechanism of the security lock. He pushed the door open and walked in. The institutional smell of all hospitals varied little, in his experience. Some smelled fresher; these tended the more acute centres. Some smelled of pee and shit, these, generally were the lodgings of the old and infirm, and invariably, the incontinent.

Psych hospitals smelled of body fluids too, but in a more insidious manner. It was as if the rankness of the surroundings, even the more salubrious private establishments, struggled to rid themselves of the stench of madness. It dripped from the walls, fogged up the windows and weighed down the air. Of course, no one ever called it that, but it was, nonetheless, what it was.

"Can I 'elp ya' mate?" The voice was deep and gruff, the accent pure South London. Rob walked forward towards the caged-in reception desk. He put his briefcase down on the floor and smiled at the old man who was sitting behind the plexi-glass front wall.

"Hello," said Rob, "I'm Robert Gorman from West Midlands Primary Care Services." Not strictly true, but he had an official looking badge which identified him as a mental health professional and was counting on his confidence and knowledge of the system to help him navigate his way into what it was he was seeking; knowledge.

"Oh?" the man replied. "What's it abart then?"

"I have an appointment with the Director," Rob lied smoothly, "could you tell him I'm here please?"

The man glanced around him, as if uncertain of protocol. He was short, even when seated. His hair was sparse and grey and overly combed. He was dressed in a light blue shirt and old-fashioned paisley tie fastened with a massive knot loose at the neck. On closer inspection, it appeared that he was not as old as Rob first thought.

He glanced down at a large flat ledger on the desk in front of him. "Got no mention of it in the diary. It would be in the diary. It's always in the diary." He rubbed his nose and blinked rapidly and Rob realised the man was a patient, one of the so-called 'trustee's', long-termers who have earned rank and privilege amongst their fellow patients. Plus they worked and didn't require payment.

Rob peered at the man's name badge, sewn on to his tunic.

"Stewie?" he said, "I think we may have met before. I..."

"No!" said Stewie decisively. "Got a good memory for faces, me. No. Not met you before."

Rob paused and studied his shoes before bringing his gaze up and smiling at the unlikely receptionist.

"If I could just talk to someone in charge, perhaps we can get this sorted out?" he asked, leaning against the counter and fiddling with his keys.

Stewie's face was blank, a tiny bit of spittle flecking his lower lip. "Umm... dunno!" he said.

Rob sighed. "Well, it was arranged some time ago and I've come a long way. Could I please speak to Dr Howard, or his secretary perhaps?" The phone in his pocket pinged again, reminding him he had not yet read the earlier message.

"Doc Howard not 'ere. 'Es on his 'olidays. Florida!" said Stewie, licking his lips, "I never bin to Florida!"

Rob shook his head in frustration.

"His secretary then? There must have been some sort of mix up…"

At that point a short, slim blond-haired goddess walked into the room. She was dressed in a similar shirt to Stewie's but it was a white one, not blue like the 'volunteer's', and open at the neck. Her name badge was one of those held on by a magnet put on the reverse of the uniform, no sharp pins in a psych unit, thank you very much. It read "MHN Rachel Jones" in blue writing. She saw Rob reading it and self-consciously brushed her hands down her uniform, smoothing out imaginary creases.

Rob tended to have that effect on women. Tall, good looking and charming, he was friendly and smart. His dark blond hair was always tidy if a little long and his deep blue eyes twinkled with good humour.

"Can I help you?" she asked, flashing a tight smile at Stewie before turning to Rob. Rob smiled back and she blushed.

"Wants to see the Doc!" Stewie told her.

"Oh, I'm afraid he is on holiday," she said, sitting down on a high stool behind her. She licked her lips. Rob hid a grin.

"Yes, so I gather!" he said, nodding at Stewie. "As I was explaining to your colleague…" Stewie gave a little snicker, "I have a long standing appointment with Steve, err… Doctor Howard. Only there seems to have been something of a mix-up!"

"Oh dear!" said Rachel.

"Perhaps his secretary may be able to help?"

"I'm afraid she has gone home for the day. You just missed her. I'm so sorry. I'm not sure what's happened…"

Rob sighed. "As I mentioned, I'm from the West Midlands Primary Care team," he flashed his ID badge, allowing her to see the official NHS logo. A phone rang beside them and Stewie eyed it in confusion. Rachel ignored it so Rob carried on, talking over the old-fashioned bell-tone.

"I'm here to interview a couple of your clients' about complaint's their families have made."

"Complaints?" She looked alarmed. "Complaints about what?"

"That's confidential, I'm afraid. I made the appointment to be able to see two of your long-term patients, err… hold on…" He flipped open the latches of his briefcase, laying it flat on a chair. He rummaged around inside and pulled out a manila file and looked inside.

"Yes, umm… Rebecca Jane Sawyer and, oh… ah yes, William David Bent."

"Well..." her tone was dubious, "umm... I'm not sure..."

"I am a trained professional," he smiled at her again, "If that's the nature of your concern. It's part of a process instigated by the Royal College of Psychiatrists, following the Bluestone Report? All complaints must be followed up..." He put the folder back into the briefcase and stood up.

"What about a chaperone?"

"You can't park there!" Stewie said.

"What?" said Rob.

"You can't leave your motor there!"

"Hang on, Stewie," Rachel said, turning back to Rob, "well... Matron is off too you see. I'm the senior on at the moment and I'm not sure I'm..."

"That's the Doc's spot!" Stewie was practically hopping from foot to foot. "The doc, he told me, no one was to use that space, see?"

Rob turned to him. "But the doctor isn't here, is he? I wish I was in Florida too actually, but since I'm not, and I doubt he'll need it anytime soon, I don't think he would mind if I leave it there for a while."

Stewie nodded his head slowly although he was clearly unconvinced.

Rachel slid a book across the counter to Rob. "Can I get you to sign in please?" she asked him, "I'll give you a temporary site badge and let you through."

She took a moment to think, "Stewie, can you go get the unit managers to get Becky and Bill ready? I think they'll be still in the dining room. I'll chaperone Linda, can you tell Maggie that?"

Stewie nodded and shuffled off. Rachel took the sign-in ledger back from Rob and put it aside without looking at it.

"Bill's quiet as a mouse these days, I'll stay with you if you want, but I only really need to chaperone Beccy."

"I can manage, I'm sure you have better things to do!" Rob told her.

"Policy," she said wryly. "No female patients to be alone with any men. Been a bit of an issue lately, what with allegations of... Oh, is that why you're here?" She flushed, suddenly defensive.

"No, no. Not at all," Rob assured her. "It's just a formality. The new Medical Director is making sure that patient choice is at the top of the list. Crossing all the 't's' and dotting all the 'i's'. You know how it is!" She rolled her eyes, she did indeed.

"I'll just wait 'til Stewie gets back and then you can see Becky. Although," she added over her shoulder, I'm not sure how much sense you'll get out of her!"

Rob smiled, nodded and picked up his briefcase.

Chapter Twenty-One

"It's him!" Rob's voice was grim and, even over the phone, Tom could hear the anguish in his tone.

"Are you sure?" Tom asked, nodding to confirm to Ashleigh that the man Rob had met, Bill Bent, was the man who had raped his mother nearly forty years ago.

There was a moment of static and then Rob said, "I'll be there in about twenty minutes."

Tom could hear the sounds of Radio Four playing softly in the background, the rain on the roof of the luxury car and the swishing of the windscreen wipers as he made his way back through heavy traffic on the M5.

"I'll get the kettle on!" Tom told him. He turned to Ashleigh. "Oh God," he said, "Oh fuck!"

"Just wait, Tom," she told him, standing and walking towards him. "Wait to see what he says." Tom nodded and took a deep breath.

"He's out late!" Ash said as she sat down.

"Good," replied Tom, "At least the kid's shouldn't be able to hear anything. I don't think I'm going to want them to hear this." Ash nodded. They sat in silence, the TV off for once, the rain outside the only sound.

After about thirty minutes, the sound of Rob's huge car swishing in the rain down the drive to the cul-de-sac that passed the front of their house alerted them. He was here.

Tom closed his eyes briefly and Ash stood, reaching up to give him a hug. "It'll be ok, baby," she whispered. He said nothing, just raised his eyebrows sceptically.

Tom opened the door and Ash said hello, proffering her cheek for the usual hello kiss. Rob obliged and gave her a wry little smile, shaking his head to rid himself of drops of rain.

"Bloody weather!" he said.

"I'll make some coffee." Ashleigh left to go into the kitchen.

"Christ, it's really bloody awful out there!" Rob took off his coat, soaked even from the brief walk from his car to the house. "She ok with this?"

Rob nodded after her and Tom shrugged. "She just wants to know, like me."

Tom slung Rob's coat on the back of a chair and they sat and waited until Ash rejoined them, sitting next to her husband on the small child-battered sofa. She put her hand on Tom's knee. "Ok, babe?" she whispered.

He nodded. Rob cleared his throat.

"Well..." he twisted his wedding ring, "I went there. I made up a story about it being an official meeting, to follow up complaints some of the relatives have made. I interviewed someone else as well, just to throw them off the track."

Tom gave a brief laugh but Ash was clearly concerned. "Why not just be honest?" she asked. Rob shook his head ruefully. "Yeah," he said, "I know, I don't like the dishonesty either, to tell you the truth, and I do know how you feel about lying... I just think... it was so long ago and if we aren't careful, we could really set the cat amongst the pigeons."

Now Tom was dubious. "I don't want you to get into any trouble, mate!" he said. "You can't afford to jeopardise your job over this."

Rob took a deep breath to answer her, but his phone pinged then with another message and, shooting her an apology with his eyes, he retrieved his mobile out of his jacket pocket. "It's Pauline!" he said, firing off a quick reply, "She's in a bit of a funk at the moment."

"Does she know about... all this? Is that why?" Ashleigh's tone was dubious.

"Yes." replied Rob, "She knows. I thought it best to be open, you know... since... well..." He paused. "I don't think that's why she's depressed though." He looked glum, "ah, she'll be ok."

"Yeah," Tom was understanding. "Anyway, you shouldn't keep this from her. There have been too many secrets already." Rob nodded but Tom could tell that Ash was unconvinced; Pauline was not always known for her discretion.

Rob seemed to pick up on her unvoiced concerns. "I just said we are looking into finding your birth parents. Nothing more. If and when we find out anything more concrete, I will explain it to her. I'm sure it'll be fine. She wants the best for you too Tom." He picked up his coffee and took a grateful sip.

"But..." said Ash.

"But what?" Rob turned to her. "She won't say anything to anyone, Ashleigh."

"No... but you said, if we found anything more concrete..."

"Yeah?"

"But we have. Haven't we? I thought you told Tom that the man you went to see was his real father."

A wail from upstairs made Ashleigh stand up. "Elliott's awake!" She went to the door and stood for a second, hoping he would settle. The wail became a full-on bawl and she sighed and headed upstairs. "I'll be back in a minute," she said, adding "you did say that though, didn't you?" Rob nodded and Tom gave a nervous laugh.

"God, Ash, give him a chance!"

Rob held up his hand to speak, but his wedding ring flew off his finger and rolled underneath the sofa. He cursed and bent to retrieve it. At the increasing volume of cries from their son Ashleigh turned and ran up the stairs, calling out to Elliott and shushing him as she went, in case he woke up Meghan too.

Rob, kneeling on the floor, reached under the sofa, pulled out a piece of carrot. He held it up, pulling a face confused and Tom laughed. He took it off him and bent to peer under the seat himself. The ring had rolled to the back and Tom strained to reach it. He pulled it out and blew the dust off it, wiping a bit off fluff of the inscription inside. He handed the ring back to Rob, who pushed it back on his finger with a grin. "I should really get it altered!" He laughed briefly, "Pauline would bloody kill me if I really lost it!"

They heard Ash pottering about upstairs and Rob looked serious again. "It's ok. Ashleigh's right. I did say that I had found him and, without a conclusive DNA result or an official confession, I'm as certain as I can be that William Bent is... he is the man I recognise from Bell Hall, the bastard I caught raping your mother."

Tom paced nervously. Upstairs the cries of his son subsided as Ash deftly changed him into fresh pyjamas and clean sheets, dumping the wet ones he had soaked with urine into the bath. They heard her washing her hands and she came back down the stairs less than five minutes after she'd gone up.

"Is he ok?" asked Tom.

"Yeah," she said, "he'd wet the bed again." Tom rolled his eyes and Ashleigh nodded. After being dry for months, Elliott appeared to have regressed, he was wetting the bed regularly these days. They had seen the GP about it, but so far, there were no clues as to why.

"He'll be fine!" said Rob, still fiddling with his wedding ring, "he's possibly just picking up some tension about all this. Kids are very sensitive aren't they? Any chance of another coffee, Ash?"

Ash jumped up again and went into the kitchen. Whilst she was gone Rob stood and turned to Tom. "Tom... I, I'm not trying to encourage you to keep secrets..." He pursed his lips, trying to think how best to phrase it.

"Secrets about what?" asked Tom.

"I don't know if this is all a bit much for Ash. I was just wondering if you should wait to tell her anything when we are more definite about it all."

Tom thought for a moment and shook his head. "She's very sensible about stuff like this. And I wouldn't feel right about... keeping her in the dark." Rob nodded and sat back down. "Sure. I guess, I was just trying to protect her."

"Protect her from what?"

"It's all so up in the air and to be honest, I'm not sure how much more we can find out."

Ashleigh returned and handed the coffee to Rob. He took it with a smile.

"Well..." said Ash, "at the very least, we want to find out where his mom was buried. And his brother. There must be something official about that somewhere." She picked up the piece of carrot Rob had found under the sofa. "Where did this come from?"

"Rob dropped his ring again! It rolled under the sofa."

"Oops! Guess the Hoover missed that one!" Embarrassed, she glanced at Rob and turned back to her husband. "Just think about that poor woman. What she went through. The hospital should be made to answer for what happened and you, Tom, you deserve some answers."

Rob was a little alarmed. "But the hospital no longer exists!"

"So? I agree with Ash." Tom put his hand on his wife's knee and she smiled up at him.

"I think we do have a right to know, even if it does upset some people."

"Shit!" Rob blurted, "Can open, worms everywhere!" Ashleigh gave a half-hearted smile but her face remained resolute.

"I think we have to know. We can't just leave it like this." She said quietly. The three of them sat in silence for a moment or so. Rob cleared his throat.

"OK," he said. Decisively, he stood and put his coffee cup down on the table to the side of the sofa. Standing quietly for a moment, flicking his wedding band, he seemed overwhelmed.

"I really don't know if that information... if we can find that out." He rubbed his nose. "All the people involved in this disappeared years ago. I think there's just a car park on the site now." He reached for his coat. "I get it though. I do. And I think I would want to know too. I'm just... shit, you know... I don't know how..." he exhaled loudly and spent a moment struggling into his coat.

"Well, this man, this William Bent," said Tom, "Can we not start there? If you recognised him? Can we not get a DNA sample from him?"

"I'm not sure he would consent, or even if his medical team would allow it. Given his lack of capacity, it would possibly be an infringement of his human rights."

"His rights?" Ash stood, her face red and strained. "If it was him, he raped a mentally ill patient, and from the sounds of it, he wasn't the only one having sex with people he shouldn't have been anywhere near. And I bet she wasn't the only one he abused either. Christ, what even makes you think he is Tom's father? She was already pregnant when he was caught, wasn't she?"

Rob held up his hand, taken aback by her anger. "Whoa, Ashleigh, don't shoot the messenger! I'm just saying, it's going to affect a lot of people."

"You, you mean. Don't you? Well I'm sorry, but it's gone beyond that now," she snapped.

Fire flashed in Rob's eyes, but he took a deep breath before he responded. "Yes, ok, fine. Of course it could be damaging to me. I never blew the whistle on the administrator and I wish to God I had. But I wasn't just thinking of that, I promise. What about Rose? The kids? What about your real mom's parents or her other family? It's not as simple as..."

"If she has other family, they're Tom's family too! He should be allowed the chance to get to know them at least."

Rob shook his head. "Ok!" He pulled the lapels of his sodden coat around him. "I'm going now, before anyone says something they may regret! I understand though, honestly. And I'll keep doing everything I can to help you find some answers. OK?"

Ashleigh tutted and turned away and Rob flashed a 'told-you-so' look at Tom which irritated him too.

"Ok, Tom?" Rob tried appealing to Tom, but he stepped towards his trembling wife, who was rigid and shaking with righteous indignation.

Tom turned to Rob. "Look, Rob, we don't want to get anyone into trouble. Especially you. We really appreciate you helping with all this. But it's just... this is too big to walk away from. At the very least, we want to know where she was buried. And my... brother. Shit, my twin. Oh God!" He sat heavily and Ash hurried over to him.

"Are you ok, sweetheart?" She sat with her arms around him, both oblivious of Rob. When Tom lifted his head, Rob was still standing in his coat, dripping rain water like tears on to their lounge carpet, his face pale and drawn.

"There must be a way we can do this without you getting into trouble," Tom stood, "but we have to do something. You do see that, don't you?"

Rob nodded grimly. "Of course I do!" he said, "look, I'll let myself out. I'll call you tomorrow." He smiled, "We'll sort it out, try not to worry!" He left and Ashleigh and Tom sat huddled together, confused, anxious and sad.

Chapter Twenty-Two

"Elliott!" yelled Meghan, "Mom, tell him!" Ashleigh came through to the lounge, tea towel in hand.

"What's going on?" she asked, wearily. She had been sleeping badly since the meeting with Rob two weeks earlier and, in spite of Rob's promise, they were no further forward. At one point, Ash had told Tom to report the situation to the police. Let them investigate she said. They'll find out what happened.

Rob had contacted them the following day but only to reiterate that he was at a loss how to proceed. He said he would look into the prospect of getting a DNA sample from Bill Bent, even if it meant that he had to take it himself. So far, he said, it was possibly best not to involve the police.

In fact, the situation had caused a rare, bitter row between Ash and Tom and both were still feeling the sting of it. Add that to the insomnia Ash was now experiencing and, all in all, tempers were fraying.

"Mom!" Meghan's voice held a trace of panic and tears and Ashleigh forced herself to focus on her children. Meg's sweet little face was all red and cross. Her gaze shifted to Elliott. He stared back at her with curiosity, more a look that said 'so what are you going to do now?' then with any contrition. In his hands he held a trophy, an award Meghan had won when she had first started competing. It was a prized possession and Elliott had somehow climbed up to the shelf above the head of her bed to get it down, had prised the metal badge from the wooden plaque which held it and had twisted it, splitting the edges and distorting the engraved name and date.

"Mommy! It's mine! Tell him!" Meghan wailed, tears spilling down her face. Elliott chortled and held his hands out, dropping the ruined pieces on the floor.

"Elliott!" Ashleigh's tone was strident but Elliott just grinned at her.

"Well?" Ashleigh kissed Meg, then turned to her son, leaning down so she was at his level. He continued to grin at her and she sighed. "Sweetie, that wasn't yours!" Elliott turned to go. "Hey, I'm not done with you, young man!" Ashleigh reached out and grabbed his hand, gently, to stop him leaving. She was astounded when he whirled around; tiny fist clenched, and smacked her hard across the face.

Although in the scheme of things, given his size, it wasn't that hard a blow, Ashleigh fell sideways in shock. She landed hard, banging her head hard against the cabinet which held the stereo in the cubby beneath the stairs.

Meghan screamed and ran to her. "Mommy!" she cried. Elliott tittered and turned, sauntering casually from the room, swinging his arms. Meg helped Ash to her feet and made her sit whilst she got her a cold wet flannel to place against the bump which had already formed on her forehead. She made her a cup of tea which she shakily brought to her mom, spilling most of it before Ashleigh could take it.

Tom came home half an hour later. He was talking on his mobile, though it wasn't clear who to, and he stopped when he saw Ash sitting with the flannel to her wound and Meghan, red-faced from crying, sat huddled beside her.

"I'll call you back," Tom said into the phone. He disconnected the call and hurried across to his wife, patting Meg's head as she shuffled over to let him sit in between them. Still, neither of them spoke and Tom leaned forward and gently removed the flannel from Ash's hand, gasping to see the bruise and swelling which had already formed.

"What the hell happened?" he asked.

"Elliott hit mummy." Meg told him.

"Elliott did that?" he said, his face reddening.

"Yeah!" said Meg.

"Well, no," said Ash. "Yes he did hit me, but I fell and smacked my head on the stereo."

Tom was relieved. "Oh!" he said, "Well... you poor thing!" He stood.

"Meg, can you go upstairs for a moment, love?" initially it seemed that she was going to object, but instead she complied, leaving the room, first kissing her mom gently on the cheek before she went.

"Tom?" said Ash.

"What, love?"

"There is something wrong with Elliott. I know you don't want to hear it, but there is." Her tone was final and there was a note of desperation in it. Tom sighed and took off his wet coat; it was always bloody raining these days.

"There isn't anything 'wrong' with him Ashleigh. He's just high spirited, that's all. He's young. You said it yourself, you fell. It was an accident."

"No, it was more than that."

"How?"

"Tom, I was telling him off because he had totally destroyed Meg's first judo trophy, just out of spite. Then, when I told him that wasn't nice, he punched me."

"He punched you?" The scepticism in his voice irritated Ash and she stood, retrieving the wet flannel from the sofa where it had left a damp patch.

"Yes," she said, "he actually punched me. Closed fist. Deliberate and hard, like he really hated me."

"He's only just three!" Tom blurted.

"So?"

"I don't know, babe!" Tom replied, standing up. "I'll have a word, but..."

"But what? You think I'm picking on him? Is that it?"

"No..."

His slow, measured response was the final straw. Ashleigh spun around and stood with her hands on her hips. "In the past ten months he has broken just about everything of value to anyone else. He has become increasingly aggressive towards me, towards Meg, at the nursery, everywhere."

The smile that had been creeping across his face to see her with her hands on her hips, a pose exactly like her mother's, slid off his face. "What do you mean, at the nursery? What's he done there?"

"I told you he bit Liam. He drew blood! He tried to stab Ruby with a pair of scissors. He's even hit the teachers. He's out of control. He's having more time-out there than all the other kids put together."

"Well..." Tom's brow was creased and his cheeks flushed. "Why is this the first time I'm hearing about it?"

"It isn't the first time at all! I've told you several times. Look at the Christmas tree incident."

"Oh God, that was months ago. Jesus Christ! Leave it to me. I'll talk to him."

"No!" she replied. "I know you think I'm overreacting, but I really think we need to take him to Dr..."

"Don't you think you are getting a little..."

"A little '*what*' Tom?"

"Carried away? Look, I know there is a lot going on, with the hospital and Rob and everything. I know you're tired. I just think..."

"You think this is because I'm tired? Next you'll be blaming my bloody period!"

"Well..."

"Oh, don't you dare!" she snapped.

"Come on, Ash, for goodness sake, stop yelling at me. This just makes me even more convinced that you..."

A frightened wail from upstairs stopped them cold. Tom sighed. A convincing scream followed. A second scream rang out and they legged it out of the room, bolting up the stairs, Ashleigh two seconds ahead.

The hall was narrow and the landing tiny. Although technically a three-bed semi, the house was rather too small for the four of them. The already cramped landing held an assortment of fresh linen's waiting to be put away, pieces of Lego, one or two match-box cars, a couple of pairs of shoes and some stray socks. The rail which overhung the stairwell was being used to air towels, fresh from the tumble dryer.

Over the top of the railing, with impossible strength, Elliott, all grim determination and gritted teeth, clearly straining with the effort, was forcing his older, heavier and stronger sister forward, trying hard to lift her legs, to make her fall head-first down the stairs.

"Elliott!" Tom yelled, as he and Ash raced up the stairs. Meg continued to resist, still screaming and Elliott, ignoring them, his manner calm and determined, maintained the pressure on her, trying to tip her over. Ashleigh reached them first and she grabbed Elliott around the waist, pulling him back, away from his sister as Tom caught Meg, righted her, standing her up. Meg sobbed in his arms. Elliott stood and watched them, the only emotion visible a blank curiosity.

"Now tell me I'm just... flaming tired!" snapped Ashleigh over the cries of their daughter. "Now tell me that's all it is!"

Chapter Twenty-Three

Two weeks passed with no more information found. Neither Rob nor Tom's numerous internet searches trying to find the final resting places of his mother and brother had been successful. They could only find evidence of Tom's existence. In the case of his twin, no records of his birth or death were available.

Tension mounted between Tom and Ashleigh. They squabbled more than Meg and Elliott did. Ashleigh was adamant that Elliott needed to be tested, possibly for ADHD, a form of Autism she explained. Tom told her to stop lecturing him; he wasn't one of the children. Ash responded by suggesting he stop behaving like one. An accountant colleague of Ash's had a child with the disorder and it apparently presented in a similar way to Elliott. Tom continued to insist that it was merely high spirits and that Ashleigh was overreacting. Quietly, Ashleigh set about cataloguing things she was worried about in relation to their son. She would keep it and show it to Tom if and when he appeared receptive.

In the meantime, Elliott's behaviour deteriorated to the point where the nursery called and asked for a mid-term parental consultation visit the following week.

They pre-arranged two sitters to leave the children with separate people; Meg no longer wanted to stay with Elliott without her mom or dad around. Tom said he thought Ashleigh's 'hysteria' was affecting their daughter. For the first time in their marriage, Ash told him to go to hell. Tom felt, at times, that he was already there.

Although he felt a little guilty, the works-do night out came at just the right time. He and Ash could use a little breathing space, he thought. The leaving do for Simon from accounts, a mate of Tom's, took place in Birmingham directly after work on a Friday, which meant that Tom went straight there with the rest of his colleagues. The plan was to get the last train back and get a taxi home from there.

At 10:30, he sent a text to say he was getting the last train as planned, and would be back around midnight. Ash replied simply 'Fine x'.

At quarter to 11 there was a knock on the door. The children were fast asleep and Ash was wary of answering. It was unusual for someone to call so late at night. She peered through the spy-hole, trying to see who it was through the driving rain.

"Tom?" Ash heard Joe's voice and she breathed a sigh of relief. She had been worried that it was Rob and she didn't want him to come round without Tom being there. She wasn't sure what to say to him at the moment. She opened the door.

She peered out into the night. "Hi Joe. Tom isn't here. He's on a leaving do for a mate from work."

"Oh, right. He never mentioned it. Never mind. Hey, are you ok?" He stood heedless of the rain, peering at her with concern.

"Yes, why?" Ashleigh was a little defensive.

"You just look a bit... blue, I suppose. Sorry, I'm being nosy! Look, it's late. I'll bugger off." He turned to leave.

"No, it's ok. Is it urgent? Not like you to call around this late. You could try calling him actually. He'll be leaving Birmingham in a bit. He said he'd be home by 12." She glanced at her wrist watch.

"No... it isn't urgent." He brushed rain drops from his dark brown, almost black hair and Ashleigh laughed. "You look like a drowned rat!" she told him.

"Cheers!" he replied, good naturedly. "I was just bored on me todd! Anyway, I was in the area, fancied a pint. Thought I could tempt him out for a quick one. Never mind though."

"You can come in for a coffee if you like? I've got a glass of wine!"

He stepped into the house and took off his jacket, considerately shaking off stray rain-drops into the dark, blustery night.

"Hum... Kate liked a drop of the old vino!" Ashleigh felt sorry for him. "You still miss her, huh? You want to swap that coffee for a quick glass of wine instead?"

"Oh... go on then!" he said, sitting on the edge of the sofa. "You've talked me into it!" He shifted a teddy wearing a pirate's outfit complete with eye patch belonging to Elliott and a book of Meg's about horses.

"Kids!" said Ashleigh with a laugh, dumping the items on the computer table. She headed into the kitchen. "I'll be back in a sec," she called.

In the kitchen, she reached into the cupboard above the oven and grabbed a small, fluted wine glass, turned and poured a second glass of her favourite Blossom Hill red. As she turned around, picking up both her refreshed glass and the one for Joe, she bumped smack into his chest. She had not heard him come up behind her and she jumped in shock, spilling some of the wine onto his pale blue denim shirt and dark jeans.

"Shit," she exclaimed, "sorry, I..."

Joe leaned in and kissed her, full on the lips. For a moment Ashleigh didn't react, then she thrust the wine on the counter. One of the glasses toppled and rolled to the side, rolling on to the floor and smashing into pieces.

"What the hell are you doing?" she asked, pushing him away.

"Ashleigh..." he murmured.

"No, Joe... I..."

"I've always fancied you." His breathing was fast and he was gazing at her like a hunter gazes at deer; his eyes sweeping her t-shirt covered chest, her face, everywhere. "Come on, you can't tell me you didn't know!" He reached for her, pulling her to him, hands around her waist, pulling her closer.

"Shit, Joe! Back off!" She tried to push him away, but he backed her into the corner of the kitchen between the pan cupboard and the cooker, his pelvis thrust into hers. She felt his hands move down to cup her arse. He squeezed.

"Get off!" she hissed. *"What the hell do you think you're doing? Please, just go! God, think of what Tom would say, you and he have been mates for years!"*

"I saw you first!" Joe's word came out muffled as he moved her face with his hand, nuzzling at her neck.

"Joe, stop! *Stop it!*"

"Careful, babe, you don't want to wake the kids, eh?"

"Don't you dare!" she hissed back, "get the hell out of my house!"

"Oh come off it, Ashleigh!" His leering eyes bulged as he used one finger to pull down the neck of the t-shirt, peering down to stare at her breasts. She slapped his hand away.

He glowered at her. "I know you and Tom at are each other's throats over all this shit with Rob. And the stuff with Elliott..."

Ashleigh concentrated on pushing him away, but he pressed forward. "He's told me all about it. How you've been nagging him. Stupid bastard. I'd treat you better than that, Ash. Come on, what do you say?" He leaned in for a kiss and she kneed him in the balls.

"Ooofff!" he yelped, scrabbling backwards, hands over his genitals. *What the fuck Ashleigh?"*

"*Get out!*" she shouted. "Get out before I really scream. Clare's in next door and she'll call the police in a flash if she thinks there's a problem!" He glared at her through narrowed eyes.

"You fucking prick tease!" he spat.

"Fuck off, you maniac. Tom will..."

"*'Tom will what?'*" he sneered. "He'll be interested to know how you invited me round, knowing he was out for the night. A little wine, a little sympathy, a little... comfort!" He moved forward again, one hand still on his balls, "Bitch," he said, "that fucking hurt!"

He reached out, grabbing her hand, trying to force her to rub his crotch. She twisted and grabbed the remaining wine glass still on the side, throwing the contents in his face. Vin Rouge dripped comically off his nose onto the pale terracotta coloured lino, disturbing, like a puddle of fresh blood.

"Get out!" she hissed. "I don't care if I wake the kids. Get out. Get out. *Get out!*"

He stepped back, nervously eying the small garden and the light which had come on in the kitchen next door, flooding the lawn.

"I'm going!" he told her, "but I won't forget this, Ashleigh!" He spun around, swiping a tea towel from the side across his face. He grabbed his coat and left, slamming the front door behind him with a resounding bang. On cue, Ashleigh heard Elliott bawling, but she stayed downstairs, unable to pull her shaking hands away from the kitchen counter. And anyway, she could barely hear him crying over the noise of her own wailing.

Chapter Twenty Four

The drive home from the meeting with Elliott's nursery school teacher was subdued. Unusually, it was a bright and sunny day. Neither of them could remember the last time it wasn't raining. The skies were blue with scattered fluffy white clouds and there was a definite feeling that winter had, at last, departed and spring was bouncing in.

In silence they made their way home. Tom called work once he got indoors, explaining that he wouldn't be able to get in for at least another hour or so, Ashleigh had the day off.

"Well?" Ashleigh's tone was sarcastic. "You still think it's just high spirits?"

Tom failed to hide his irritation. "I don't think there is anything seriously wrong with him, if that's what you mean!"

"Were you not listening? Ms Howarth said..."

"I heard what she said, Ash, I'm not bloody deaf."

"Tom, he's out of control. He's violent, he's antisocial, he's..."

"He's our son!"

Ash shook her head in exasperation. "I know that! Don't be so dense Tom. I think we need to help him! The teachers at the nursery think he needs help. I'm not saying I don't love him or that I think he's a lost cause. I'm saying that, if we ignore this, there could be... oh I don't know, real consequences."

They glared at each other for a long moment. Eventually, Ash broke the stand-off, turning away abruptly and walking the short distance into the kitchen. After a moment, Tom followed her. He pulled out a chair at the small round table, scraping the legs against the floor. Ashleigh winced at the sound.

"Oh for..." Tom's frustration peaked and he slammed his hand down on the table. "Bloody hell, Ashleigh!" She gave a quiet sob, turning away quickly.

"You must admit, you are being..."

"Being what?" she asked, quietly.

"Being a little oversensitive?" His tone was softer now and he could see her shoulders heaving as she sobbed into the tea she had just made. "Just milk in mine please," Tom joked, "I'm trying to give up tears!"

He heard a little laugh and she sniffed, surreptitiously wiping her nose with her sleeve.

"Classy bird!" he said with a grin.

"Sod off!" she told him, though with a watery smile on her face. He reached across to the top of the fridge and grabbed a piece of kitchen towel, handing it to her where she sat next to him at the table. For a moment, silence once again enveloped them. No traffic noise. No kitchen sounds or kid or hamster sounds or even garden or neighbour sounds.

"Isn't it quiet?" Ashleigh whispered. Tom grinned and nodded. He coughed and took a noisy sip of his tea and finally was rewarded with a proper smile.

"That's better!" he said, putting his tea down.

"Look, Ash, I agree, Elliott has... changed... lately. And it's true that Meg seems nervous around him."

Ashleigh opened her mouth, but Tom interrupted, adding quickly, "yes, and the comments from the nursery. But I just think, if we blame it all on him, that could do more harm than ignoring it. It's just a phase."

"Meg never got like this!"

"No, but she's a girl! Boys are different."

"No?" Ashleigh's tone was sarcastic but he could see she was still joking. "How? I never realised that! *Really*? Are they, like from Mars or something?"

"Maybe!" he replied, seriously. "Ok, let's agree that we need to monitor his behaviour and agree a plan for when..."

"For when he's what?"

"Well... like you said. If he gets aggressive, we deal with it, there and then. Backing each other up. You know, trying to be consistent. We really need to be consistent. And, we should ask the nursery to do the same. He loves going there. If we try telling him they get upset when he does something... naughty... and tell him he can't go unless he, you know, behaves, maybe that will sink in. He'd hate to miss it. He would be gutted."

"You don't think..."

"What?"

She hesitated, unsure how to voice her concerns without upsetting him further. "Well, your... visions... whatever they are..."

He narrowed his eyes. "What about them? You think I'm harming my kid?"

"No!" She reached across and covered his hand with her own, he pulled away. "Look, we don't know why you've had..." She broke off, seeing his contemptuous stare. "Oh, Tom!" she said, "I'm not blaming you! It's just odd, the timing. Don't you think?"

"No!" His brusque reply made her look away and he softened his tone. "OK, it's possible that he's picking up on something, I don't know, some tension or something. Still, we need to be sensible, how we manage it I mean." Ashleigh nodded.

Tom continued, "OK, so, we agree between us before hand, how to manage him. Back each other up. Make it clear that he will lose out if he continues but that it doesn't change how we feel about him. Yes?"

"OK. Yes, of course. That's a good idea. God, it's so hard isn't it? He's like two different people. Like a split personality. One minute he's wonderful and the next he's a little devil! It's like having twins! I wish... Tom? Tom? Hello? Anybody in there?"

Tom was staring at Ashleigh like he had seen a ghost.

"What?" she asked. "Are you ok? Tom?"

He seemed to be staring through her almost, head cocked, absolute astonishment on his face.

"Are you having a vision? Tom? Oh shit! Tom?" She stood and pulled his arm.

"Twins!" he said, slowly turning to face her.

"Yes?" she replied, "What about twins? Tom, you're scaring me!"

Tom seemed to space out for a moment or so, and Ashleigh was on the verge of calling an ambulance when he spoke.

"I'm a twin!" he said.

"I know love..."

"I think he..."

A sharp bang on the door made them both jump. Tom stood up shakily, holding onto the table to steady himself. He went to answer it and came back with a small manila envelope in his hands.

"Who was it?"

"I don't know. This was on the mat."

"What is it? Are you ok?" said Ashleigh.

"Humm... yeah, I think so. Hang on, I'll tell you in a bit."

"Open it then!" She nodded at the packet and stood. Walking across to the kettle, she shook it to check the water level and switched it on to make another drink. Without asking him, she made him a second one, busying herself putting in milk and sugar for Tom, before turning around and walking back to the table. He was sat reading, his brow furrowed and jaw clenched.

"Who is it from?" she asked, taking a sip of tea and wincing at the heat.

"Joe. Odd!"

Ashleigh blanched. She had not told Tom about what had happened on the Friday before. By the time he got back, half cut and shattered, she was in bed and thought she should leave it a while. Although Tom was generally slow to anger, he would no doubt be furious with Joe and she didn't want a scene whilst he had been drinking. The Sunday had been filled with trying to stop world war three breaking out between Elliott and Meg and then today, they'd had the parental consultation. She was in two minds if she should say anything, but was certain at least, that it would at least have to wait until after they had seen the nursery.

Privately, she acknowledged, the thought had also crossed her mind that Joe would tell it differently and after all, Joe had known Tom years and years longer than she had.

"Tom..." Wringing her hands, she stared down at the table.

He read the letter, confusion on his face before he dropped it to the table. She leaned forward and picked it up. She held it for a moment before she read just the first line. It said 'I need to tell you something and I'm not sure how to say it...'

Ashleigh gulped. "Tom?" she tried again.

"What the fuck, Ash? You kissed him?"

"No... I... No!" Ashleigh felt a blush suffuse her face and she held her hands up, unsurprised to notice they were shaking.

"He came round, late, when you were out..."

"Yeah, so he says. He also says you planned it that way."

"Bastard!" She rose and stomped to the far side of the room. "Fucking bastard!" Her face was red and heated and she could hardly get the words out.

"Ashleigh?" The pain in Tom's voice broke her heart, but at the same time, she was furious that she hadn't told him before this. And more than that, that Tom would believe that weasel over her.

"How could you believe him? He assaulted me!" she spat. "He turned up, said he didn't know you were out. He said he was bored, missing Kate or some crap. Said he wanted you to go for a pint. I felt sorry for him, I told him he could come in for a quick coffee."

Tom's face was bereft. She took a deep breath and continued.

"Tom... he... He went on about how he was missing Kate and how they used to drink wine. I'd had a glass so offered him one instead of a coffee. He said yes so I came in here to pour it and he..."

"He what?" Tom's voice was dangerously low and she frowned.

"I turned around. After pouring the wine. And he... he was just there. I hadn't heard him come in. I... without any warning, he leaned in and kissed me. I... I was so shocked, I spilled the wine on him. I shoved him off and said, 'what the hell?' or something like that." She blinked back tears.

"And?" he asked; his voice so quiet she almost missed it.

"He tried to... he put his arms round me. I shoved him off, he groped me a bit and..."

"He groped you? I didn't think you even liked him!"

"Oh for God's sake! I didn't! I don't! And yes, he groped me, but I kneed him in the balls and he backed off. I shouted, woke up Elliott, naturally! I told him that if I screamed Clare next door would automatically call the police. He left. End of story."

Tom stood and walked towards her. "Did you kiss him, Ashleigh?" The quiet menace in his voice startled her and her breath caught in her throat. She gasped.

"No!"

"Did he hurt you?" His voice had lowered again and Ashleigh gulped.

"Did he?" Tom was sounding almost conversational and she felt a shiver of fear run down her spine. Not fear of her husband. She had never felt anything but safe around him. She wouldn't stay otherwise. But the blankness on his face and the coldness in his eyes reminded her so much, at that precise moment, of their son.

"Why didn't you tell me?"

Another knock on the front door made them both jump again. Had Joe come back? Tom turned and Ash caught his arm, afraid of what he would do. Seconds later it was accompanied by a shout through the letter box and Elliott's little voice carried through the house, floating towards them like a paper aeroplane.

"Mommy, Mommy, Mommy!" The letter box slammed shut. Ashleigh took a deep breath, sighing with relief and went to the door. Tom stayed at the table. Pam, their neighbour had sat for Elliott whilst Meg was at school. She was bringing him back as arranged. Ash opened the door and Elliott bolted in.

"All ok?" Ashleigh asked Pam.

"Oh, yeah... Little monkey! Full of energy!" laughed Pam, a twist of the lips enough to share that he had been hard work, fond of him though she was.

"Daddy!" Elliott shouted, delighted that his father was home, spying him through the door. He barrelled through to his dad and threw himself on his lap. Tom held his son tightly for a moment. He stood with the child in his arms. Ashleigh thanked Pam and said goodbye, closing the door before she could be engaged in meaningless conversation or asked if she had been crying.

"Ta-ra babs!" Pam waved through the window and headed back home.

"Bye! Thanks!" called Ash.

When she walked back into the kitchen Tom was sitting at the table with Elliott standing on the chair beside him, frantically regaling him with all he had done at Pam's, everything single thing he had eaten and everything he'd seen on the TV.

Once more, Ashleigh was frightened by the look on her husband's face. It was the same look Elliott had had lately, when he was just about to destroy something precious.

The first Ash knew about it was yet another knock on the door, later, after the kids had been bathed and put to bed. Tom, saying only that he needed some fresh air, had left the house, slamming the front door behind him. He walked past their front window, head down against the ever present driving rain.

The sight of two police officers, full uniform, all sombre faces and professional distance, nearly scared the life out of her.

"Mrs Bearing?" The male officer was tall and thin. He had a face marked by so many acne scars his skin was eerily like every photograph she had seen of the surface of the moon. His mousy brown hair was greasy and had no discernible style. In contrast his colleague was impossibly young, slim and stunningly pretty. She had hazel eyes, perfect skin and brown hair that glinted in the light; natural auburn highlights glowing in that – 'I know damn well *I'm* worth it' kind-of-way.

"Are you Mrs Bearing?" The male officer repeated. Ashleigh nodded dumbly.

"Oh my God!" she said.

"We're here about your husband." He said. Ashleigh felt her jaw drop, felt like her face was melting like a Spitting Image puppet which had been left too long under studio lights.

"Tom!" she said stupidly.

"Yes. I'm so sorry. We..."

"Tom!" she repeated.

"Mrs. Bearing?" Ashleigh faced the female officer.

"Oh my God!" said Ashleigh to the ugly policeman.

"Mrs. Bearing?" The female officer spoke again.

"Huh?" Ashleigh replied.

"Can we come in?" The blank professional coldness was replaced with a more sympathetic look. "Mr. Bearing... Tom, he's ok."

"What?" Ashleigh felt like she was swimming underwater.

"He's at the police station!" The female officer cleared her throat. "Unfortunately, he was involved in an altercation. An allegation of assault has been made. He's been arrested."

"He's ok? Right? He's ok?" Ashleigh was aware her voice had risen several octaves.

"Yes."

"He's... what? He's under arrest?"

"Yes," said the male officer. "We've been trying to call you."

"I thought he was dead!" Her voice rose with each word until she was almost shouting, glaring at the male officer. The raw anger in her voice changed the expression on the ugly policeman's face. She could almost hear him thinking, 'well, he's obviously not the only nutter in the house!' but he replied with a studied professional detachment, "No! He's not dead!"

"You said... You made me... I thought he was *dead*!" She took an indignant step forward. Involuntarily the male officer took a step back. The female officer stepped forward.

The next door neighbour's door opened and light spilled out, making prisms of light dance in the rain drops.

"Ash?" she called, peering out.

"No!" said officer pretty, "No. He's not hurt. Sorry if we gave that impression." She glanced at the neighbour but ignored her.

She glanced at her colleague. "Mrs. Bearing, your husband has been arrested for assault. He asked that we contact you. We can give you a lift to the station?"

"Ash?" repeated Clare, stepping out into the rain, pulling an over-large coat around her and pulling the hood over her head.

"It's ok, Madam," said the male officer. "Please, go back inside."

Clare ignored him this time and she walked forward across the small soggy lawn which separated the two houses, putting her arm around Ash. "Is everything ok, love?"

Ash struggled to speak. Instead, she turned back to the WPC.

"Who?" she asked. The word came out as a whisper and she coughed to clear her throat.

"Sorry? Can you repeat that?"

"Who? Err... who did he assault?"

"A Mr. Umm..." PC ugly consulted his notes, "ah yes, a Mr. Stanley. Joseph Stanley."

"Oh fuck!" said Ash.

Chapter Twenty Five

He stood on her doorstep, as distant as a stranger. "Can I come in?" he asked. "Please?"

She nodded and stepped back to allow him access. He looked bloody awful. His hair was greasy and unkempt. His skin was sallow and spotty, a sure sign he was eating crap again. His clothes, though clean enough, were creased and held the unmistakable sign of a man living out of a suitcase.

"Kids ok?" he asked.

She nodded. "And... your mom? Rose, I mean. Is she ok?" He shrugged. Nodded. Sighed. "Actually, no, not really!" he said.

"Tom..."

"He's out of hospital, Ashleigh." She closed her eyes. The charges Joe had made against Tom had been dropped; suspiciously fast after his arrest, in spite of the fact that Joe had spent four days in hospital with two broken ribs, a busted nose and moderate concussion. Neither Tom nor Ash had heard from him since.

"How's Elliott?" Ashleigh knew he was asking after more than his son's health.

"He's ok," she said cautiously. "He seems a little subdued. The nursery rang yesterday. I nearly panicked but they said he had fallen asleep and wouldn't eat or anything for the whole session."

"Why? What's going on? Why didn't you call me?"

She was slighted by the tone. "Because when he came home, he was starving! He ran around all evening and slept fine again all night. He's ok, Tom. Really!"

He nodded. "Sorry!" he said.

"It's just so... weird!" she said, after a moment.

He nodded again and she smiled.

"Tea?"

"OK!"

Together they walked into the kitchen and Ashleigh made some tea. Tom took his usual seat at the kitchen table.

The silence was uncomfortable and Ash cleared her throat. "How's work?" she asked.

"Ok." She nodded.

"Actually, the shit has hit the fan!"

"What about?"

"Lynn and Max. They were caught..."

Ashleigh laughed and put the tea down on the table in front of him.

"What?" said Tom, "they're both married! They were having sex in the store room, Jose caught them. At it like rabbits he said. Both completely starkers!"

"Oh bugger!" Ash exclaimed. "Can't say I'm surprised though!"

"Why?"

"That day, when Lynn called me in, the day you had the... that fit, I saw them looking at each other. I thought something was going on then."

His face darkened and she sighed. "What?" she asked.

"Interesting to see how worried you were about me!"

"*Really*?" Ash's tone was that of their daughter's; sarcastic and rude. "*OMG!*" said Ashleigh, still parroting Meg. "Don't be so bloody stupid!"

He shrugged and Ashleigh glared at him, shaking her head.

Several moments passed. She tried again. "You said you wanted to talk?" She picked up her drink and reached to the top of the fridge to grab a packet of biscuits. He nodded.

"I need you to know..." She waited, hands cupped around her tea.

"Ashleigh... the other day, I... Oh God!"

"You didn't believe me!" she said softly.

"About Joe?"

She nodded.

"I... I did Ash. I remembered something. He's done it before."

"What?"

"Come on heavy to my... well, a previous girlfriend. I believed him and we split. This time... oh God..."

"I can't believe you put him in hospital," she said.

"I didn't mean to. I just... I went round there. He was so smug. He said you had come onto him once before, when you'd been drunk. He said... oh, it doesn't matter. He's a lying bastard. I just lost it. I hit him and before I knew it he was in bits on the floor, blood everywhere."

"God, Tom. That's not like you."

"No... Ash, that's not why I wanted to talk to you."

"It isn't?"

"No." He took a deep breath.

"I don't think he's dead!"

Horror dawned on her face. "Who?" she asked, "Joe? He's dead? Oh my God...!"

"No!" said Tom, scratching his head. "No, not Joe. My twin. Sam. I don't think... I don't believe he is dead."

"Oh fuck!" said Ashleigh again.

Chapter Twenty Six

The second Tom stepped foot in the psych unit he felt physically sick. It wasn't the smell of the place. It wasn't the bland stares and numb despair of all of those he saw there and that included the staff. It wasn't even the fight and endless red-tape he had had to get through to get in to see William Bent. It was that William Bent himself, obsequious and foul, insisted that Tom *was* his son.

He proudly acknowledged that he had been at Bell Hall during the period in discussion. He nodded and shrugged when asked if he had had sex with patients and he told Tom, pride in his voice, that he had at least five other children, that he knew about.

Tom remained calm, fighting to keep from spewing his guts or punching Bent. He had promised Ashleigh that much. He looked everywhere but at Bent as he scratched and sniffed, boasted and lied.

The room was huge, bare and depressing. Bars at the windows and locks on all doors made Tom feel like he had wandered into a prison. It was hard to tell the difference between the staff and the in-patients to Tom's untrained eye. Even the staff were sat around and one, wearing jeans and a checked shirt, was sat, texting furiously on a mobile phone, her legs swinging over the arm of the chair like Meg did when she watched TV. It was only when she stood and answered a land line phone with the words 'Nurse Kowalik, Evergreen Ward!' in a marked Polish accent so sluggish with apathy, that Tom realised she was a member of staff, albeit a disillusioned one.

His visit was swift though it felt like a lifetime to Tom. Small talk was awkward, to say the least, and he spent most of the 30 minutes he was there watching Bent as he shifted and sniffed and scratched. At times the man seemed to forget Tom was there. His right eye blinked almost constantly and Tom felt as if Bent was winking at him.

Other patients wandered around, their faces frighteningly blank. Other sat huddled or rocking. Hardly anyone was wearing shoes. *Is that how the residents can tell who is who? Ah*, thought Tom, *the staff are wearing shoes.* A man dressed in dirty pyjama trousers and a greying too-short white t-shirt stood by the barred window. His bare feet were almost blue with cold. He reminded Tom of an extra in that film with Robin Williams as a doctor and Robert De Niro as the catatonic patient who woke up for a while. Tom shuddered.

It was only as he went to leave that he remembered to ask for a DNA sample. He had been coached by Clare, their neighbour who worked in the lab at Worcester Hospital, on the taking and processing of DNA samples and he had come prepared.

Bent's eyes flickered around the room, deviously. "Does it hurt?" He reached inside his baggy green t-shirt and scratched under his armpit.

"Ummm... no. I don't think so!" Tom had failed to ask that question and found to his shock that the concept of causing pain to the creature who was potentially his father, was surprisingly attractive. He exhaled loudly. Bent glowered suspiciously.

"Oh... I don't think so! Anyway, it's the only way to find out for sure." Tom tried to instil some confidence into his words.

Bent's body language had changed and he visibly withdrew.

"Well... err... I suppose I could go the court to get permission. A court order or something!" Tom's tone was casual.

"Court? No need for that. Shit. Whadda I gotta do?"

"I use this stick thing to take some cells from the inside of your mouth and send it to the lab.

"To the police?"

"No," Tom replied shortly. "To a private lab. It will not get to the police through me. I just want to know..." He took a deep breath, "I just want to know."

"What'll I get?" He peeked at Tom though his greasy hair. With really long, dirty fingernails he scratched at his neck where the skin was red, blistered and sore-looking. Flecks of skin sloughed off and drifted to the floor like tiny flakes of snow. Tom watched repulsed as Bent scrapped some debris from his fingernail, pausing to examine it carefully and flick it onto the floor.

"What do you mean?" Tom eyed the shell of a man before him.

"What will I get, if I let you do it?" Bent's wheedling tone was nauseating and Tom found himself cringing, as if he could hear the same manipulation being used on his mother.

He pulled back sharply, and for some reason, this had an effect on Bent. He sighed and opened his mouth to reveal teeth that were yellow and black with a thickly coated green-ish grey slab of tongue floating in a sea of saliva and bubbles. Tom swallowed down puke which had risen in his throat.

"O' on 'en!" said Bent with his mouth still open.

With shaking hands Tom reached into Bent's open mouth and scraped the swab one on his cheek. Bent's eyes opened wider when the stick scraped the soft skin but otherwise, he stayed still.

Tom withdrew the swab and stuck it into a receptacle, snapped off the top and sealed it inside. Hands still shaking, he dropped it into a clear plastic bag already pre-labelled with the case information.

"That it?" said Bent, licking his lips.

"Yes." Tom stood and Bent grinned at him.

"So... will you come back?"

"Why?" asked Tom.

"If I'm your daddy!"

Tom could not bring himself to reply. He stood, regarding Bent for a long moment, straining to see any similarities yet desperate not to. Without further words he turned and left. He walked straight past the nursing staff and out, signed the visitors log, threw the temporary ID badge at them and almost ran back to his car. Bent shrugged and turned back to the main TV room. He flopped down in a battered, stained seat, scratching mindlessly at his neck. Tom did not look back.

The constant computer searching was giving Tom a headache and the smell of his mother's cooking was proving to be an effective dietary aid. He felt like shit. Weight was falling off him at an alarming rate and when Rob turned up, unexpectedly, whilst Tom and his mother ate dinner, he commented on it.

"You don't look well, son!" Tom glared at him balefully as he forced himself to eat the cottage pie his mother had made.

"Well... I'm eating, aren't I?" he retorted.

"Tom!" His mother's gentle rebuke reminded Tom so much of when he was young that he smiled and picked up another forkful of mince. He ate that, then set the cutlery down, forcing himself to swallow the final mouthful.

"What?" he said, defensively. "I can't eat if I'm being watched!" He stood and took his plate to the bin, scraped the remains away and put the empty plate on the draining board beside the sink.

When he turned, Rob was seated at the table, whispering to Rose. A flush heated his cheeks.

"You're going to ask him for a DNA test?" He stood hurriedly. "Is that really wise? Think of the repercussions! I'm not talking about me... what about the kids? How would they feel if... What about Ash? Come on, Tom. You know where he is. You know what he did. Let it lie now. Look at what this has done." He spread his arms wide, indicating that Tom was already estranged from his wife, suggesting that the search for the truth of his birth was the cause.

"You know it, Tom. He..."

"I've already been to see him," Tom said quietly. "He's already had a DNA test." The shock on Rob's face matched that on his mother's.

"Oh, Tommy!" she whispered, "Why?"

"I need to know!"

"And how do you think that will that help you?" She sounded hurt.

"But how?" Rob pursed his lips, "How did you manage to get the test?"

"Oh. I went to see him. He freely admitted to... well, the possibility."

"Did you send the test to the hospital already?"

"It's not a hospital test," Tom told them, "you can't get paternity tests on the NHS apparently. I paid for it." He laughed wryly. "In more ways than one, I guess you could say!"

Rob sighed and rubbed his eyes, "I don't understand why you can't just..."

"It will answer at least one question. If that... that *creature*, is my father or not. Then I will find out where my mom was buried. And my twin, unless..."

"Unless what?" Rob sat back down.

"I want to be sure."

"Sure of what, sweetheart?" Rose was trying hard to be impartial and supportive, and Tom's heart contracted with love for her. He smiled at her and she shook her head. "Oh, love," she massaged her temple as if she had a headache too. "I doubt we'll ever know..."

Rob's eyes were narrowed. "Sure of what?"

Tom held his chin up high. "I want to know if he is really dead."

Rose gasped and Rob looked stunned.

"Of course he is! What makes you think he isn't?" he looked wildly at Rose. "Don't you trust me? Tell him, Rosie!"

"Tell him what? How would I know?" Rose was suspicious. She narrowed her eyes, "Don't *you* know?"

"Well, yes I... I saw him. I told you! I saw his body. Look, it's all too late, Tom. Yes, it's tragic. Yes, it's gross. But you, you're ok. You have your health. Your family." His tone turned towards the bitter, "You're a lucky man." He bowed his head. "A lucky man!"

"You said, you always said you were there. When he died. Isn't that true?"

Rob glanced at Tom, then at Rose. "Yes... I mean, yes." His voice gained in strength. "Tom, he's gone. So has your mom. And that man... Bent, he's nothing to do with you! Not anymore. Let it go. They're gone."

"Then where?" Tom was resolute.

"Where what?" Irritation made Rob's tone short.

"Where have they gone?" Tom spread his hands wide. "If they're both gone, then they're gone. I can accept that, if I know for sure. But where? If they're dead, they must be buried somewhere and someone knows about it. I will keep searching, Rob. Mom. I will keep on looking, till I find out for sure."

"Oh, love!" His mother's face was flushed and upset.

"I'm just trying to stop... I don't want you to get hurt." Rob put his arm around Rose, who leaned in to him, sniffing.

"I know. Mom, I need to find out. Rob, I will do what I can to make sure this doesn't fall back on you. I promise. But I have to find out." He walked towards Rose and kissed her powdery, scented cheek. "I'm off to bed!" He paused at the door. "Night, Mom," he said, "night, Rob!" He left, listening to Rob sigh as he went.

Chapter Twenty Seven

"Bentley? Bentley?" Frustration caused her to stumble and she almost fell over. That damn dog. Bloody typical. He never ran off, except apparently, now, he did.

Lead in hand she roamed around the empty park calling for her dog, glancing nervously at shadows and peering around corners. He was nowhere to be seen. Tutting loudly she kept going, calling for him.

Greenwich Park was one of the most magical places in the whole of London as far as she was concerned, except when it was within a few minutes of closing time and the sodding dog had disappeared. Street lights blinked in the blackness beyond the park, illuminating the main road through Blackheath and into London via Peckham and Camberwell.

The vista beyond the park was one of the reasons she loved it here. To the far right, the River Thames sparkled in the night, the faint hum and groan of river traffic still audible from here, given the right conditions. To the left, beyond the ornate white dome of the Greenwich Observatory which glowed like a beached alien spaceship, lay the beautiful, quirky Borough of Greenwich and, beyond that, an expanse of the east of London; laid out like an exotic quilt. She walked on, still tentative, calling for the dog.

Sighing with relief, she heard a faint barking in the distance and headed towards it. Her car was at the top end of the park, near to the main Blackheath road and the playground, where the barking seemed to come from, was at the very bottom, close to the road which led into Greenwich proper. She sighed. *Bloody animal*. It was a long walk back up the hill and she was tired and hungry.

She rounded the corner, shouting out for Bentley. He was a Golden Retriever, for heaven's sake, really not that easy to lose. In the distance, she spied the almost luminous fur of the dog sitting beside the children's swings. The sand pit was sinister in the murkiness, the roundabouts and slides dark, monstrous and scary. She swallowed.

"Bentley!" she called with relief. "There you are. Come here!" Instead he lay down, head on his front paws. Thoroughly exasperated she walked towards him. Still he didn't move. Dusk was falling fast and she calculated how long she had been looking for him. *There was no sign of anyone else in the park, bugger. Maybe they were already locking the gates? Should she call out to see if she could catch someone's attention? Oh God, how embarrassing if she got locked in.*

She strode towards her dog, irritation quickening her steps. As she approached him, she tapped her thigh to call him. "Come on, boy, come on, boy!" She could hear him whimpering.

"Bloody hell, dog!" She was almost beside him when she saw the rope which tethered him to the side of the swing. She scanned the playground for someone who may have done it, but still, there was no one in sight. Thinking someone had tied him to keep him safe, she reached out, fear of being left in the park and having to call the police to be rescued making her fingers clumsy.

The sudden blow to the side of her head was accompanied by a dull *thunk*.

"What the..." was all she had time to say before she fell to her knees beside the dog. Bentley stood and shook himself, barking just once. A second blow from behind knocked her flat to the ground and she went fully down with a decidedly ungraceful 'Uuugghhhhhh," before landing splat, face up, beside her faithful dog. The dog barked again, a single sound shattering the damp stillness of the night.

The wound on her head was a mortal one and she lay dying. Grey and pink brain matter splattered across the nearby swing like party custard. The dog whimpered softly and bent to lick her face. He tried to pull himself free, but he was still tied to the rail of the swing. He lifted his head, his ears pricking up only when he heard the sound of rapid footsteps running away. Patiently, the sound receding, the dog lay back down beside her and waited.

Chapter Twenty Eight

In contrast to his earlier, highly vocal doubts, Rob was animated, excited. "I found him!" he declared. "I've only bloody found him!" The front door was still open where he'd barged through, pulling Rose with him to the front room where Tom sat listlessly watching the seven o'clock news. His laptop was open on the sofa next to him and his mobile by the side of it. He was waiting for a reply from Ash, having texted her two hours ago to tell her he was miserable without her, without his kids. She had not replied.

The two and a half months he had spent at his mother's was killing him, he was convinced. Sucking the soul out of him, through her relentless cheer, optimism and cajoling. It was bloody annoying.

"Tom!" said Rob, standing in front of him, waving a pale yellow coloured letter.

"What? Who?" He dragged his eyes from the news, yet more boring shit about the bloody phone hacking scandal. Like anyone gave a crap.

"Your twin!" Rob was practically hopping around.

"What?" asked Tom stupidly.

"Oh my goodness!" said Rose, hands fluttering at her throat.

"Tom, listen to me! I've found him! He *is* alive. You were right! He was taken to hospital, after your mom died. I... I didn't know... He was taken there and dropped off. Ended up being adopted by a doctor or something. Anyway, it seems that he's in the USA. In America! Well, that's where he was last seen."

"America!" Rose gasped. "Oh, Tom, oh, love!" she said.

"How?" Tom shoved the laptop away from him and stood up. His hair was sticking up in all directions; he was unshaven, un-bathed and a stone lighter than when he had first started searching.

"How?" he repeated. Rob sat on the edge of the armchair that had been his father's.

"I found Karen through work. She was the manager of the unit at the time. I went down there and kept hassling her until she told me everything. I told her we were going to go to the police and she panicked. She said she thought, well, we all thought he'd gone. When your mom died, we thought that Sam had died too. But he hadn't. She said, she told me, one of the mental health nurses saw him and he was still breathing. They took him to St Anne's hospital. It's not there now. Anyway, she said he survived. He was adopted by a doctor and taken to America when they emigrated. He's *alive*, Tom! You were right!"

"Sam?" said Tom.

"That's what they called him. At the hospital apparently, after one of the doctors who was treating him."

Oh, fuck!" said Tom.

"Thomas!" said Rose.

"Oh, fuck," he repeated.

Ashleigh answered the phone as soon as it rang. She was crying.

Tom, frightened by her tears, was diverted from telling her for a while.

"Tom?" she sobbed.

"What is it? What's wrong, love?" Tom was anxious and pacing.

"I miss you!" she said, "please, Tom?"

"What? Ash, what?" he replied.

"Come home?"

Tom whooped and grinned at his mother. "I'm on my way!" he said in the phone. "I've got something to tell you, Ash! Get the wine out love! We're celebrating!"

"Oh my God!" Ashleigh was stunned. "He's alive? All this time? Oh God, Tom! Where is he? Does he know? Can you meet him? Oh my God!" He pulled her close.

"I know!" he said.

"It's like something you'd see on one of those true life movie channels!" Tom laughed and kissed her deeply, unperturbed by the giggles of their daughter who watched them.

"Who's alive, Mommy?" Meg asked, when they surfaced for air.

"My brother, sweetie!" Tom told her with tears in his eyes. "I have a twin brother! And he's alive!"

Chapter Twenty Nine

Ashleigh sat in the small, cramped garden, fanning herself with a magazine. It was the middle of the school summer holidays and the start of Tom's annual two week break. Ashleigh had the time off too. This year, like the last, they were making do with mini-trips and short breaks to accommodate their finances; this year especially, since they were saving for a trip to the USA.

In spite of the news that Rob had found Sam, actually getting in touch was proving harder than they had expected. Sam had been taken to Wisconsin initially and the family had moved around some. The final address they could identify for him was in Massachusetts, in New York State although there was some query about his name.

Rob had continued his efforts on Tom's behalf and both he and Ash were very grateful. Privately, Rose was less so, but since it was not something she could stop, she tried to be supportive.

The smell of smoke drifted across from the house whose garden backed onto theirs. Ash glanced at her next-door-neighbour's garden. She had washing hanging out on the line. That would not go down well, it would stink. Ashleigh stood and went indoors. She sat at the kitchen table. The sounds of summer drifted in through the open patio doors, of kids playing on the small eight foot trampoline with their neighbours' children. Screams of joy and youthful enthusiasm rang throughout the small cul-de-sac.

Ash and Tom were sat in the kitchen, out of the heat. Tom was ploughing his way through yet more paperwork that Rob had dropped off. The quest seemed endless to Tom and something of an anticlimax. So far they had no communication from Sam himself and Tom was getting increasingly frustrated.

Finally, he opened a letter which was addressed to him personally. On the outside of the envelope was a lurid yellow post-it note in Rob's handwriting. 'Think this may be it! R.' it said.

"What's that?" said Ashleigh, eying the envelope warily.

Tom shrugged though his eyes were shining. "I don't know," he replied, "Rob left it for me to open!"

He ripped the flap open and pulled out a single flimsy sheet of yellow paper.

Outside they heard the sound of a child crying, but the tone suggested annoyance, not fear or pain, so they stayed put. Then they heard Meghan's little voice, all reason and calm and smiled at each other. She should work for NATO.

Tom unfolded the letter. He read it and frowned.

"What is it, love?" asked Ashleigh. "Is it from Sam?"

Tom shook his head slowly. He met her gaze. "It's from his lawyer," he said bleakly.

Two days later, the telephone call was pre-planned by email to account for the time differences between the UK and the eastern side of the US. At exactly four PM Tom and Ash sat by the phone, having arranged that any urgent childcare issues would be managed by Clare next door. They dialled the number and waited through a seemingly interminable series of clicks and stops until at last they heard a dial tone.

"Marvin, Brooks and Hellier," announced a sexy, throaty deep voice at the other end. "Madeline speaking. How may I help you?"

Tom cleared his throat. "Erm... can I speak to Mr. Brooks please?" he asked.

"Which Mr. Brooks?" He grimaced.

Ashley scanned the letter. "Hugo!" she whispered.

"Hugo Brooks," said Tom.

"Hold the line please." More clicks, static and another ring tone.

"Hugo Brooks!" The tone was quiet and professional.

"Mr. Brooks? My name is Tom Bearing and I'm calling as arranged? From England? About my brother? About Sam?"

"Ah, yes, Mr. Bearing. Thank you for calling. You are in Worcester, England I gather! What a strange coincidence! It's a lovely part of the country. In the circumstances however, I'm not sure offering you congratulations is really in order." His tone suggested bad news and Tom's heart sank.

"Is he... is he dead?"

"No." Brooks cleared his throat. "I'm afraid I have to tell you... Your brother is in prison." There was silence at the end of the phone. "Mr.

131

Bearing? Are you still there?" They could hear him tut and sigh and Tom shook his head.

"Tom!" whispered Ash, "Answer him!"

Tom's expression was bleaker than she had ever seen. "Ask him what for!" she whispered.

A further pause. More line static. "Murder!" replied Brooks and Tom together.

Chapter Thirty

"Well, how do you explain it?" Ashleigh had been hissing under her breath for some time and Tom was beginning to understand how someone could really lose their rag and not really care about the consequences.

All around them the competitors were warming up, some almost impossibly small and slight, Meg amongst them.

"Will you flamin' stop having a go at me!" he whispered back through clenched teeth, watching as Meg danced across to Sian. People were beginning to stare at them and they self-consciously lowered their tone. Nigel, Ashleigh's trainer was frowning at them. Tom took a deep breath, he went to continue but Ashleigh cut across him, spitting out the words. "Not here!" she said.

Fuming, he looked back at the action on the mats. Beside him, Elliott was playing with Ashleigh's mobile phone. In fact that was the match that re-lit this particular fight; Tom wouldn't give him his to play with in case there was a call or email about his brother.

Meg stepped up against a much taller child, a boy, and bowed low to him, as per the tradition. The fight began with its usual ceremony and silence momentarily enveloped the hall. Gradually, people began to shout encouragement to the fighters, although they seemed oblivious. Meg was holding her own and Elliott stood, entranced as Meg won point after point.

Ashleigh searched the benches where they sat, lifting coats and bags. With a sigh she leaned forward. "Elliott, where's my mobile?"

He ignored her, caught up in the fight. Ash rolled her eyes and started searching again. Tom was too caught up in his irritation to help her and she glared at him.

Over to the far side of the room, Sian was hoping around from foot to foot in front of her mother and trainer. Neither Ashleigh nor Tom noticed her colour suddenly change, her face turning whiter than a polo mint. Sian's mom leapt up, catching her daughter as she fell. She and their trainer helped her to the bench, where she lay next to her mom, leaning into her shoulder. Several people ran across to see if Sian was ok, but by this time, she was fast asleep. With no alternative, the trainer pulled Sian from her next fight and Caroline took her home.

"Elliott, where did you put my phone?" Still searching, Ashleigh turned to Tom. Can you call me to see where it is?"

"It's on silent for the fight!" he replied, not taking his eyes off Meg.

"Shit," Ash muttered, under her breath.

For several tense moments Meg hunched on the mat, skirting her opponent, seeking a weakness. With a sudden lunge she flipped the other girl onto her back, holding her effortlessly as the girl lay trapped beneath her like a butterfly in a net. The whole thing took less than one minute.

With a cheer, Meg won the round and after bowing to her partner, danced back to her parents, eyes glowing. She was through to the finals!

Standing, Ashleigh peered down under the benches, still trying to find the mobile phone. "Bloody hell!" she muttered as Tom reached out to hug Meg.

"Well done sweetheart!" he whooped. Meg grinned and reached down, picking up Ashleigh's phone from underneath the chair of a woman so huge, she spilled over the sides of the seat. She smiled at Meg and turned back to the match. Meg handed the phone to her mom.

"Bugger!"

Rolling his eyes, he turned to his wife. "What now?"

Ashleigh turned the phone to him. The screen was cracked. He turned away unable to hide the smug look on his face. What did she think Elliott would do with it, for God's sake? What did he do with everything these days?

Tom tuned out as Meg was called back for the next fight. Since Sian had had to withdraw the placement was altered, meaning Meg would instead compete against the girl who had been due to fight Sian. She was older than Meg and bigger by far. Meghan gulped and turned back to her parents neither of whom noticed.

She walked back to the mats nervously, glancing back just once.

"Tom, send me a text?" Ashleigh was playing with her phone, checking to make sure it still worked. With a sigh, Tom pulled out his own phone and unlocked it. As he did, it vibrated in his hand as he received an incoming email.

He scanned it quickly. It was from a social worker who had worked in the states, herself a twin, who he had contacted via an organisation for adoptee's. She had agreed to meet him to talk about her own experiences, both of being a separated twin and her work in the USA.

He turned to his wife, a grin on his face like a space hopper.

"Did you text me yet?" She shook the phone and tutted. "It's not come through. Bloody thing..."

"No!" He sat forward, unable to contain his excitement.

"What?" Ashleigh lowered her voice as the large woman in the seat in front turned around and frowned at her.

"What is it?" she whispered.

"Amanda Whiting, that social worker Rob told us about? She's agreed to meet me!"

Ashleigh rolled her eyes. A cheer went around the room and Tom glanced around to see why, but Ash leaned down to him.

"Is that all you can think about?" She sat back shaking her head and folded her arms.

"It's important, for Christ's sake!"

"It's not the only thing!" Ashleigh nodded at their daughter competing twenty feet away from them.

"Don't lecture me, Ashleigh. You knew this may happen. You encouraged it."

"Hey, take it outside, eh? Some of us are here to support our kids!"

Elliott turned bodily around and faced the man who had spoken, his head on the side, examining the man like he was a science specimen. The man looked away, whispering something quietly to his wife sitting beside him, clearly talking about Elliott. She tittered. Ashleigh bridled and turned to face them.

"Something else you wanted to say?"

The man smirked at her. "Why don't you concentrate on the reason we're all here, you know, *the kids*? Remember them? Instead of staging your own fight!"

Tom went to stand up, but Ash pushed on his shoulder to make him sit. Tom pulled Elliott towards him, sitting him on his lap. Elliott was still staring at the man.

With a final glare at Ashleigh, the wife of the man who had spoken pulled his arm to sit him back down. Shaking his head, he did so, ostentatiously turning to face the fighting.

"Arse!" Tom whispered to Ash, but she didn't smile.

"Mommy!" said Elliott pulling Ashleigh's hand. She turned to Tom like she wanted to say something.

"What?" he whispered.

"I don't get you!" Ashleigh's face was sad.

"Why?" Tom replied.

"Mommy!" Elliott said, still reaching out, pulling at his mother.

"Elliott, sit still!" Tom turned to his wife but she turned away.

Tom sighed and rolled his eyes, trying to stop Elliott squirming on his lap.

"I know this is a big deal for you," she reconsidered her words, "well, ok," she said, "for all of us. But there is a time and a place Tom."

"All I said was that I'd had an email!"

"Yeah, that's all you ever say these days. You don't talk about anything else." She reached out her arms to Elliott who scrambled across to sit on her. She winced as he dug his foot into her groin.

"Shush!" More people in the crowd were getting annoyed and Ashleigh blushed.

Another cheer distracted them and as one, everyone turned to face the competitors. The six fighters turned to each other and bowed. The referee, smiling, shook Meg's hand and she turned to try to locate her parents in the throng of supporters. She had won. She bowed low to the ref, again to her opponent and raced over to them.

Their daughter, still dressed in her ghee and obi, hair loosened from her high pony tail, was chattering and laughing with glee. All around them, people stopped her to congratulate her and she loved the attention. Elliott was quiet, he sat thoughtfully on his mother's knee. They stood, gathering their things together. Ashleigh put Elliott down to make him walk.

"Ummmm!" Elliott reached his hands back to his mother, clenching and unclenching his fists like a baby rooting for food, constantly pulling at her clothes to get her to lift him back up.

"Walk, Elliott," she told him, "You're a big boy now!"

"*Mommy up!*" Elliott shouted.

"...and, and did you see me at the end? OMG! It was amazing!" Meg was breathless with excitement.

Tom nodded and smiled, although he hadn't. Beside him, the fat woman looked back, throwing a sceptical look at Tom and Ashleigh.

When Meghan had bounded off, racing across to a friend, crowing about her victory, the woman turned her bulk to face Ashleigh.

"She only won because Sian didn't compete." Her voice was calm and quiet; she was stating a fact, not being a bitch. Ashleigh glanced around, trying to locate Sian or her mom. She really hadn't noticed they'd left. Neither of them were to be seen, even their trainer had disappeared.

"She was taken ill," the woman told them. "I've just had a text from Caroline, her mom? Sian got kicked in the head just before she went sick. They've taken her to the hospital. They think it might be a concussion." She picked up a jumper off the back of her seat. Tom and Ashleigh were speechless.

"Oh God, poor Sian!" Ashleigh was rooted to the spot, hand over her mouth in shock.

"Still," she said, nodding towards Meg, "she did do bloody well!" She smiled at them. "Even if she did beat my son! It's a shame you missed it." She lumbered away and, red-faced, Tom waited with Elliott as Ash went to get their daughter.

Meg had won all her fights today. Tom and Ashleigh's however, continued in the car and long after they got home. Both were aware that their children were in bed above their heads, by now, neither was able to moderate their tone to take that into account.

"I'm sick of it, Tom! It's been going on for nearly three years now." Ashleigh was clearing the kitchen after their tea.

Tom rolled his eyes and stalked off back into the lounge. "Jesus, Ashleigh, give it a rest, you sound like a fish wife!" The regret was instantaneous as he saw the hurt in her eyes. Sighing, he scratched his head.

"Well..." Her face red and furious, she turned around, banging a cup so hard on the side in the kitchen that the handle fell off. "Shit!" She snatched up the pieces. "Well," she continued, "it's better than sounding like a flaming lunatic!"

"What did you say?" He thundered back to the kitchen and Ashleigh turned to face him.

"Do you have any idea what it's like to live with someone who, I don't know, one minute is all calm and rational, the next he's... ranting about murder and rape? Shit, it's a wonder no one had you committed!"

He stared at her, aghast. "Is that what you really think?"

She shrugged and turned away, aggressively wiping the kitchen counters.

She sensed him watching her and her shoulders slumped. "No." she said quietly. "I didn't mean that." Dropping the dish cloth and leaned back against the counter top.

"It's just..." She scrunched up her eyes, trying to find the words. "I *was* worried. God, I'm still worried." She grimaced at the understatement of her words, scratching the back of her head then rubbing her nose which she did when she was upset. "I was praying that we would find out something about your brother, for you. I knew how much it meant to you. But now..."

"Now what?"

"Now... well, it still doesn't explain everything that happened to you, does it? And don't give me that crap again about it being 'a twin thing!'" She continued over his dark stare. "You didn't even know for sure that you were a twin until last year. And you still can't even see him. Jesus, after all the time you spent looking, you're no nearer the truth now. All you know is he's in prison."

"I know which prison!"

"Yeah ok, big deal. You know which prison. Which state. So what? He's still refusing to see you. He won't let you write to him. He doesn't want to talk to you. All you do is run up the phone bill talking to his solicitor. Can't you see that it's just dragging it out?"

"His lawyer."

"What?"

"He's a lawyer, not a solicitor."

She rolled her eyes. "Oh! Sorry! Look Tom, I'm not saying give it up. I was just saying... I don't know, try to keep it in perspective. You have a family here. The episodes, the visions, whatever they were, they seem to have stopped. Can't you just... leave it. Give it a while? Maybe he'll change his mind, if you stop pushing."

Tom said nothing. He just stood by the kitchen table, arms folded, watching her.

She barked out a sharp laugh. "God, sometimes I feel like I don't even know you anymore. You know what; I almost think it would have been easier if you had had a breakdown. Instead of all this crap. At least I would be able to understand it more."

"Fantastic. Thanks babe. Good to know I can count on my wife!"

"God, this is impossible! You're like, I don't know, two different people." A snort of derision escaped from her throat as she realised what she had said. Still Tom didn't react.

"Tom?" Her tone now was conciliatory, but Tom could only close his eyes against the truth of her words.

"I am!" he told her quietly. "I am Tom, part of your family. And Tom, part of his."

Ashleigh was silent for a long moment. She nodded slowly before she resumed her cleaning.

Like most people, they were totally ignorant of the workings of the legal system. Tom had never even been to a prison before. Like most men, there was still the mild, hang-over lure of police procedure, high-speed pursuits and convicts held over from his childhood. He still felt the pull, like his own son, of a speeding police car, ambulance or fire engine as it raced past them. Elliott always insisted on watching until they disappeared from sight.

It was the same reason people gaped at road crashes, gathered to witness house-fires or watch gruesome crime dramas. That morbid fascination of human nature.

Tom was still reeling over the knowledge that he had a brother. A live one. The search for the place where his mother's remains were hidden was still a work in progress, but had definitely taken a back seat. The connection to Tommy, however unsavoury his character, was what caused this seemingly endless row. If Tommy / Sam would only agree to talk to him, to see him, it would all get sorted.

He continued his research. He was currently engrossed in a book called 'Identical Strangers' by separated twins Elyse Schein and Paula Bernstein. These two were living proof of the strange and wonderful connection between those who shared a womb. The facts in their case, and for Tom and Tommy, were stranger than fiction. Elyse and Paula were lucky though, as far as Tom was concerned. They met whilst still young enough to work through the questions such disclosure demanded, yet mature enough, and with a future to be able to properly entwine their respective lives.

Did they look alike? Sound alike? What did Tommy know about his background and how much had his childhood and the circumstances of his birth and his adoption, shaped his future? Unanswerable questions. Still, Tom kept asking and Ashleigh was beginning to show her frustration.

"You don't even know him!" Ashleigh stormed at him. "He's a murderer! A monster!"

"I know," he replied wearily. "But he's still my brother. You know who your family is. You've always known. I never had that Ash. Everything I knew was based on a lie."

"Not all of it!" her tone was bewildered. "Tom, think about it. Before you do anything. Just think about it."

"What is there to think about? It's not like I'm suggesting he come to live here, if he ever gets out."

She narrowed her eyes. "He's never getting out!" She stomped around the room, collecting abandoned toys and clothes the children had dropped. "He killed two people. That we know of! One of them was a police officer. God, I hope they never let him go!"

"Thanks!" Tom slammed his cup down on the coffee table. "Thanks a fucking bunch, Ashleigh!" He stood and stomped over to her furiously.

"This is my brother we're talking about. My only real family."

She took a step backwards, hugging the toys and clothes to her chest.

"Then what are we, Tom?" she spat back, *"scotch fucking mist?"* She let out a single sob and staggered over to the couch. She sat heavily, still holding the things she had collected. When she looked up at him, her eyes were brimming. "We can't carry on like this," she whispered. "It's tearing us apart!"

"According to you, these days, everything is enough to tear us apart." The bitterness in his voice brought fresh tears to her eyes and she blinked. "If you want me to leave again, Ashleigh, just say it."

She leapt up and gasped. "No!" she cried, "I don't want you to leave!" Tears spilled unchecked down her cheeks.

"Well... that's not what it sounds like!"

140

Ashleigh glanced upstairs as the floor boards creaked. She didn't reply. Instead she turned on her heel and stalked out of the room. He heard her stomp upstairs to put away the stuff she'd collected and to check on the kids.

When she came back down she was quiet. She walked into the kitchen. He heard the fridge open and heard her mutter softly to the hamster.

"You know what he did."

"So?" He stood and went to fetch a beer from the fridge.

"How can you still want to see him?"

He sighed. "Because he's my brother. I need to see him."

"But... he's a rapist. And don't bother telling me he wasn't convicted of that. It doesn't change anything. How would you feel if it was me or Meg? Or your sister? Don't you think that would make a difference?"

"It wasn't though. And it's not as simple as that, Ashleigh. Maybe there is a reason why he's like he is. Maybe, if I'd been the one to get taken to the States, it would have been me in prison and he would be the one fighting with his wife for the right to see his only brother. Don't look at me like that. It could be."

"He's not your only brother, what about Peter? Ashleigh turned away, watching Graham Norton laughing on the TV.

"Tom, he killed people. For God's sake, he's just lucky he's not in Texas. He'd have got the death penalty. They kill everyone there!"

"How do you know that?"

She shrugged. "It was on a film. Apparently it makes a difference in what State the crime is committed. I don't really understand it but there you go."

"He isn't lucky at all, Ashleigh." He turned away, picked up the TV remote and un-muted the sound.

The rest of the evening was spent in silence; a truce of sorts, watching re-runs of *Friends*, the least contentious thing they could find to view. Tom drank too many beers and spent a restless night on his own, sleeping on the sofa.

Chapter Thirty One

The first visitation order arrived just before Christmas.
Arrangements were made via Hugo Brooks, the American Lawyer, who
had sorted everything. "There is no guarantee," Brooks told him, "that he
will go through with the visit." Tom didn't care. He had to try.

The visit was timed to coincide with Tom's Christmas leave in five
weeks, so for the main part, Ashleigh would have to manage the frenzy
alone.

Rob had offered to be on call in case of emergencies although
Ashleigh could not envisage any situation which would see her calling him
for help. The extent of Rob's involvement was still something of a bone of
contention between her and Tom. Anyway, Rob had taken to calling daily,
to see if there was any news.

He drove Tom to the airport on December 19th. Tom was due
home around midday on the 24th. In case there were delays, he planned
ahead, shopping for a present for his wife before he packed. He left it,
gift-wrapped in the garage, in a box on the bench where he kept his tools.

They pulled up at Gatwick and sat in the car. The engine was still
running to keep the heating on, sitting for a moment outside the main
entrance; Tom quietly contemplating his forthcoming journey as Rob sat,
fiddling with his wedding ring. It was bitterly cold and Tom was wrapped
in a big coat, scarf and gloves. Finally, he exhaled loudly and went to get
out of the car. Rob turned to face him,

"Good luck!" he said. "Tom, Pauline and I wanted you to have
this!" He pulled the ring up to his knuckle then, taking a deep breath,
reached into his coat pocket. He handed Tom a roll of bank notes secured
with an elastic band.

"What? No!" said Tom, "Hey, thanks though. We..."

"Please, take it. We just want... we want to help and we are
family. Anyway, go on; you don't want to miss your flight!"

Tom hesitated and, taking the money, nodded his thanks. He
slipped the roll of notes into his breast pocket; it was reassuringly heavy.

He felt choked up and smiled at his uncle, pausing briefly before he climbed out of the car and hauled his travel bag onto his shoulder.

He patted the inside pocket of his jacket once again, checking for the ticket – his and Ashleigh's present to each other this year – his passport and other travelling papers. And, now, the money. In his suit case was a letter from the Connecticut State Prison, approving him for a series of visits to inmate number 5488960, James Tomas Harper 3rd.

With a last fleeting glance at the car he stepped away, heading inside to the massive departures hall. He heard his uncle drive off, the distinctive throaty sound of the powerful engine purring off into the early morning. For a while he heard nothing except the sound of his heart beating in his chest, his pulse rushing in his ears, even as he was surrounded by hundreds of people; some striding purposefully, others milling around as if just killing time. Gradually, other noises intruded and he felt himself calm.

He stood up straight, spent a moment orientating himself, striding confidently to the Pan Am check in desk. He was on his way.

His journey to Connecticut was arduous. He was exhausted by the time he arrived and bewildered thanks to the time delay. He fired off a rapid text telling Ash he had arrived in the state and was heading straight for the Motel. He arrived, checked in and flaked out.

His first meeting later in the day was arranged with Mr. Brooks at his office. Tom arrived feeling incredibly nervous. The secretary he had spoken to initially was at the desk. Despite being aged, Tom estimated, around her late 30's, she was smartly dressed in a pale blue satin blouse straining slightly across her ample chest. She wore expertly applied make-up, including a pale pink, glistening lipstick and an incredibly glamorous hair-style with copper highlights and soft, flattering curls. She definitely lived up to the promise of her sexy telephone voice. She gave him a warm smile and asked him to sit whilst she contacted the lawyer to tell him his client's brother had arrived.

Tom's palm felt sweaty when Brook's held his hand out, but he fought the urge to wipe it before they shook.

"Sit, sit!" Brooks gestured to the chair opposite his desk and Tom sat, sitting at the edge of the seat. He waited as Brooks stepped back around the desk and took a seat.

There was a file on the desk in front of him, thick with bright yellow paper. A note was clipped to the front and with it, a post card with a US stamp on it. Brooks plucked the card off the front, pursed his lips and slipped it into the file.

Tom cleared his throat and Brooks smiled.

"So... You've come a long way." He meant purely the geography, but the significance felt bigger to Tom. It was more than just miles he had travelled. And he wasn't there yet.

Brooks was stocky and well-built. His voice and accent were all-American, laid back, confident, but his appearance was that of a native of the med. His hair was thick and curly around his collar and he had a growth of dark hair around his chin which suggested a need to shave at least daily. The olive colour of his skin was smooth and Tom was reminded of on actor from the TV, but he couldn't think of the name. He wore an expensive looking suit and small round Harry-Potter-type specs.

"Mr. Bearing?" Brook's voice broke through his trance and Tom jumped. He cleared his throat again. Mr. Brooks smiled at him. He was a nice bloke. "Can we get you a coffee or something?" he offered.

Tom shook his head but realised coffee might help him focus.

"Umm... actually, yeah, please. Thanks," He said. Brooks picked up his phone and murmured into the handset. He replaced it on the cradle gently and Tom realised it was an old fashioned type, complete with circular dial. He smiled.

"My wife's idea of a joke!" explained Brooks. "She thinks I'm something of a fossil!" Tom laughed weakly.

"So... how was your flight?" Brooks was clearly working to make Tom feel at ease and he appreciated it.

They spent a moment or so talking about the journey until there was a knock on the door and the secretary entered, carrying a tray with drinks and biscuits on it. She winked at Tom as she set the tray down on the desk.

Brooks laughed, "Thanks, Madeline!" he said as she left. Tom could hear her shapely thighs swishing together as she passed him in a waft of sultry perfume. Aware of Tom's reaction to his wife, Brooks decanted the drinks from the tray, hiding a smirk.

The room was on the dark side, but plush and comfortable. Books lined two full walls, heavy thick works that Tom took, correctly, for legal tomes. There was a patterned rug on the floor, old and expensive and a tiffany-style coloured lamp on the desk which glowed green through its hooded shade. The room smelled of books and a faint trace of perfume. The other main wall, behind Brooks, was all-window and through it, Tom could see the foreign skyline of the town beyond.

"Mr. Bearing? May I call you Tom?" Tom turned back to the lawyer, who passed him his coffee and nodded. He declined sugar and cookies and set the cup down on the desk in front of him. Brooks did the same.

Opening the file, he cleared his throat. "These are very unusual circumstances," his tone was serious. "I must admit, it's a first for me."

"The twin thing?" replied Tom. Brooks nodded and skimmed the file. He stopped at a page, hesitated a fraction of a second but took a breath and, releasing it through his nose, turned the file around, laying it open in front of Tom.

The file was open at a page of pictures. Tom was uncertain if he wanted to see but Brooks smiled at him, a smile of understanding and support.

"I imagine you would like to see what he looks like," he said in a quiet voice. Tom took a deep breath and forced his eyes down to the paper in front of him. He pulled the file closer.

The pictures were of Sam's – now know, of course, as Tommy – arrest. Mug shots. Cold hard light. Lines painted on the wall to his side and behind him to mark his height. A number held on a board in each shot identified the offender. Side profile. Full face. No expression. No reaction. Tom swallowed and sat back. It was his own face. Only the hair was different. And the eyes. Something hard in Tommy's eyes. Tom's own eyes closed and darkness followed.

"Tom? Tom? Are you feeling better?" Tom nodded and sat up. He had listened carefully to Brooks though he heard nothing. After an hour or so the room seemed be swimming round and round and he struggled to keep his eyes open. When he awoke, sometime later, he sat up, finding himself on the couch in reception. He was covered by a soft blanket of some description in spite of the warmth of the room.

Embarrassed, he sat up, wiping his mouth and pushing the blanket aside. The secretary had gone and Tom looked up to see Brooks sitting in a tub chair opposite him, reading intently.

"It's just the jet lag!" Brooks offered kindly. With a wry smile, Tom nodded and sat up. He rubbed his eyes.

"What happens now?" His voice was thick with sleep. He cleared his throat and made to stand.

"I'll make some more coffee!" Brooks stood and walked away, telling Tom over his shoulder, "maybe it would help if I went over the details again?"

Tom nodded, then, realising that Brooks could not see, he called after him. "Yeah. Ummm... Yes, please. Cheers."

When the coffee was made Brooks led the way back into his office. Tom sat in the same seat, this time feeling ready for the meeting. Shit, jet lag was a nightmare.

Tom asked few questions because he didn't know where to start, and anyway, Brooks was thorough and patient. He had not expected Tom to understand the American Penal System and he didn't. He guided Tom through the various stages, the initial arrest, the discovery of the body, the court case, the appeals and the sentence.

"Tom?" The gravity in his voice made Tom's stomach flip. He waited. Time seemed to zoom out, like a camera that was focussed on one place which panned at top speed back to show the world.

"Say it!" he told Brooks.

"That he received a death sentence?" Brooks put both hands on the desk in front of him and knotted his fingers together. Tom nodded.

"Yes," said Brooks. "He was sentenced to death on March sixteen, 2012." Tom nodded although he felt something like a ball of ice settle in his stomach. It was what he was expecting. He had seen it in the vision at the judo comp a few years ago. He felt a moment of relief to know that he wasn't going mad. Shit, he wondered if Ashleigh would appreciate that.

That did not explain however, that somehow, even though he and his twin had never met, they shared a connection great enough that Tom would feel consequences of the catastrophic decision to send his brother to death row.

"Tom?"

Brooks cleared his throat. "I'm so sorry..."

Tom shook his head. "I... knew, I think." He paused, seeing the question on the man's face. "Don't ask me how!" he said, "I just knew." He took a breath. "So... can I see him?"

146

"Tom," repeated Brooks. Something in his tone hit Tom. He started to tell Brooks that it was ok, he really had been expecting it, but his lawyer's face stopped him.

"What?" Tom's voice was barely a whisper.

"I'm so sorry," Brooks said again. "His date... He is officially scheduled to die in just under four months."

"*What*?" Tom stood, pacing the room, stunned. "But he's here, in Connecticut. They have repealed the death penalty haven't they? I read it on the internet. Doesn't that mean they don't execute people here anymore? Anyway, four months gives us time to..."

"Those rules, they don't apply to him." Brooks exhaled loudly. "It's more complicated than that. There is a lot of stuff I can't get into. Bottom line, his date has been set. I'm so sorry."

Chapter Thirty Two

Christmas without his family was hard. Tom felt torn into a million pieces as he spent a fortune on the phone with Ashleigh and the children. Explaining his absence to them, to Ash, was heartbreaking, but, he reasoned, there was little choice. Four months was no time at all, he stayed to try, with Brooks, to change his brother's mind.

Without the money from Rob Tom would have been unable to stay and even now, Rob, unbeknown to Ash, was still funding the trip. Tom just told her he was being economical, but the truth was Rob was paying funds into a pre-paid credit card for Tom on an almost weekly basis.

Back home, Ashleigh was struggling to cope. Even Meg was hard work, but that wasn't surprising. As for Elliott, nothing seemed to impact his behaviour, not the threat of losing presents, trips out or being confined to his room. The 'naughty-step' was almost his second home.

Finally, Ash caught him squeezing all the water out of the hamster's water bottle clipped to the side of his cage. She realised it was why the bottle always seemed to be empty, no matter how many times she refilled it. She lost the plot, shouted at Elliott and smacked him on the bottom.

He was five now, as confident as his sister and as capable of talking, although he seemed to prefer a state of moody silence. When she smacked him, for the first time ever, instead of crying he narrowed his eyes at her, but said nothing.

"Elliott, that's cruel!" Ashleigh was struggling to be firm but fair. Still, the child said nothing. Meg wandered into the room, eating a chocolate from the tree. Ashleigh glanced at her, but Elliott's eyes never left her face, burning with a fierce intensity which left her breathless.

"Mommy?" Meg's voice was tentative, she was still wary of her brother.

"It's ok, Meg," Ash turned to her daughter, giving her a weak smile. She turned back to Elliott, feeling stronger.

"Well? Do you have anything to say?" He stood still and quiet and Ashleigh swallowed. Shit, she would be glad when Tom got back. "Elliott?" He lifted his head and turned his face away.

Exasperated, she snapped again. "Go upstairs!" she said, louder than she'd intended. "Now!" He watched her for a long moment before he turned, glanced once at the hamster guzzling his water and stalked out of the room. Ashleigh fought to keep herself from shivering.

Tom listened to the litany of complaints from Ashleigh through gritted teeth. Frustration that he was unable to see how to help his brother, who so far still declined to see him, coupled with mounting irritation at Ashleigh for moaning at him across thousands of miles, made his jaw ache where he clenched it so hard.

He rubbed his head, feeling the headache which had been present for days now, threatening to overwhelm him.

Spending his days mostly with Hugo and his unlikely wife, Madeline, Tom found himself becoming embroiled in a virtual battle to save his brother. Yet Tom knew that Tommy was guilty. He'd seen it for himself. He'd felt it.

He spent hours reading. A handbook from the Connecticut Department of Corrections had been given to him detailing the intake process, how to give inmates money, discipline in the prison etc, but not how to talk to a twin you have never met, and persuade him to see you.

Research, at this point, had proven largely useless. None of it gave him any idea of how to talk to Tommy. What to say. The stack of photographs he had brought were still in their envelope. He hoped to be able to show them to his brother, but was beginning to suspect he wouldn't get the chance.

According to Brooks, Tommy was counting down the days with remarkable calm. Tom found this hard to believe. Tom had bought, with Rob's money, a cheap tablet PC to access all the information he needed and to keep in touch with Brooks and his team.

In fact, the internet had given Tom some hope. Brooks had tried hard not to lecture Tom about the death penalty and its various statistics. Most of the extraneous stuff, such as the gender bias on death row (predominantly male), the incidence of mental health problems such as depression and suicide attempts (three times that expected in the general population), the inequities relating to race (overwhelmingly black or ethnic) and income (i.e. none!), Tom learned all via the web.

Brooks was an expert on the death penalty. He could spout fact after fact about it, who was killed, who was waiting to be killed. Why such and such a person had been given the death penalty. Tom argued that, to a non-national, a big part of the problem was about the 'right to bear arms'.

Not, Brooks told him, that that was necessarily a bad thing, but that when that law was passed, it was in the days when a pistol took half an hour to load and firing it was something of an occasion. The law had not kept pace with the 'arms' in circulation in modern times. That, Brooks argued, was the main flaw.

In Tommy's case, he killed the lay-preacher with a candlestick - that was bad enough. The nail in his coffin, however, was to kill a police officer with his own weapon. Game, set, and match to the state.

No one, Brooks told him, could get out of that one. Not, he added evasively, that Tommy was trying to.

The days raced past in a blur. Tom felt increasingly remote, barely eating, drinking too much and sleeping little. His conversations with everyone but Brooks were short and tense. On New Year's Day, Tom received a call. Brooks invited him to his home in Hartford, Connecticut. Initially, Tom declined. Pulling out his secret weapon, Brooks put Madeline on the phone and, using her best sexy-phone voice, persuaded him to reconsider.

He arrived bearing a bottle of wine and a bunch of flowers for Maddy. She greeted him at the door wearing a soft shift dress, hair done and made up to the nines. She smiled and kissed his cheek. She smelled delicious. Behind her, Brooks stepped forward and shook Tom's hand.

"Umm... thanks for the invite!" The place was not especially big, but it was bright and cheery. Blues, beige and white created a sea-side feel and, glass of crisp white wine in hand, Tom felt himself relaxing for the first time in weeks.

In the past two weeks, the case had been thoroughly outlined by Brooks. He had worked hard to simplify the complex American penal system. All the initial processes during the arrest were correct. Tommy had been caught 'bang to rights'. No grounds for appeal there.

Not to say that Brooks hadn't tried that route, after all, there were just a few inmates on death row in the state, he had some considerable experience. The appeals, in fact, had been arduous and methodical. All possible arguments were explored, even that of insanity.

The last time Tom and Brook's had met Brooks had explained that, subject to the mental state and wishes of the defendant, there were still a few appeals that could be made. With time running out and the date of the execution looming, Tom struggled to understand.

The last thing Brook's had said to him was 'We're not done yet!' and Tom had nodded, too emotional to respond. He had spent New Year's Eve alone in his starkly modern, bland brown and beige hotel room, watching the fireworks burst across the skyline at midnight and wishing he was with his family.

"Tom?" Madeline's voice broke through his thoughts and he turned to her. "I was just saying," she said, sashaying into the kitchen and smiling at him over her shoulder, "I've made a little light dinner. It's ready whenever you are."

Brooks steered him into a room off the hall and Tom realised it was a home office. In contrast to the one where he worked, the room was bright and colourful. Clearly Maddy's hand at work in here. A large desk was cited in front of the window with a view of the small, neat, winter-dark yard out the back.

Flowing terracotta drapes framed the window, pooling onto the floor. Matching cushions sat on the two fancy leather seats, a small Indian-wood table between them. Wall lights illuminated them from behind, despite the daylight, casting a warm, creamy glow over the space.

Brooks bid him to sit and Tom did, placing his wine on the table between them. They made themselves comfortable for a few seconds. Tom nodded at the garden. "I thought it would be warmer in the US!" he said. Brooks gave a wry nod in response. The heating was on and the room was pleasantly warm, highlighting the bleakness of the garden outside.

"Tom," Tom recognised the tone and he felt the ice re-form in his stomach. To delay what Brooks was about to say, he picked up the wine and took a big gulp. Brooks waited until he placed the glass back on the table before continuing.

"Are you ok?" Tom nodded for him to go on. "Tom, he has agreed to meet you." Tom's eyes flew to Brook's face, unsure of how to feel.

"He has?" he said stupidly. Brooks nodded.

"That's great!" Tom sat forward. "Hey, that's fucking great!" He stood, nervous energy suddenly filling him. He turned to face the lawyer. "When?" he asked.

"Very soon, given the circumstances." Brook's' voice was quiet and Tom thought for a moment.

"But?" he asked, "I sense there's a 'but'." Brooks said nothing for a second and Tom found himself pacing, the thick lovely carpet muffling the sound. He turned back, "Yeah, ok, it's getting a bit hairy, but when you've filed more appeals..."

Brooks sighed. "Tom, there *are* no more appeals. There isn't going to be a reprieve." Tom closed his eyes against the words, feeling the walls spin as if he had drunk the whole bottle, not just half a glass.

He rubbed his eyes and found his voice. "I thought you said..."

Brooks stood too. He walked over to Tom and paused. "I did. But now... there are no more appeals, because Tommy... he doesn't want them."

Tom's eyes flickered wildly. "But... he will! That's ridiculous. He wants to meet me! You just said he did. He'll want to, I don't know, have some time to..."

Brooks held up his hand. "Tom," he said, "you don't understand..."

Tom stood, feeling breathless, his head cocked to the side, waiting.

"He has been assessed by the state as competent. The state, therefore, must accept his wishes and so must I, much as I dislike it." Tom stared at him, afraid to open his mouth in case the Chardonnay came spewing back up.

Exhaling sharply, Brooks turned to face the garden. The dead heads of the flowers and pale lime colour of the grass showcased the dismal atmosphere in the room.

Brooks turned back. "He's agreed to meet you the day before his execution. He asked me not tell you before. I feel shitty for springing this on you. Tommy..."

"What?" Tom's heart was in his mouth.

The lawyer continued, "Tom, he wants to die and we have to let him."

Chapter Thirty Three

She wished it was all over already. The day was rapidly turning into a nightmare for Ashleigh and she fought to maintain her composure. And it was still days and days to Christmas. So far, she had resurrected the poor bloody Christmas tree three times, washed unknown substances off Meg's judo stuff (Elliott refused to say what the substance was and all Ash knew was it was oil of some description from the garage).

She had consoled Meg when Elliott had torn the head of her favourite ragged old teddy off, furious with Elliott but unsure how to deal with such wanton destruction. She was determined, this time, to get Tom to acknowledge that the child needed help. Jesus, she would be glad when she went back to work. She would be glad when Tom came home. She... Oh crap!

Hearing a piercing scream from the kitchen, Ashleigh sighed aloud. She plastered a smile of parental patience on her face and headed into the room, ready to separate the warring factions.

She walked in, dumping stray cups and beakers by the sink, before she turned to her children. Meghan was sobbing, pulling at Elliott's hair and his jumper, trying to make him turn around whilst he, with one hand, kept her at arm's length. Reaching out, Ashleigh caught hold of her arm, her tone cajoling, ready to try to mediate this new fight.

She succeeded in pulling Meg away from her brother and Meg turned and collapsed, wailing, into a chair at the dining table. Ash reached out for Elliott, trying to see what he had broken now. Horror froze as a bubble in her throat, making her feel like she was choking. His sturdy little body facing the draining board, in his hands Elliott held Harry the hamster, dead and dripping from being drowned in the sink. His fur clumped and his jaw open impossibly wide, Elliott was squeezing the creature hard around the middle.

"He's dead!" The satisfaction in Elliott's voice hit Ashleigh like a slap. She recoiled, stepping backwards and knocking the cups off the drainer in her haste to get away. He looked at the hamster and then at his mother. He gave a small sigh of satisfaction, turning to give her a strange, wry little smile. *"Did you know hamsters can't swim?"* he asked her, "I checked!"

By now Meg had stopped wailing, but tears continued to roll unchecked down her face, dripping onto the glass table top. She gulped and shuddered, trying to control herself. Ashleigh went to comfort her daughter, but neither of them could speak. Behind them, Elliott dumped the dead hamster on the draining board and snatched up a toy car off the floor. He raced past them waving the car around. "Vvvrrooommm!" he shouted.

The journey back to the UK passed without Tom realising, most of the time, where he was. He was herded through customs in the US, herded onto the plane, herded off and corralled to the line to collect his luggage.

'Go home,' Brooks had told him on New Year's Day. 'Go see your wife. Hug your children. Don't make any hasty decisions.' The words echoed in Tom's head as he sat on a bench outside Gatwick, oblivious to the snow falling. By the time Rob reached him, Tom's lips were blue with cold and he was shivering.

Rob climbed out of the car and walked over to Tom. "Earth to Thomas!" he laughed, clapping him on the shoulder.

The laughter died on Rob's lips. "What is it?"

"He's going to die!" Tom was bereft.

"Well... I thought you said, well Ash said, because he is in Connecticut, they don't do that anymore."

"Well," Tom's voice was grimmer than Rob had ever heard. "They do now!" he replied.

Rob dropped him off outside, he thought it best to give Tom some time with his family. He drove off, watching as Tom hesitated on the doorstep of his own house, hand poised to open the door. He seemed frozen there.

Ashleigh had heard the car. She flung open the door and threw herself at Tom, almost knocking him over.

"Oh you're back, you're back!" She pulled him inside and he stood numbly in the small hall as Ashleigh wrapped her arms around his neck.

Interpreting his lack of action as tiredness and jet lag, she called to the children to tell them he was home, cautioning them to be calm, daddy was tired.

Their little faces lined up before him. God, they had grown even in the few days he had been away. Meg was pulling him into the lounge and Ashleigh was behind him, pulling his coat off and removing his scarf.

"...And, and, I got and iPod for Christmas, Daddy! It's purple! Mom says you'll help me put the music I want on it. Will you?"

"Will I what, love?"

"iTunes, Dad. Will you help put the music on my iPod?"

Tom finally managed to focus on her face. "What iPod? When did you get an iPod?"

"Daddy! I just told you, I got an iPod for Christmas. A purple one!" Over the top of her head he looked at Ashleigh. 'Rob and Pauline!' she mouthed at him. He rolled his eyes.

"Oh, Daddy!" Meg flung her arms around his neck. "I've missed you sooooo much!" He kissed her and she stepped back, clapping her hands with glee that her father was home. Elliott stood a few feet back, watching them with careful eyes.

"Hello, matey!" Tom held his arms out for a hug and, after a notable pause, Elliott walked forward slowly, into his embrace.

"God, Elliott, you've grown so much!" Tom held the child back, staring into his eyes. Elliott gave a half-hearted smile before he turned and looked at his mom, almost as if asking permission to terminate the hug. Tom looked again at his wife, she shook her head and shrugged.

"Did you bring us any presents, Daddy?" said Meg, bouncing up and down.

"Duh, no, I forgot!" Tom stood and winced as his back clicked.

"Meg, Elliott, let Daddy sit down for minute. He's been travelling for hours and hours." Ashleigh's voice was firm and both children stepped back.

"Daddy, would you like me to make you a cup of tea?"

"Can you do that?" he replied.

"Duh!" she parroted, "of course I can!"

The rest of the evening flashed past. Tom made it until eight o'clock before exhaustion took over.

"Go to bed, love." Ashleigh was kind and in control. "We can talk about it tomorrow. The kids are going to my Mom's for the day so we'll have some time to ourselves." He nodded, too tired to do anything more than stumble upstairs and fall into bed. He was asleep in two minutes.

"I need to tell my Mom." Tom's face was haggard. He had slept until noon by which time the children had gone. He hadn't even heard them complaining that they wanted to see him.

He spent an hour unpacking his bag, sorting dirty washing and toiletries, piling everything onto the laundry basket in their bedroom. Ash sat on the bed watching him. She gave him a summary of the days without him. Although he had only been gone a few days longer than planned, still, it left a hole in her life that she struggled to fill.

"We spent Christmas day with my parents," she said, picking through some of the items he had brought back from the hotel; tiny soaps, miniature sewing kits and travel-sized bottles of shampoo and conditioner. "In the end we stayed the night too. It seemed easier. Elliott really seems to get on well with my dad. My Mom can't cope with him of course, but still... Dad is cool about it. He says that all he needs is a firm hand and a lot of love.

"Oh, and Joe? He rang. I nearly had a heart attack! He wanted to see if you were back. Apparently Mark told him what was going on. I didn't want to talk to him. I just told him you were staying a bit longer and put the phone down." Tom eyes searched her face. "That's all," she said. "I don't think he wants to walk away from your friendship."

Tom continued his unpacking in silence. "Thank you for the Christmas present you hid!" She fingered the silver heart at her neck. "I love it!" He smiled. "I saved this for you!" Reaching into her bedside drawer, she pulled out a box beautifully wrapped in red and gold paper with a fancy ribbon around it.

"I just wanted to say... I... I'm sorry you didn't get to see Tommy." Tom took a breath and turned and sat on the edge of the bed. He held the parcel in his hands for a moment. "Go on!" she urged, "Open it!"

He ripped it open. Inside was a square white sleeve. He slid it off and opened the box wide. Inside was a watch with a dark tan leather strap and a large dark face. "It tells the time in two countries!" she said, "so you can work out what time it is where Tommy is!" She was so excited and pleased by her gift.

"Thanks." Tom tried to seem happy.

"What's wrong?" Her face fell. "Don't you like it? You can change it; it's from Argos in Town."

"I love it," he told her. "It's just..."

"Just what?

"It's just... Tommy doesn't have any time. He's been given an execution date."

She gasped, her hands flew to her throat. "Oh," she said, "but, I thought you said they didn't..."

Tom leaned forward, as if he was going to be sick. He sat back up. "I did say that. That's not the problem. In Connecticut, they don't execute people anymore. Life means life there."

"But... I don't understand," Ashleigh's big brown eyes were filled with tears. "Then how...?"

Tom laughed; a harsh, mirthless sound which exploded from him. "Oh, well, apparently," he spread his hands wide; "apparently my brother has *volunteered* to die. And it means the state has no choice but to execute him."

Chapter Thirty Four

Travel arrangements were rapidly made. Ashleigh spent five days sorting washing, ironing and re-packing. Rob and Pauline again came through with more money which went a long way to easing the worry, in that respect anyway. Ash was dismayed that he had taken money from his Aunt and Uncle without telling her. He couldn't worry about that now.

Tom went to work with a leaden feeling in the pit of his stomach. The execution was two weeks away. He had been offered special leave – paid – which thankfully meant they could still pay the mortgage and bills, though at this point, Tom didn't care about anything except getting back to the States to try to see his brother.

It seemed to Tom and Ashleigh that everyone knew. Neighbours crept around, mining for details. Bugger subtlety, no one bothered to hide their curiosity. Friends they had not seen for years appeared out of the woodwork. Most were supportive, some less so.

'I hope you're there to see the bastard fry!' Tom was told, more than once.

Behind closed doors, he and Ashleigh clung to each other like drowning men. Nothing Ashleigh said could bring a glimmer of hope to him, but it did not stop her trying. The children, even Elliott, crept around, keeping quiet and being as good as gold. Neither of them had a clue what was going on, but they knew their Daddy was hurting and that meant they were hurting too.

Tom got through the morning by rote. Jose, quietly and with no fuss, sorted out anything Tom had missed. Time dragged and by lunch, Tom felt like he was being fried. He sat heavily in the canteen, watching as it filled up. His packed lunch sat on the table before him. Jose joined them and sat down, shook open *The Sun* Newspaper and peeled the foil off his sandwiches. The smell of spicy chicken filled the air.

Gradually the noise level rose as colleagues joined them. Tom barely registered the change in numbers. Normally, the office staff ate at

159

their desks or went into town. The senior managers never ate in; usually they were out on the road or in meetings which were catered. Today though, it seemed that everyone was in the canteen.

Tom forced himself to eat a sandwich. The tomato had made the bread soggy and wet. He put it back down and struggled to swallow the lump in his mouth. He pushed the lunchbox away.

To his left, Amanda, the big boss's secretary, asked him if he would like a cup of coffee. Only Jose was engrossed in his lunch. Everyone else was watching Tom. He nodded and she stood and walked back into the kitchenette. A low hum of conversation ebbed around him until Amanda brought the drink back and placed it in front of him. He shook his head. Never before had he been this interesting!

"Thanks," he said, nodding at the coffee. She smiled. Across the table, Rich cleared his throat.

Tom sat up. "Go on then!"

"Is it true?" Rich spoke quickly and sat forward, eager to hear the answer. Almost in unison, so did everyone else.

Tom gave a snort of disbelief. He had told no one here but his line manager. Now everyone knew. Well, bollocks, he thought, he had nothing to hide.

"Is what true?" he replied mildly. Rich looked at the man sitting next to him, one of the accountants, Marlon something. *Fucking stupid name.* Marlon shrugged and turned back to Tom.

"About your brother being in prison in America." Tom nodded slowly.

"Shit," breathed Marlon.

Amanda turned to face the group crowded around the table. "Come on everyone, maybe he doesn't want to talk about it." Tom scratched his head and sat back in his seat. It was now or never. "Yes. It's true. I just discovered I have a twin. Yes he's in prison, and yes he's on death row."

"In what state?" Jose's paper was laid down on the table covering his lunch.

"Connecticut," Tom replied.

"Phew!" Rich pretended to mop his brow. "At least he's not in Texas!"

Tom snorted a laugh. "You think?"

"Well, yeah." Rich turned the group, "they're like, really extremist there. Highest execution rate in the States. Only the Middle East kill more of their own people." His tone was confident and the group appeared rapt with excitement.

"What did he do?" Tom strained forward to see the person who had answered the question. Her name was Francesca and she worked in the offices. He knew her only by sight, this was the first time they had ever exchanged words. She too was leaning forwards; eyes alight with excitement, a pale blush staining her cheeks. Tom blinked, feeling his guts clench.

"He... murder." Almost as one they appeared to be holding their breath. He sighed, exhaling loudly.

"He killed a man who attacked him. Head injuries, I believe. Then he... a policeman – well, a trouper I guess – he responded to a call the man Tommy killed called, you know, before he killed him. Well, anyway, there was a fight and Tommy killed the cop with his own gun."

Silence descended as his co-workers digested the information. Next to him, Amanda swallowed. "Oh, my God!" she whispered.

"Have you been able to see him?" Jose's voice was quiet, deferential. Tom shook his head. "Does he know about you?" Jose continued. This time, Tom nodded.

"You're going back there sometime?" This came from one of the drivers. Simon was half the size of a barn, fat but with enormous bulk, covered in tattoos and with a skin-head hair cut. His face was fleshy and yet there was something about him which signalled enormous strength.

Tom cleared his throat. "Yeah," he said, "in fact..."

"What?"

Tom couldn't see who asked this so he addressed the group in general. "What no one has asked is if he is actually going to be executed. He is." All around the table, jaws dropped in astonishment. He took a deep breath and continued. "His lawyer, a great guy called Brooks, he's tried to explain it all, but..." His voice trailed off. Amanda reached out and patted his arm. Her eyes said, 'stop, if it's too much, just stop,' but Tom shook his head slightly, he was ok.

There was silence in the room for the moment. After a second or so the water boiler in the kitchen kicked on, its low droning buzz like a stuck bumble bee filled the air for a moment before it settled back down.

"Connecticut has executed people before. I think the last one was a guy called Michael Ross, in about 2005, Brooks said. He killed a bunch of girls. Since then, the local government, well, the State, I suppose, they've stopped executing people."

"So Tommy, is that his name? Hey how weird is that, he has the same name! – what, he'll just sit on death row until he dies?"

Tom shook his head slowly. "No," he said, carefully. "I found out, just before I came home... Tommy..." He reached out and took the coffee off the table, took a slug and put it back down. Before him, the small crowd were hanging onto every word. "The system in the states is really complicated." With a laugh Tom realised he sounded just like Brooks.

"The Federal Government, like who the country elects, you know, like, Clinton, Obama, they can still execute prisoners in non-death penalty states. Not sure how... something to do with the Federal Government. Otherwise each state can sort of, decide for itself if it has execution as a punishment or not, and for what crimes. Some criminals, they know this and make sure they're not caught in the more... umm... strict ones."

"Like Texas?" Rich was trying to helpful. Tom smiled and nodded.

"I still don't get it." Jenny from accounts sounded like Ashleigh and Tom sighed. "I thought you just said they don't kill prisoners in that state anymore?" She looked around the table. "It doesn't add up!"

A few people nodded. "There is another rule..." Tom paused and rubbed his hands across his eyes. "Apparently, prisoners who are given life sentences can... 'volunteer' to be killed." Using his fingers, he indicated quotation marks around his words. Slowly, his hands descended back to the table. Silence greeted this statement. Around him Tom could see some of the group look at each other as they considered this.

"Why?" Amanda, this time.

Tom shrugged. "Maybe they think it's better than spending the rest of their lives in a cell twelve feet by ten? I don't really know. Needing permission to shower. No company. No daylight. No... *hope* I guess."

"That's nuts!" Marlon shook his head in disgust. "That's gotta mean they're mad, don't it? The prisoners, I mean."

Again Tom shrugged. "No, apparently not. No state is allowed to kill someone who is, umm, mad! They have special docs assess those who 'volunteer', to make sure they are sane enough to kill."

"Fucking hell, that's crazy!" Marlon shook his head. A few of the group nodded, sharing his view.

The door to the canteen opened and Tom's line manager stood there. Max was clearly taken aback to see so many of the staff all crowded around the canteen table. Then he saw Tom and his eyes narrowed.

He walked over. Everyone ignored him. "Alright, mate!" He put his hand on Tom's shoulder. Tom turned; he hadn't registered who it was.

Lynn sat quietly opposite Tom. She did not even acknowledge Max as he sat. He wondered if they were still seeing each other.

Tom cleared his throat. He appreciated his boss's sympathy but he needed to talk about it. "Oh, yeah. It's no problem."

"You don't have to..." Max's head nodded towards the crowd and Tom smiled.

"Nah, its fine. They're just curious. I guess I would be too."

"So, your brother, has he been examined by this doc?"

Tom nodded.

"He's volunteered?" Tom turned at the horror in Amanda's voice. He felt his breath catch in his throat. All he could do was nod again.

"Oh, love!" Amanda turned to him and threw her arms around him. "Oh, Tom, you poor thing!"

Max turned to Jose and whispered in his ear. Jose whispered something back and Max sat back, revulsion on his face.

"Yes," Tom turned to the speaker. Another of the drivers, a tall thin man called Andy. He always seemed edgy, hyped up, as if he was on drugs. A thin sheen of sweat shone on his upper lip.

"And, what, he's sane enough to be executed?"

"Apparently."

Excited conversations broke out between various people sitting together. Across the table, Jose eyed him.

"You ok, mate?" His voice was kind and Tom felt a lump in his throat. He shrugged.

Jose shook his head slightly. "Tom, mate, if there is anything I can do. You just... you just gotta say."

Tom smiled his thanks and picked up his coffee.

"I'm sorry man." The voice came from the far side of the table. Tom leaned forward to see who spoke. "It's Mick," said the man. "I'm really sorry, Tom. That's really fucking rough. To hear you've got family you never knew, then to hear all this. Man, that's rough." Tom laughed at the understatement.

"Yeah, well..." Simon spoke in a clear, confident voice. "Don't do the crime if you can't do the time!" His tone was hard, matter of fact. He sat back.

"Yeah, but he is doing the time!" Amanda spoke up, directing her words towards Simon.

Simon shrugged. "Sorry," he said to Tom, "I believe in an eye for an eye, you know what they say."

"I guess, if he killed in cold blood, it's hard, but..."

Tom remained silent, watching the debate unfold before him. Rich took a bite of his sandwich and chewed thoughtfully.

"I dunno," he said, through a mouthful, "I guess it's one thing where someone is choosing to die. But when it's the decision of the courts, you gotta think, well, I mean, Americans, they know the score. It's not like here, is it?"

Jose said something under his breath.

"What?" Tom watched the man blush.

Jose coughed self-consciously. "I said, 'an eye for an eye makes the whole world blind."

Several people nodded, others shook their heads.

Max leaned forward, one hand on the table. He addressed the group, "Yes, I guess you could argue it either way. But, well, look at the law here. Murderers kill and they're sentenced to life. But what, they're out less than ten years, less in some cases."

"Not Hindley!" Francesca was pleased with herself.

"Murdering bitch!" said to almost unanimous nodding.

"Well, she killed kiddies." To Max the argument was clear.

"But why make an exception for her, and not oh, I dunno, someone who killed as many people, but is less... famous?"

"It's not right!" Amanda exhaled.

"No," continued Max, "it isn't. But then, I mean, look at our laws... kids can have sex and get married at 16. They can be made to fight for their country at 16, but they can't vote for the government that sends them to fight for that country until they're 18." He snorted a laugh of derision. "What the hell's all that about? Does that make any sense to anyone?"

"I think..." Tom's slow, measured tone made silence descend rapidly around the table. He scratched at his neck. "I think," he continued, "I would still take the UK legal system over the American one."

"Why?" Jose looked up.

"Because then they wouldn't kill his brother!" A wave of nervous tittering rippled around the group.

"I dunno," said Tom thoughtfully. "Maybe," he considered his colleagues around the table, "maybe it is that simple. It's just... I... I wish there was time..."

"Oh shit. I wish I knew what to say, Tom, it's just so awful." Amanda had tears in her eyes.

"Will you watch it?" A collective gasp went around the room. Francesca gazed at him, a light in her eyes telling Tom that death, in all its forms, held a fascination for her. *She was just the sort to write to someone on death row, weird fucking bitch.* Still, the others in the group were waiting for his response.

He shook his head. "No. He... he won't let me," he told them.

"But... if he did, would you?" Francesca was practically panting. Jose flashed her a strange glance. He raised his eyebrows at Tom, grimacing. Tom nodded in agreement.

"Yes," he replied. "He's my brother. Of course I would."

Chapter Thirty Five

He did not seem like a five year old. Furtively, the boy crept behind the large empty shed. Beyond his garden, the vast expanse of fields, dry and dusty, lay still and barren. Birds flew in perfect, lazy circles over his head. He watched them for a while. Weeds, some taller than the child, wafted in a soft breeze and sunlight, dappled through trees, made him squint.

Quiet as a mouse, patient as a Marine, he stalked the cat; pausing when the cat paused, moving when she moved. At one point, the cat sat abruptly, taking a long break to wash her face. Languid in the sunshine, she stood, stretched and yawned. The boy held his breath, was she about to take a nap?

He pursed his lips in disappointment but she moved on. Her gait changed and he sensed a shift of purpose. The twigs and foliage moved aside noiselessly as she hurried now, her body slinking past. Sunlight made her coat gleam as if she had been illuminated. He grinned with joy, then froze, still as a statue, as the cat halted. She moved on and so did her stalker.

He was quieter than a mouse. He was a better hunter than Indiana Jones. A better wizard than Harry Potter. He was stronger than a... a... Synonyms escaped him and he shook his head, still squinting. He ground his teeth in frustration. Where had she gone? Had she seen him?

He spent some ten minutes or so creeping around the garden. He loved the garden. In the past, it had been immaculate. A lawn cut so precisely that he knew its lines were straight, straighter than his ruler he took to school. The borders used to be a riot of colour, of scent. Big bushes, cut into shapes, like a horse once. He loved to hide between the bushes and jump out to scare people. That was fun.

It was even better now. He had the whole place to himself and, messy though it was, it was better suited to his games, his mood.

Ah, the cat! She lay behind the shed in a puddle of sunshine. The inside of the shack was dark, but it didn't frighten him. Nothing frightened him. And no one. Silently, he crept up to the animal, but she heard him. She lifted her head with a soft mew. Damn. Never mind. Still, practicing his stealth, like the best soldier in the world, he crawled towards her. His belly scraped across the ground and twigs and leaves stuck to his t-shirt. He ignored them. He liked the scraping noise as he wriggled across the floor. The cat looked away and lifted a paw to lick it. She looked once more at the boy and lay back down in the glorious sunshine.

He reached her and held out one small hand for her to sniff. She stretched her neck, sniffing his fingers, but could sense no food. Nothing worth moving for. She yawned again. He could see her little pink tongue. Her pointed teeth.

He wriggled and shuffled and sat beside her, stroking her down the entire length of her body. She arched her back, still prone on the ground. He continued petting her for a moment or so until the sun moved and shadows lengthened, dulling their small shelter.

The cat sat up, pressing against his legs, mewing softly. He smiled and reached down, lifting her and holding her to his chest. He could feel her heart beat. He continued to stroke her and she preened under his touch.

Without warning, he twisted, ramming the cat underneath his thigh. She yowled and wriggled frantically, struggling to get free. For a moment, he just held her there, trying to stay clear of her claws. The noise she made! Like a tiger! Like a lion!

He reached across to the edge of the border, no longer full of blooms and colour, but stony, dull, full of weeds. He picked up a rock and held it, enjoying its heft. It was almost the same size as his little hand. Still the cat, mewing and spitting beneath him, wriggled and fought. Good thing he was wearing jeans. Otherwise he would have been scratched to pieces.

Casually, preparing his aim, he brought the rock down on the top of the cat's head. She froze briefly before she yowled again, spitting and hissing. Her claws scrabbled against his denimed leg and scratched on the dusty path, but he was strong. Stronger than a... stronger than superman! Ha! He hit the cat again. Her skull split open, fur tore and blood seeped out. He watched, fascinated as it dripped, glossy and vibrant onto the dry earth beside him.

Still she moved. He brought the rock down again, then again and she shuddered and lay still. He waited; always make sure, he thought, that's what hunters do. She was still. He took a deep breath and, twisting, slung the cat to the over-grown border which marked out the path. He shoved and shoved, jumping clear of the blood as it dripped off her. He pulled reeds and small branches; covering her until he was sure he couldn't see her from the path.

He picked up a large dock leaf and studied it for a moment. He used it to swipe at the drops of blood decorating the path. Green from its veins left marks like crayons on the ground. Satisfied, he was a real warrior; he stood, brushed mud and dust from his hands, from his clothes and turned as he heard a voice calling.

"Kitty?" The voice was faint and he smiled. He walked slowly back around the side of the shed, strolling, pretending to search diligently amongst the tall weeds and wild plants.

He reached the back of the house. The woman stood with her back to the door, peering out towards the field, one hand shading her eyes from the bright sun.

"Any luck?" she asked, hopefully.

He shook his head, lower lip quivering; the very model of sadness. "No!" he lied, innocent and wide-eyed. "I think she's run'd away."

Chapter Thirty Six

His flight was booked, his bags packed, his agenda clear.
Brewstairs had been fantastic about it all. They were still paying him, even though he was about to take yet more time off. They had given him a card yesterday, signed by everyone, his last day before the trip on Monday.

Dressing in an old tracksuit, he cleaned his teeth and went downstairs. The children both sat at the kitchen table eating breakfast. Ashleigh was washing up. Both kids were chewing noisily, competing to see who could be the loudest. Ashleigh shrugged. What the hell, at least they weren't fighting. Tom smiled and flicked on the kettle, made himself a coffee; Ash shook her head when he waggled the cup at her. He walked to the fridge and poured milk into it. He glanced at the empty space on top of the fridge where the hamster had lived and glanced at his son. Elliott stared back, still munching, almost as if defying Tom to mention it.

He pulled out a seat and sat with a sigh. Both kids swallowed at the same time. "Me!" said Elliott, "I won!" Underneath the table, he was swinging his legs. He kicked Meg and she yelped.

"Apologise Elliott!" said Tom mildly. Elliott glared at him and said nothing. He dunked his spoon back into the bowl of Cheerios before him and scooped up a load, spilling milk on the table in the process.

"Elliott?" The child looked up at him. "I said, apologise." Tom's voice was quiet and calm. Elliott paused, spoon halfway to his mouth. He regarded his father for a moment. Ashleigh was looking at them, as was Meg. Elliott smiled and turned to his sister.

"Sorry!" he said, in a sing song voice. Tom picked up his coffee and took a sip. It was still boiling hot. He shifted his gaze towards the garden. The lawn was muddy and puddles of water were trickling towards the borders.

"It's such a mess out there!" Ashleigh sighed, seeing his gaze. Tom nodded.

"Well, it *is* still winter," he reasoned. Her turn to nod.

"Want some toast?"

"Yes, please, love." He twisted his cup around on the table, lifted it and blew on the surface.

"Daddy?" Tom turned to his daughter.

"Yes, sweetie?"

"Alex at school..." She looked suddenly engrossed in her nearly empty bowl.

"Yes?" Tom released a small sigh. "What, love? What about Alex?"

A red flush crept up her neck. "He said..." She swallowed. "He said... that your brother is a murderer."

Ash and Tom exchanged a 'what-the-fuck' glance and Tom cleared his throat. "Well..."

"Kids, go get dressed!" Ashleigh's voice was sharper than she'd intended and she stopped and turned, plastering a smile on her face. In her hands she held some dirty clothes, about to stuff them into the washing machine.

"No, Ash," said Tom, "if they're talking about it at school, we should explain it to them ourselves."

"But they're just kids!" She leaned down and flung the clothes into the drum. Standing, she rifled through the hamper on the side. She pulled out some jeans.

"God, Elliott, what the hell have you been doing in these? They're filthy!"

Tom interrupted. "Yes, so? No lies, we always said that, didn't we?"

Meg looked from one parent to the other; sensing that at this point staying quiet would get her more answers. Ash sighed and turned away. She threw in some wash tablets and pushed the button to start the washer. She turned to the sink and picked up a dish cloth.

"Ash?" Tom held his hand out towards her and, reluctantly, she put down the cloth and stepped across to the table. She sat in between the children, using a tea towel on the table to wipe up the milk that Elliott spilled.

"Is it true, Daddy?" Meg's tone was guileless.

"Yes," he told them. "It's very hard to explain. Erm... I never even knew I had a brother until, well, until just before last Christmas. Then, when I looked for him, well Uncle Rob and me, we found out that he had been taken to America at the same time I was taken by Nanny Rose and

Granddad Malc. My real mom, she couldn't keep us. She was too ill." Ash raised her eyes at him, sympathy on her face.

"Anyway, my brother, he did something bad, really bad and got sent to prison. He... is, oh bugger!" His shoulders drooped and Ash reached across and patted his hand.

"In America, if you kill someone, sometimes they... well, they order people to kill *you*. To try to put right what you did wrong."

Meg's eyes were wide and her mouth agape. "But, it's wrong to kill people!"

Elliott sifted his gaze between all the members of his family as they talked, but Tom noticed his eyes were curiously blank. He probably didn't understand. He was only five.

"I know," Tom replied. "But it's different in America. They have different laws to us. Here, if you do something really bad, well, then, you have to go to prison."

"Forever?"

Tom huffed. "Well, sort of. Sometimes they let you out if you are really good in there."

"Oh!" Meg paused, considering. "Well, I suppose that's good then. Can't your brother come to England instead? Then we can get to see him!" Ash shrugged nonchalantly. Tom swallowed a flash of irritation.

"No, love!" he said to his daughter. "I'm afraid not."

"Is it the same in other countries?"

"You mean; do they have the death penalty?" Meg nodded.

"Well," Tom was careful not to frighten her, "most countries don't have the death penalty anymore. It's called capital punishment. Some do. In some countries it's far worse than America." He paused as Ashleigh shot him a warning glance. "I mean," he qualified, "some countries have very different laws to ours. We're lucky here. In England, the government, they're the people who make the laws..."

"I know what the Government is Dad, I'm like, not a baby!"

He smiled. "Well, then you know that in this country, the government make the laws, basically, according to what we, the people, decide."

"Huh!" said Ashleigh, "Well, at least that's the theory!"

"So," Meg's little face was scrunched up in concentration. "...If all the people agreed, the government could decide to start killing our people again?"

Tom considered her statement and nodded slowly. "I guess so," he said.

"But," Meg shifted bodily to face him; her eyes flew between her two parents. "But," she stuttered, unable to speak the words fast enough; almost breathless with indignation, "what if they make a mistake? What if they kill the wrong person?"

"Ah," said Tom, "Clever girl! That's the million dollar question! I don't know, sweetie. I guess I do believe that's happened. Even in this country, in the olden days, before the government changed its mind about execution. I think that's one of the reasons they stopped. In case they make a mistake. They can't exactly take it back, can they?"

Ash looked at her children. "This is a really hard time for Daddy," she told them. "He's going back to America soon, to try to see his brother before..." She looked helplessly at Tom.

"Before the state decides it's time to... execute him."

"How?" Tom turned to Elliott.

"What do you mean, how?" He reached out and tried to stroke his son's hand, but Elliott moved out of his reach. "Do you mean, how can they do that?" Tom shrugged. "Oh God, I don't know. I don't really understand it myself."

"No," said Elliott, his eyes shining. "I mean, will they shoot him? Or stab him? Or... or... they could poison him. Couldn't they?"

Ashleigh scraped back her chair and stood, tea towel in hand. "Enough!" she said.

The children stayed with Ash, Tom went alone to his mother's. All the way there, he rehearsed what he planned to say. At this point all she knew was that Tommy had been found and that he was in prison. She had changed the subject at that point, silently giving Tom permission to put off the inevitable.

He pulled up outside the house, peering out at the soft, yellow glow from the street lights. Evenings were already getting lighter. Tom took a deep breath. As he walked to the front door, he saw his mom peering through the curtains. She watched him walk up the path. He smiled and waved, but she did not move. Using his key, he opened the front door and walked in.

"Hi!" he called out, slipping off his coat and hanging it up. "Mom?" He walked down the hall into the front room. Rose was still at

172

the window. Seated on the sofa were Peter and Helen, his half brother and sister. It was only the second time he had seen them since they all learned of his adoption.

Tom frowned, but Peter stood, clapped him on the shoulder, his usual greeting. Helen smiled and offered her cheek for a kiss. He obliged and stood up.

"What's going on?" he asked, sitting on the chair their father always used. "Mom?"

"Hullo, love!" She walked towards her chair, placed across from the TV. In the background, the TV showed one of the dull documentaries his mother preferred. Her bloody Sky recorder was filled with them. She wasn't particular; wildlife, stories about people born with weird and wonderful diseases, documentaries lamenting the sorry state of the country, she watched them all. The sound was turned down, the voices of the interviewer and interviewees a muted drone. He glanced away.

"Should I turn it off?" asked Peter.

Rose shook her head. These days, the TV was always on when she was home. It made the house seem less empty.

"I'll make you a coffee, shall I, love!" she said to Tom.

"No, thanks, I've just had one. I'm fine."

She nodded and sat back in her chair. Peter cleared his throat. "Mom's told us about... your brother. About Tommy."

Tom looked at him and nodded. "Oh, Tom, I'm so, so sorry!" Helen's words came out in a rush and Tom blinked.

"Me too," said Peter.

For a moment they all stared at the TV. Some serious academic appeared to be postulating about the rampant escalation of crime in the UK. "He's a law professor!" Rose told them. Her three children nodded.

Peter cleared his throat. "We just wanted to... to say, look, if there is anything you need. Anything we can do. To help, like!"

Helen nodded. "Yeah," she said, shuffling forward to sit on the edge of the seat, "anything at all."

Tom felt a lump in his throat. He smiled at them, unable to speak for a moment.

"How bad is it?"

Tom took a deep breath and turned from Peter to Rose.

"About as bad as it gets," he said slowly. Peter, Helen and Rose waited. The lamps were on in the room, but it seemed to Tom that he was encased in darkness. "He's on death row," he said, "they repealed the death penalty there some years ago..."

"Does that mean they won't kill him?"

Tom shook his head, no. Helen gasped. "Oh my God!" she said.

Tom sighed and looked at Rose. "I'm going back," he said, "On Monday. Its... he... oh God..."

"You don't have to talk..."

"No," said Tom, "It's ok. It affects you. You're all my family too." He took a deep breath. "Although he is in one of the states where they don't use the death penalty anymore, he is... he has..." He swallowed. "Sometimes, lifers, they can choose not to accept life in prison..."

Helen glanced from one to the other, confusion on her face.

"It means, he has volunteered to die. He's refused any more appeals. There is nothing the lawyer can do now. Tommy wants the state to kill him."

Checking his new watch, Tom clocked the time. Almost half past five. Rose and Helen were both crying, even Peter was visibly moved as Tom showed them the photograph of Tommy that Brooks had given him.

A knock on the front door made Rose jump. "Oh," she said, patting her heart, "that nearly frightened me to death!" She stood and walked out the room. Helen, Peter and Tom smiled at the faux pas. Peter shrugged, "That's our Mom!" he said. Tom laughed. Helen did not.

Rose walked back in followed by Rob. "Hi all," he said breezily, shrugging off his overcoat.

"Peter, Helen. Hi Tom, how are you doing, mate?" he asked, sitting on the arm of the sofa.

"Oh, you know..." Tom shrugged and smiled.

"Yeah," Rob's tone was subdued now. He leaned forward and kissed Helen. "Looking gorgeous as ever!" he told her. She laughed and swatted his arm playfully.

"You old flirt!" she replied. "How are you?"

"God," he said, loosening his tie "Work is a bitch! So... what's afoot?"

Tom gave him a wry smile. "I was just telling everyone about... about Tommy."

Rob nodded soberly, the smile slipping off his face. He had heard all about it on the way back from the airport. He had even cried with Tom before he dropped Tom home. He was his ride back to Gatwick again in two days time.

"It's just awful." Rose's hands were fluttering at her neck. Helen nodded.

"It's unimaginable!" she said.

"Yeah!" Peter's voice was gruff.

"It can't be real!" Helen continued. "I mean, in this day and age. It's so barbaric."

"But, if it's his choice? I suppose it would save the country a ton of money?" Rob tried to be the voice of reason.

"Well," Peter considered, "I guess it's his life. But... you just got to think, how bad must it be in there, for him to want to take that route? He's a young man still."

"Yeah," Helen looked around the room, "where there's life and all that!"

"Well, I'm not giving up!" Tom was standing now and pacing around the room. Even with the lights on, the glow from the TV cast a blue hue over him, making him appear alien and strange.

"I'm going to keep on until he agrees to see me. I'll be there until... until it's too late." His voice broke and Helen stood and rushed over to him.

Rose shifted in her seat. "I mean," she said, "fancy! Fancy having someone like that in the family! It would have killed your dad."

Helen made more drinks and she carried them through on a laminated tray with pictures of puppies on it. She distributed the drinks.

"What time you taking the kids out?" She asked Tom.

He looked at his watch again. "In a bit," he replied, "I'll just finish this." They were all quiet for a moment or so.

"Sorry, Tom, love!" Rose sounded tearful and Tom smiled.

"It's ok. No one knows what to say. I sure as hell don't." He took a sip of his coffee, wincing as it burnt his tongue. "Ow! That bloody hurt!"

Peter's eyebrows raised but said nothing. There were far worse pains out there.

"Well," Tom finished his drink. "Actually, some people do seem to know what to say!"

"What do you mean?" Helen blew on her tea.

"Oh," said Tom, "You'd be amazed just how many people have an opinion. I was told that I should kill him myself, keep in the family, as it were! Actually, some people in the states think that the family of the victims should do the execution, if they're the ones the state are trying to please. Hugo – that's Tommy's lawyer – he said he thinks the judges and senior politicians, those who deny appeals and the like, they should be the ones who give the drugs. So they know exactly what they're doing. Not just... delegating the dirty work to someone else."

"Is that what... lethal injection?" asked Peter. Tom nodded.

"Oh my God!" said Helen with a shudder.

"You're not planning on watching it, are you?" Peter sounded horrified.

Tom nodded. "Hugo said Tommy had agreed to see me, but that he was totally against me being there when.... You know. But... well, if I can, I will."

Rose moaned, hand across her mouth and Tom rushed across to her. "I'm sorry, Mom," He sat on the arm of her chair.

"I know you hate hearing all this. I'm so sorry."

"It's not that, love," she told him, stroking his face gently. "It's just... you live, all your life thinking one thing. That we should give as good as we get. It's what the bible says. It's what we have all been told at school." Her family regarded her, waiting. "Well, it is," she insisted. "An eye for an eye."

"Yeah," Tom tried to keep the sarcasm out of his voice. "I seem to have heard that already!"

"No, love," Rose sat up straighter in her chair. "You don't understand. I always knew, and your father did – Malcolm I mean – if anyone hurt any of you, our kids, anyone we loved, we would want justice."

"And...?" said Tom carefully.

"This thing, this awful thing that the America's want to do," she took a shuddering breath, "oh yeah, I know you said it's his choice, but its suicide. That's all it is. State assisted suicide. And it's wrong. It shouldn't be allowed. Oh, Tom, love, this is going to hurt you, so much, and there's not a damn thing I can do to stop it." Her voice broke and she left the room in a rush, as tears erupted and spilled down her face.

No one spoke for a while. The TV flicked in the back ground. Pictures were held to the camera and, in the absence of conversation, the muted voices of the speakers was just audible. "...and we never know, from one day to the next, if he's going to show up." The face of a good-looking young black man appeared on the screen. 'It was a hate crime, pure and simple. And nobody gives a [beep].' A woman with blond hair so stiff and still it seemed more like a helmet, spoke up. "That's what makes it hard. The not knowing. It's what relatives always say."

"Yeah, well, sometimes it's just as hard when you do know for sure. That they're dead, I mean." Another woman, small and dumpy, was framed in the screen. She had a beaten look of sorrow about her; her shoulders drooped, as did her mouth. Her eyes were lifeless and dull. "My mother," she took a shaky breath, "she was found in Greenwich Park in South London. By kids. Little kids. She'd been beaten around the head so badly they had to use her teeth to confirm her identity. They wouldn't even let me see her at the morgue. They said it was for the best." A sob escaped her throat and the camera swung to the blond stiff presenter.

"This woman," holding a picture up at the camera the presenter said grimly, "she was just walking her dog, minding her own business and someone killed her."

Rob held his breath. The reporter leaned forward unctuously. "What was the motive? Robbery?"

The dumpy woman, the murdered woman's daughter, sniffed. "No. She had nothing on her. They didn't even take her phone. She was just an ordinary woman, a public servant, working in the healthcare sector and some [bleep] decided it was her time to die. For no reason. She never hurt anyone in her whole life. She worked for years with mentally..."

"Oh shit!" Peter interrupted, reaching for the remote. "I really don't think we..."

"Turn it off, Pete," said Helen.

"Wait," said Rob, "your mom's recording this isn't she?"

He stood and faced the TV, Tom peered around him. "That's what I mean," he said quietly.

"What?" Peter looked at him.

"All this... this violence. We think it's nothing to do with us. But it has. All this arguing about the death penalty and life meaning life. An eye for an eye... it's all shit. None of us really understands any of it. None of us care enough to try to change it. We just moan and whinge. 'Oh, it's all so terrible, oh, they should throw away the key.'" He stood, his face red and angry. "What about when it *does* affect you, eh? Then it's too late. It's too fucking late to do anything."

Peter stood and took the remote from Rob's hand. "It's ok, Tom. Come on, sit down." He turned to Rob. "Don't worry, Rob," he told him, "he's not having a go at you. Let's turn it off, eh?" He clicked the remote and the screen went black. Rob stood frozen, his face glued to the TV.

"Rob?" Tom sniffed. He called to his uncle, "Are you ok?"

Rob turned slowly. "What?" Alarm rippled through Tom's voice. "What is it?"

"I..." He stared at Tom, his eyes shining with a blazing intensity. "Oh, umm... I... I just decided! I'm coming with you. To the states!"

Chapter Thirty Six

The arrest sent shock waves through the entire community. It was all anyone could talk about. The involvement of the police, to those in the mental health profession, suggested that the burden of proof had been satisfied.

Patients were moved with little or no thought for the effects such action would have on their already fragile mental health. Close it up, cover it up, pretend it isn't happening. That seemed to Rob to be the mantra.

His role, in the ever shifting landscape of NHS care, had morphed into one of gatekeeper. He shuffled patients around, using his vast experience of the health economy as it related to mental health services. Staff, those who remained, were re-deployed. Some lost their jobs, but then, so many in public services were in the same position currently, the loss of a few more front-line mental health staff was a drop in the ocean. It went unnoticed by the local press. Thankfully.

Rob was afraid he would be called to give evidence. It was looking likely; he had already asked to give a statement. He tried to keep his head down. Things were bad enough without that. Besides, he didn't know Dr. Blue. He'd never actually worked with him.

Working in the same service, albeit it on the periphery, Rob was as shocked as everyone else by the allegation levelled at the senior doctor and by the arrest which followed. Dr Ashkarahn, Dr. Blue, as he was known by the patients, had been charged following the gruesome suicide attempt by one of the psych patients who had alleged that she had been assaulted and she named Dr. Blue as her attacker.

Rob kept his statement as brief and factual as possible. There was not much to tell. He had been in the unit, doing a quality assessment visit. He was in one of the rooms when the patient appeared to decompensate, meltdown in other words. She had kept rocking and moaning and all she could say was 'Dr. Blue, Dr. Blue'. Short, sweet and to the point.

Dr. Blue was on bail and a GMC review was on hold, pending the outcome of the police investigation.

Rob shook his head and turned back to his report. Sometimes, this was a shitty, shitty job.

Chapter Thirty Seven

People were definitely staring at him. Ever since the local newspaper had printed something about the story, just over eighteen hours ago, they were staring. Rob said he was imagining it. He kept his head down and pushed his way through the crowd. People turned in his wake to watch him, whispering and pointing. Rob followed, staying mute. Neither he nor Tom spoke as they passed through the departures hall. In fact, they couldn't even if they had wanted to, it was so rammed.

He caught sight of the Pan Am desk and looked back to Rob, nodding towards it. Together they shouldered their way through. The woman at the gate, so overly made up Tom thought for a moment she was a mannequin, went through the motions; checking in luggage, checking papers. She smiled at Rob, but then everyone did. Still mute, they picked up their hand luggage and headed towards the waiting room. There was no inclination to indulge in duty free. It was not that sort of trip.

Once on the plane, the hostesses were especially attentive. Tom wondered if that was because they too recognised him, or if it was Rob's charm again. Either way, he kept his head down, conversation to a minimum.

Every seat was filled. The only babies in sight were at the far rear of the plane, thank God. Tom couldn't cope with squalling kids on top of everything else today. His own had been bad enough.

Throughout the take-off procedure, he and Rob focused on the small window. Tom was on the outside, closest to the window, Rob was in the middle. The isle seat was taken by a little old lady. She fell asleep almost as soon as she was seated and didn't move until the belt-on sign came back on at the end of the fight. She snored loudly; otherwise they wouldn't have known she was there.

As they took off, once the ping announced the 'belt-on' restriction was removed, Tom and Rob both relaxed. Rob accepted a glass of wine, Tom declined. He thought he would throw up.

"How did you manage to get the time off?" he asked Rob at last.

Rob shrugged. "I told them I had an emergency family situation." He peered past Tom, out of the tiny window. Below them, West London spread out like a studio photograph. Lights twinkled everywhere. Tom could see some landmarks he thought he recognised, although mostly, all he could see was the M25 below them, spreading out for miles and miles with red tail lights showing cars bumper to bumper on both sides. "The biggest car park in London!" he said to Tom.

Rob sat back, drinking his wine and reading the in-flight magazine advertising the airline and all sorts of pricey goodies. He flicked through it like a seasoned traveller.

"You been to the states before?"

Rob shrugged. "Yeah, just once. A while ago. Business."

Tom laughed. "I thought you worked for the NHS!" he said, "what sort of business would send you to the States?"

"Just some research. Boring stuff." Rob seemed a little evasive and Tom apologised.

"Sorry, mate. I'm just... making conversation. I didn't mean to be nosy."

Rob laughed. "It was a bust!" he told him, "I made a right twat of myself." He shrugged again. "It's not really worth talking about to be honest!"

"Ok." Tom nodded.

He stared out of the window at the changing landscape. They were over water now. He drifted off into his own thoughts. Tom's last day at home had been spent checking, double-checking and checking again. He had spoken to Brooks on the phone last night. Brooks no longer tried to persuade him not to come. Tom was staying with Hugo and Maddy this time. They would not have it any other way. Tom kissed Ash, lingering over their embrace. She locked her arms around him and held him tight.

"Oh, love..." she'd said. He had just nodded. She didn't need to say anymore.

An air hostess with the most enormous breasts ever, came over with some food. She glanced at the snoring woman in the aisle seat, but decided not to wake her. She deposited a tray in front of her anyway. Tom went to refuse his, but Rob stopped him with a glance. "You need to eat," he told him. The hostess laid their trays on the lap pad in front of each seat, smiling at Rob, leaning across the sleeping woman, whilst she deposited Tom's.

"Can I get you anything else?" There was a definite offer in her tone and Tom watched his uncle to see what he would do.

"No, thanks. That's great," Rob answered, smiling politely.

"Hey," she said, "don't I recognise you?" Tom groaned inwardly, but she was looking at Rob.

"No, love!" Rob said with a laugh. "No one ever recognises me!"

"Hummm... you seem familiar!" she pouted sexily. "Sure you're not off the TV or something?"

Both Rob and Tom laughed and opened their meals. The cartons were like something from a take-out kebab shop. Inside lay some congealed eggs, a strip of something that was supposed to resemble bacon, and a lone, watery tomato. A half slice of buttered bread was squashed in a clear plastic envelope and a mini packet of biscuits, the colour of dirty-water, completed the feast.

Rob nodded at his neighbour. "Wonder where she's going," he said. Tom smiled.

They both snapped the cartons shut. Rob settled down for a nap. "Better make the most of it," he said, grimly, "I doubt there'll be much time when we get there. If I snore like that," he added, gesturing to the woman, "feel free to shoot me!" Tom smiled but didn't answer. He turned to back to the window.

As they disembarked, the hostess with the big tits sidled up to Rob. She pressed something into his hand. Tom walked on. He was used to Rob's effect on women and for the first time, he wondered why he stayed with Pauline. They collected their baggage and made their way to the Am Track train station, to make the final leg to Connecticut. Despite their rest on the long flight, both were shattered when they arrived. Tom walked wearily into the local station and almost immediately spotted Hugo and Maddy.

"Hey you!" Maddy enveloped him in a big hug. He and Hugo shook hands and Tom introduced Rob.

"I know you said it was ok," Tom said, "but we really can stay in a hotel. It's a lot to harder to put up with two house guests, not just one."

"Rubbish, rubbish. We wouldn't dream of it!" Hugo was exactly as Tom remembered. Dressed in cargo-pants and a blue chambray shirt, solid utility walking boots on his feet and a thick padded ski jacket over his arm, he seemed as far from an anti-death penalty lawyer as Tom could imagine.

They shuffled towards the huge Station Wagon in the short term car park. Hugo threw all their luggage in the boot and Tom and Rob climbed in the back seat.

"You ever been to the States before, Rob?" said Maddy, turning around in the seat to talk to them.

"Yeah, just once," he replied, watching the scenery pass out of the window. "Long time ago though." She nodded and turned back to the front.

Tom whispered to Rob, "What did that air hostess give you?" Rob was puzzled. "When you left the plane? She gave you a bit of paper!" He saw realisation dawn on Rob's face and he shifted, scrabbling in his pocket to find it. He unfolded it. It was her name and phone number. It ended with a smiley face and the words, 'call me!' with an 'X'. Tom laughed and Rob pulled a face and scrunched the paper into a ball.

They drove in silence for the remaining five miles it took to get to the house that was to be their home for the next week or so.

"Hey, you guys rest, ok? I'll give you a shout in a couple of hours. Get you something decent to eat. You must be starving!" Maddy took off her coat and Tom saw Rob's eyes widen as her stunning figure was revealed. Tom and Hugo exchanged a furtive grin.

"Great, thanks." Tom turned to Hugo. "Is there any news?"

Hugo shook his head. "Not really, no. It's been pretty quiet. Why don't you rest up and we can catch up properly when you've got your breath back?"

A huge yawn split Tom's face, his jaw cracked and Hugo laughed. "I rest my case!" he said, leading them up the stairs to show them their rooms.

When he awoke, for a moment or so, Tom couldn't work out where he was. The sound of his ringtone woke him and he forced his eyes open, thinking he had overslept for work. He pulled out the mobile. Shit, he had completely forgotten to text Ash to tell her they arrived safely. Bugger. He pushed the green button, but the call disconnected. Sighing, he waited a moment then dialled her phone. She answered even before it rang.

"Tom?" Her voice was high and anxious and he felt like a shit for not calling her.

"I'm so sorry, baby," he said, "we're here. We're both fine and..."

"I was bloody panicking! I've got the bloody papers outside, the kids racing around like sodding lunatics, and you, you couldn't even bother to tell me you got there ok."

He heard tears in her voice and felt even worse. "I am sorry," he paused. "Did you say the papers are there? What do you mean?"

"The newspapers?" Sarcasm dripped from her voice and Tom looked at the receiver like he was going nutty.

"The papers?" he repeated stupidly.

"Yes, Tom, the papers. And the *BBC* and *Chanel Four*."

"What the hell is going on? Are you ok?"

"No I'm bloody not ok!" Now she was crying in earnest. "It's a flaming nightmare! I've kept the curtains closed, they just peep in, like they have every right to poke about and stare at you. It's awful."

"Oh God, sweetheart, I'm so sorry. What the hell do the media want? Jesus, from one little article in the local paper to the national press camping out in our little street. Bet the neighbours bloody love that!"

"How should I know?" She sniffed into the phone. "There was another thing in the *Worcester News* yesterday. An interview with someone called Rich? From your work?" She was calming down; he could hear it in her voice. Tom wasn't.

"What?" He swung his legs over the side of the bed, running a hand through his hair. "I'll fucking kill him!" Pacing the room he tried to rein in his anger. "What does it say?"

"Oh God, erm... he said something about you finding out you newly discovered twin brother is on death row about to be executed. There's a picture of you and him. I think it was from that night out, maybe from that leaving do you went to in Birmingham? It's a crap picture, but you can tell it's you."

"Shit!" Tom was still pacing. "I bet it was him told them about it in the first place!"

"Probably," she said, "although I know lots of people in town are talking about it. The kids say everyone at the school knows now."

"Holy fuck!" he said.

185

"Ummm," she replied, "that's kinda what I thought! Tom..."

"What?"

Static interfered again and for a moment, both thought the connection had been lost.

"Tom," Ash repeated.

"What?"

"Are you worried... that you'll feel it I mean? When they... when he dies?"

His mouth dropped open and he stared at the phone. "Well..." he said bringing the handset back to his ear, "I wasn't. I bloody am *now*."

Rob gaped at him, "*Chanel Four*?" he said, "The *BBC*?" He whistled through his teeth. "Holy shit!"

Both men cringed, the same thought clearly occurring to them at the same time. "Rose!" they said together.

"Who's Rose?" Maddy walked in dressed in a long beige coloured flowing shirt, dark brown, skin-tight trousers of some description clinging to her shapely legs. Her lovely face was glowing in the soft light and as she leaned forward, Tom caught a hint of the seductive perfume he recognised from their first meeting.

"My mom." He caught a look from Rob and qualified his response. "My... step-mom I guess."

Maddy smiled at the her two guests as she lay a tray of food on a massive square foot-stool-cum-table in between two huge squashy sofas. She sat, one leg curled up underneath her. Tom felt a moment's unease, wondering if she too would fall for Rob's charms, but so far, she seemed immune.

Maddy turned to her husband. "Would you rather I left you to it, honey?"

"No," he sat with a sigh. "You're involved in the case too. Besides," he rested his hand on her knee, "I feel better when you're next to me!" She grinned and leaned across to kiss him, her hand cupping his face briefly. Tom could see her long finger nails were painted a luminous apricot colour.

The food sat untouched. Tom sat on the edge of his seat as Hugo explained the current position.

"So, basically," Hugo sat back, "nothing much has changed since you were here before. Tommy is still adamant about his decision. And the state, well, the state are thrilled."

"Why?" Tom's tone was puzzled.

"Because it gives them an excuse. Aside from the cost – executions are prohibitively expensive – it's a win / win for the local politicians.

"Fuck!" Tom blushed. "God, sorry, Maddy!" He ran a hand through his hair again.

She laughed; a gentle, sad sound. "Oh, hey, don't worry about me!" She patted her hair, "I can cuss with the best of them!"

Hugo gave her a wry grin. "She can too!" he said.

The following day, a heavy wind blew around the house. Tom and Rob arrived downstairs at the same time. A small, dark-skinned pretty maid, complete with black dress and white frilly apron looked up and smiled as they entered the kitchen.

"Hello!" she said, "I'm Gloria. Maddy has gone to work. Hugo is on the phone in the office. Can I get you some coffee?" Tom smiled as he recognised her accent as pure New York. He'd heard it on *Sex and the City* which Ashleigh loved. She told him every time it was on that it was based on her life, 'sex and the shitty!'

"Yes, please." He and Rob sat at the huge oak table and waited, self-consciously as Gloria served their drinks.

"Morning, morning!" Hugo bustled in, carrying a stack of papers.

"Morning, Gloria, how are you?" he asked, taking a seat at the table opposite Tom.

"I'm good, thanks," she fetched him a cup.

"Your mom better?"

She nodded, smiled and returned to the kitchen, calling, "Do either of you guys want cream and sugar?" Both craned their necks to look at her, shaking their heads.

"I'll start in the den today." She said to Brooks. She picked up a small flat bucket and left, calling back over her shoulder, "let me know if you wanna eat, ok?"

Hugo waited while she left and sipped his coffee. He gave a sigh of pleasure. "Greatest part of the day!" He grinned at them.

"That's posh, a uniformed maid!" Tom gestured to Gloria's departing back.

Hugo grinned. "She's from an agency. They make them wear the outfit. Maddy and I kept arguing about who should do the housework. Paying for a maid slash housekeeper is good for our marriage!" He sipped his coffee. "Ooohh, definitely dollars well spent!"

Rob and Tom laughed and picked up their own drinks. "Wonder if Ash will go for that?" Tom joked. The look Rob gave him suggested not and Tom shrugged.

"Right, Tom," Hugo pulled on his serious face. "I have the visitation order here." He turned to Rob. "I'm really glad you are here to support Tom at this point. It's not going to be a fun trip. Obviously, I can't get you in to see Tommy. There's just no time to get a visitation order sorted."

"Sure," Rob spread his hands out, "I didn't expect to be able to see him. I just wanted someone to be here for Tom."

Tom turned to Hugo. "So... when will I meet him?"

"Tomorrow."

"Wow!" Tom rocked back in his seat.

"You ok, mate?" Rob's tone was concerned.

"Yeah, I'm fine. It's just... it's getting so real." Tom shook his head. "I can't believe I'm going to get to meet him. After all this time."

Hugo smiled. "I just wish the circumstances were different."

"Oh God, yeah," Rob's eyes flashed with anger. "Don't we all, mate. Don't we all."

Rob sat in the backseat all the way to the prison. The Houseman Correctional Facility in Hartford was nearly an hour away from Hugo's home. The journey was torture for Tom. Hugo spent the time pointing out facts about the legal system he had spent so many years fighting.

"How many clients have you had, umm... executed?"

Tom twisted in his seat to look at his uncle. Rob shrugged.

"Eleven." Hugo glanced at Tom before he responded. Rob nodded.

"Wow, that's hard."

"Uh huh!" said Hugo.

Tom stared out of the window, not really seeing anything. "How many have you saved?" he asked quietly.

"It doesn't quite work like that," Hugo explained. "The appeals process is interminable. Some prisoners on death row are there for years. Decades, some of them, caged like animals. That's one of my fundamental problems with the death penalty." He sighed.

"I'm just one small cog in a very big wheel. Still, you know what they say... all it takes for evil to prosper..."

In the back Rob grinned.

"What?" asked Tom.

"The saying, 'all it takes for evil to prosper, is for good men to do nothing.' You've never heard that?" Tom shook his head and Hugo sighed.

"You know, the UK, it has its good points. So does America. Land of the free. This is one serious anomaly which goes against the grain. I'm not a religious man, but my arguments against the death penalty are still less legal, more moral. The system is fucked. It's corrupt and biased and it stinks. I'm not excusing the crimes that put people in jail. Shit, don't get me wrong. I don't want to walk amongst baby killers, rapists and psychopaths any more than the next man. But the way the penal system works, it just ain't right. Bribes. Positions of power. Sex. Apathy. Ignorance. Fuck, it makes me sick."

He and Tom exchanged a glance. Tom was giving him permission to continue and by now, Hugo was unstoppable.

He glanced at the side mirror and indicated, pulling out to overtake another car. "I could tell you, for instance, I could name people who have been executed, some very bad people, and others, shit, no doubt as innocent and you or I, executed because their legal representatives were inept. Forget those who are merely corrupt, bought off. If you had a lawyer who slept through your entire trial, and woke up too damn late to argue your case, well, tough. Under federal law there is no automatic right to have a lawyer at all, so you had one who was tired, or stoned, or drunk - Tough. And... it's just not a comfort, for me at least, to know most of them are guilty."

Rob leaned forwards, pulling on the back of Tom's seat. "But... that doesn't make sense!"

"No," replied Hugo tartly, "But then, it doesn't have to. Who cares about these guys? Oh yeah, right, there are people like me. Those of us who oppose the death penalty out of principle. We... we try, and we try and we fight." He shrugged. "The reality is; we're pissing in the wind." He overtook another car, their speed gradually ramping up.

"I mean, do you really give a crap if the rights of some scum who murdered and raped children, tortured teenagers or who set fire to their wife because God told them to, do you care if his rights are violated?" He exhaled loudly, still speeding down the freeway. Surreptitiously, both Tom and Rob took hold of the handles above their seats. The clung on as the car sped up.

Hugo didn't notice their nervousness. He carried on, driving faster and faster as his anger grew. "The rule about mental health? I could quote dozens of cases where defendants had an IQ way below what the government says is legal to execute. But, execute them they did."

He sat back and rubbed his eyes with one hand, the other clamped to the steering wheel, his knuckles white. "Fuck..." he said. "Tom, I'm sorry. I just..."

"Don't worry about it. I don't know anything about the law. I never really needed to. Well," he pulled a face as Rob smirked at him, "I didn't before I beat the crap out of a friend who assaulted my wife." Hugo threw his a questioning glance.

"Long story!" Tom pulled a face. "The thing is... I don't know how I feel about the... you know, the rights and wrongs of execution. I've learned more about the legal system in this country and my own in the last twelve months than I have in the past forty years. And I'm not religious either, so I can't claim their arguments as mine. But... my God, this is just so fucking mad. My brother, my real brother, a man I never even knew existed until recently, he's admitted that he did things... really horrible things... and he wants to die. Not only that, he wants the state to kill him." He shook his head, puffing out his breath.

"All this stuff, the faults in the system, the people here who just don't care, who keep it all going, yeah, I get it, it's like trying to push water uphill. But... the thing is Hugo, none of it is relevant to me. To my family. Tommy's not mad. He's just... bad. And I don't know which is worse. He did some bad shit and he held his hands up. He'll never leave prison and frankly, no, I wouldn't feel too great about introducing him to my kids. To my wife. But..." he took a deep breath. "Oh God, I wish... I wish I'd met him before. Before all this. Now it's too late. How the fuck do you get your head around that?" He looked at Hugo. "Do you know? Can you tell me? 'Cos I sure as hell don't get it." Hugo shook his head slowly; neither did he.

When Tom was at school, in year eleven, he had had his first major fight with a lad in the year below him, a kid called Nick. This kid was enormous. He was well known for bullying and the schools were pretty much useless to do much about it. Nowadays, the schools were more vigilant. Much harder on bullying, in theory at least. Long story short, Tom had been trying to stop Nick picking on Helen. Tom had squared up to Nick but, by the time the show-down was imminent, he was crapping himself.

You know how everyone says stand up to bullies? That really they're cowards and if you could fight back, they'll back down. It's bullshit. The playground was packed. Nick was in one corner, flexing his hands, Tom was in another, concentrating hard on not puking or wetting himself. He danced around Nick for a while, but Nick just grinned and advanced with deadly intent. Tom, cheered on by his mates, his brother and Helen, charged at him, head down, knocking him flat. Nick went down with a massive thud. Tom was amazed.

His relief was short lived. Nick stood, the muscles in his neck bulging, his eyes hooded and furious. He launched himself on Tom and beat the living crap out of him. Tom had never been so scared in his life. The fight was stopped by the head teacher. All Mr. Brains (yes really, he'd shown them all his birth certificate to prove that was his name) saw was Nick beating the crap out of some kid smaller than him again. Hell, all the kids were smaller than him. Most of the teachers too. He rushed up to intervene, but Nick was so enraged he threw a blind punch at the head teacher who rocked back on his heels. Nick was promptly expelled. Job done.

As they approached the prison, Tom remembered the fear as he stared at Nick stalking towards him. His bowels felt as if they had turned to water. His knees were knocking together and sweat dripped from his palms. He was panting. He would rather be facing a one hundred people like Nick, right now, than face this.

Hugo grabbed his briefcase from the boot and locked the car. He spoke quietly to Tom. "Are you ready?"

Tom turned to him. "Yeah." He took a deep breath, hiding his fear. "Yes. I'm ready," he said and turned towards the prison.

Chapter Thirty Nine

Hugo explained the procedure in all its ugly technical detail, because Tom had insisted. He had listened with rapt attention. He could not afford to miss a thing. Tommy would, Brooks explained, have been moved to a 'holding cell' a day or so before the actual execution date. Visiting in the prison was a painful affair. It was intended to be. Nothing in any of their literature could prepare him for the reality of prison. It looked, smelled and felt like the gateway to hell.

This visit was a privilege, Hugo told him, not a right. The warden had granted leave for under the 'special circumstances' rule, but he could rescind the offer at any time and for any reason. Tom understood.

Tom was led into a room, its walls a dirty grey-green colour. The only window in the room was around six feet off the ground and was more of a slit than a window. A thick wire mesh was screwed over it, secured at points around the edge with bolts spaced an inch apart.

Tom shook his head, trying not to gag at the smell. Shit, he'd thought the psych hospital was bad. There seemed to be a fug of odour in the room, it made his eyes water and sting.

Hugo nodded to a seat stationed in the middle of the room. In front of the two plastic chairs positioned there, bolted to the floor, there was a screen. He thought it resembled the old offices of the DVLA in Worcester where he used to go to renew his car tax disk.

The booth was maybe six feet wide, separated from the other side by a solid Perspex shield. Deep scratches were carved into the plastic wall. The legend 'Fuck you cunt,' seemed to be a fairly popular theme. Tom sat and Hugo placed his briefcase on the chair next to him, opened it, and took out an envelope.

"I'll just say hi, then I'll give you some time alone. Ok?"

Tom nodded, shell shocked; the mere process of getting this far into the prison had almost blown his mind. He kept clenching and unclenching his fists, feeling his nails dig into his skin. His breathing was even shallower now and he felt beads of perspiration pop on out to his forehead. He looked blindly at Brooks.

Hugo smiled and patted his shoulder. "You'll do fine, mate," he said, snapping the case shut. Tom concentrated on his breathing. In his mind, he saw Ashleigh's face. For a moment he felt the warmth of her last embrace and he closed his eyes. They flew open as a door clanged on the other side of the booth.

Two guards advanced into the room their faces resolute and closed. The first was built like an all-in wrestler, with a square jaw and a buzz cut. His colleague was slimmer, lean almost, with a wiry strength which emanated from him like an odour. Between them, a man dressed in cheap blue jeans and a faded orange t-shirt walked, his ankles shackled together.

Tom saw the number 5488960 stencilled on the left side of his chest. He exhaled loudly and Brooks glanced at him. 'Be cool,' his eyes said. Tom licked his lips. A third guard followed the inmate into the room, as wide as he was tall almost. He wore a uniform so impossibly starched he seemed to walk as if he had an ironing board running through the back of his clothes.

None of the guards looked at Tom or Hugo, they focussed on their job of escorting the condemned man to what would be one of his final human contacts before he shuffled off this mortal coil.

Tom Hanks, in the film 'The Green Mile', was a man of compassion. As were most of his colleagues. Tom could see nothing humane about the men who pushed and pulled Tommy into the room, one of them pressing his shoulder to sit him down. They could have been robots for all he knew.

Deftly, the leaner of the guards unshackled the prisoner and latched the foot cuffs to a bolt underneath the booth on the far side. No one spoke in all that time; none of the guards addressed Tommy at all. Tom could see more guards in the corridor behind. *Shit, did they think they were here to try to break him out?*

Tommy's two main escorts, their movements precise and economical, stood, almost at attention and stepped sharply backwards, to the rear of the room where they stood, backs ramrod straight, arms folded loosely in front, staring forwards. The third man left the room, standing almost to attention, just outside the door.

Tom swallowed. The man on the other side of the plexi-glass shuffled until he was sat back in the hard plastic chair. Only then did he look up.

"Hi, Tommy. You ok?" Hugo's voice held a tenor Tom had not heard before and he glanced at him in surprise. Although the tone was kind, he was all business. Tom stared across, greedily taking his first look at his brother.

Tommy shrugged and lifted his cuffed hands up to scratch at his neck. It was red and sore.

Hugo waved the envelope at Tommy, who nodded, clearly he was expecting it. "How's the war wound?"

"OK, thanks," Tommy replied.

For a moment Tom was reminded of the meeting he had had with William Bent. He blew out the breath he seemed to have been holding in. It made his head spin.

"OK. I'll be right outside, if either of you need anything." Hugo picked up his briefcase and turned to go. He nodded at the guard on the other side of the door, through thick, reinforced glass. The door opened and Hugo left. He didn't look back. The guard took his place again, watching silently through the reinforced glass.

Moments passed. Tom and his brother spent the time appraising each other, seeing likenesses and differences. At last, Tommy grinned.

"Fucking weird or what?" he said.

Tom grinned. "You're telling me!" They fell silent again. Tom cleared his throat. "So... did you know?"

Tommy's eyes narrowed. "Know what?"

"That you... that we were adopted."

Tommy shrugged. "Yeah. I was told by my Mom when I was seven. She said they'd chosen the wrong kid." There was no bitterness in his voice. He was just stating a fact.

"Huh, nice!" Tom felt a moment of panic. He had no idea what to say. How did you cram a lifetime of memories and questions into the only two hours they would ever have to talk? The spectre of death hung over them like a veil. It was hard to see clearly. The room was hot and airless, but Tom felt a cold sweat sweep over him, even as perspiration dripped down his spine.

He tried again, "I was only told about 18 months ago." Tommy nodded.

194

"Thanks for agreeing to see me." Again Tommy nodded. Tom sat back in his seat. "Did you know about me?"

Tommy shook his head. "Nah." He sniffed and he lifted his hands, his cuffs rattling to wipe his nose. "Brooks told me. I always knew I was a twin, but they told me you'd died, at birth."

Tom pulled a face. "Yeah, that's what I was told when I first learned about the adoption." Tommy looked away and Tom struggled to maintain his composure.

"Why did you agree to see me?"

Tommy shrugged again. "Dunno. Curious, I guess." Tom smiled. Tommy's head was low; he was tracing something scratched onto the table in front of him.

"I... I wish we'd met before," Tom continued.

Tommy pulled a 'whatever' face. He reminded Tom of Meghan. "Why?"

"Because..." A small laugh escaped from Tom's lips. "I just... I wish I had had the chance to get to know you."

"Yeah," he muttered, "I guess."

"Is there anything you want to ask me?" Tom leaned forward, his elbows on his knees. Behind Tommy, one of the guards shook his head slowly. Tom gulped and sat back up. He cleared his throat, but Tommy remained silent.

"Not really," he said.

Tom tried to suppress his mounting frustration. Half an hour of their time had passed already and he was learning nothing. Tommy seemed less bothered to see him than he was about reading the graffiti on the table in front of him.

"Well..." said Tom, his tone measured and firm, "I'll tell you anyway. I'm married, my wife is called Ashleigh. We have two kids; Meghan - she's 12 now, and Elliott - he'll be six soon. We live in Worcester in the UK. I work in a factory in Droitwich. We make packaging materials. Job's pretty boring but it pays the bills." He stared at Tommy through the barrier.

"When I learned about you, I... I had no idea what to do. I spent ages, *months*, trying to find you. My uncle helped. He's outside. They wouldn't let him in. Rob, he's called. I was adopted by Rose and Malcolm Bearing and I have a brother called Peter and a sister called Helen. They all live in Worcester too."

Tommy looked up, interest lighting up his face. "Hey, I've been to Worcester in the States! And that name..."

"What name?"

"Bearing. I seem to recognise that."

"Yeah," Tom laughed. "I was 'Yogi' all through school!"

A smile creased Tommy's face and for a second, Tom could see the face of his son reflected in his brother.

"The war wound?"

Tom's face showed his confusion.

"Brooks asked me about the war wound?" Tommy explained.

Tom nodded.

"I had a tattoo done, a while ago. On my shoulder, at the back." He lifted his left shoulder to indicate the tat's location.

"Yeah?" Tom didn't understand where this was heading.

"It was Yogi Bear!" Tommy grinned at Tom's expression. "It got infected. I ended up with septicaemia. It was rancid! I nearly died. Man, that's some fucking strange shit ain't it?" he asked.

Tom laughed too. "Why Yogi Bear?"

Tommy shrugged, scratching his neck again. "Dunno. Just felt... just did. The name kept coming to me. Freaky, eh?"

"I felt you." Tom's voice was so quiet Tommy leaned forward to try to hear him. The massive squat guard behind him leaned forward and pulled him back into his seat. Tommy didn't react but he sat back compliantly.

"What?"

"I felt you," Tom repeated, "I... saw you. I don't know how. Sometimes, it was like I was dreaming and I could see stuff, some really heavy shit, I could see you in the chapel when you..." His head bowed and a wave of dizziness over took him.

"Whoa!" Tommy laughed again, a strange sound which echoed around the room.

"Mad isn't it?" Tom grinned. Tommy laughed.

"Like the accent man!" Tommy grinned. "Had another visitor talked like you a while back. It's real cool!"

Tom nodded. "So... you got kids?"

Tommy's face closed down and he turned away. "Yeah," he replied, "just one now. Never seen him though."

196

"Shit, that's rough." Tom was aware of a change in his speech pattern, he was sounding like a native. He laughed and Tommy raised his eye brows, clearly not seeing anything funny.

"Not that you've not seen him." Tom was flustered. "Just... you know, all this. The whole thing I suppose. I've no idea what to say to you. My wife, she's back home dealing with the press. Can you believe that? The fucking press are camped out on our doorstep. It's wild. I mean, this is all going on over here all the time... mostly, people in the UK don't even notice it. Unless, they're like, serial killers or something."

He glanced at his brother's face and saw nothing to make him stop talking. "And the kids, shit, they're *so confused*. My daughter, Meg, she's desperate to meet you. Elliott, he's... he's different. He's very quiet. Doesn't say much. But, well, he's only little. A baby really."

"Yeah," Tommy's voice was low and husky. "You can't expect them to understand. Fuck it man, I don't and I'm the asshole in here."

"Tommy..." Tommy appeared to notice his brother's change of tone, but he said nothing, just waited for Tom to finish.

Tom took a deep breath. "I'm so sorry. About... If we'd been able to stay together... maybe..."

"Nah," Tommy gave another of his trademark shrugs. "Not meant to be. Things are they way they are for a reason."

"Brooks is still... he can still appeal..." He hated the pleading note in his voice.

Tommy shook his head. "No." His voice was so quiet Tom strained again to hear him. Tommy continued. "It's too late. It's fucked up, yeah, but it really is too late. For me anyway. I can't live... I can't carry on like this. Anyway, you know, fuck it, I did all what they said, and more. It's best for everyone, if I... I have to end it, man. You just gotta let it go. There ain't nothin' we can do at this point."

"But," Tom was wild-eyed, "if we had more time. We..."

"No, Tom." He opened his arms as wide as the restraints would allow. "There's no point." Shrugging, he tried to gesture around him, but the restraints were too tight. "Look at me! And please, don't tell me that you wanna be there. I would hate that." He barked a short, sharp bitter laugh. "Not for me." He shook his head. "It would be fucking worse for you. At least we met, eh? At least we had that."

He glanced behind him at the guard and nodded. The guard watched Tom through the opaque shield, otherwise he didn't move.

"It's time," Tommy told him. "I'm sorry, bro'. Shit, ya know, it's the first time I've said it and it's true! Look, this... this is all such bullshit. In here I mean. You could say I'm taking the easy way out." He shrugged one final time, "...and maybe I am. But it's just what I have to do. I can't spend the rest of my life in here, eating food that been pissed on. Body searches. Cooped up. It's not living."

"Tommy please..."

Tommy continued, ignoring his brother's impassioned plea. "Oh yeah, and don't go watching all them prison dramas and shit like that. Fucking *Shawshank* shit. It ain't like that for real and it'll just do your fucking head in!" He remained seated whilst the guards unlocked the leg shackles from the booth attachment and locked them back together. Standing, Tommy leaned forward.

"Take care of yourself, Tom." He looked him straight in the eye. "It was real nice to meet you," he said. The guards stepped forward, each taking hold of an arm and led him out of the room. Briefly, at the door Tommy paused, looking back. He winked once at his brother and was gone.

Chapter Forty

The River Severn had flooded its banks again. Worcester was on the national news for reasons other than the impending death sentence of Tom's brother. Ashleigh, head down against the wind, walked down the tow path past, past the Diglis Hotel and on, towards the cathedral. She was alone. The car was parked miles away, at the playing field near Perdiswell and she had walked all the way, eyes stinging from the rain. As yet, the water wasn't that high, although it lapped at the top of the banks, the threat of worse to come.

She reached the point where marks on the wall showed the height of the floods from time to time, jumping as a dog appeared at her side, her tail wagging and sniffing her ankles. She turned at a voice behind her.

"Bella, come here!" The woman turned to face Ashleigh and she saw a flash of recognition in her eyes. Not only had Tom's picture been in the paper in the past week, so had hers. Just once though. Apparently it was enough. Flushing, she reached down to pet the dog.

"She's lovely!" she told the woman. She was short and dumpy, red hair blowing around in the wind brushed against her face. She reached up and tucked it back behind her ear.

"Yes," she laughed, "she's great. She's sulking because I won't let her in the river when it's like that!" She shivered as a cold wind almost blew them to the side.

"God," she said, pulling the front of her aging blue wax jacket tighter across her large bosom, "it's pretty wild out here isn't it?"

Ashleigh nodded. "It's pretty wild, alright," she said. The woman nodded, her smile suggesting she understand the deeper context of Ashleigh's words.

"Bella," she called, "Come on, come on." The woman smiled at Ashleigh. "Take care of yourself," she told her. The dog, a collie of some sort, bounded out of sight and the woman sighed and went to follow her.

She limped slightly. Ashleigh nodded and began the long, lonely walk back to her car.

"You and your bloody walks! You missed Tom!" Her mother's voice was faintly accusing and Ashleigh closed her eyes. "He called while you were out walking in the rain!"

"Well... I'm sure he'll ring back." Ashleigh pulled off her coat and scarf and walked into the sitting room. Meg was sat on the sofa watching Sponge Bob.

She scanned the room, "Where's Elliott?"

Her mother pulled a sour face. "He's upstairs," she replied.

"Why?"

"Because he was getting really aggressive. Your dad took him up to give me a break."

"Oh, Mom!" The peace she had felt during her walk along the blustering, swollen river dissipated and Ashleigh made herself swallow an angry retort. Her mother turned, walking across the large room and calling up the stairs.

"She's back, Steve," she said.

His voice drifted back down the stairs, 'alright, Maggie. We'll be right down, love."

Ashleigh went through the kitchen and switched on the kettle. Her mother leaned back against the counter, watching as Ashleigh helped herself to a coffee.

"He's out of control," said Maggie.

Ashleigh ignored her, pouring milk into the drink. "Ashleigh? You can't keep ignoring it. It's not going to just go away."

Ashleigh turned in a huff. "I know!" she snapped. "I know, mom. But... right now, we have other things to worry about. I have the bloody press camped outside my house. They shove cameras in my face, none of the neighbours are talking to me. The kids are getting picked on in school. It's a flaming mess. And if that's not bad enough, my husband is several thousand miles away, about to witness his newly-found brother get executed."

"Oh, no," her mom gasped, "he's never going to watch?"

Ashleigh moved her neck around, trying to free it of an ache she had had for weeks.

"No," she shook her head. "I mean... well, they won't let him be there to watch... Tommy, he's refused. But Tom will still be there. Outside the prison. He'll know exactly what's going on. Jesus Christ, how can this be happening to us?" She put her head in her hands and her mother rushed to her side.

"Oh, sweetie!" she crooned.

"I... I'll be glad when it's all over," whispered Ashleigh. "Oh God, I know Tom would hate me for saying that. It's just... oh God, I wish it was all over and that he was already dead."

Blindly she reached out to her mom who folded her up in her arms, shushing her and trying to make her feel better. Neither of them noticed Elliott in the doorway, watching them talk. He slunk away before they realised.

Chapter Forty One

"They're here."

Tom heard the flat note in his wife's voice and he swallowed. "I take it you mean the DNA results?"

"Yeah."

"Well... finally. It's about bloody time." Since the lab had lost the first samples, Tom had revisited Bent again, an occasion as odious as the first.

Ashleigh heard him as he exhaled down the phone, then the line went dead. "Tom? Tom?" static filled her ear and she held the receiver away, cringing as the noise shrieked out of the mobile phone. "Are you still there?"

"...and it took hours to get in, just through the admin process. They took my finger prints." He laughed bitterly. "God," he said, "now my finger prints are on file in the UK and in the USA!" Silence for a moment, Tom looked at the screen of the handset, it was still connected. "Ash, are you still there?"

"Yes," she sounded beaten. "Did you want me to open it?"

"What? Oh, the results? Shit, I don't know. No..." he said, slowly. "Leave it for the moment."

"OK. So, how was it?"

"I was just saying, by the time I got through to see him, it was late afternoon. The place was fucking *rank* Ash. It was awful. We had, like, two hours. It went so fast." He swallowed a lump in his throat. "Fuck it, Ash, it was just brutal."

She nodded and realised he couldn't see this, so she cleared her throat and spoke into the phone. "Yeah, yeah, I'm sure it was."

"He doesn't look like me that much. You can sort of see that we're brothers, but I don't think anyone would believe we were twins." He fell silent for a moment, Ashleigh waited.

His voice sounded tinny and far away, and not just in terms of geography.

"Are you ok?" she asked him softly.

"Yes. No. I don't know. Better than him, I guess."

"Did he say anything about..."

"His crimes?" Tom finished the sentence for her. "No," he said, "although Hugo told me he was suspected of other murders too. Around the same time. They're not following those up though." He gave a short harsh laugh. "Not really any point they said!"

"No." She hesitated. "So... will they let you be there when..."

"No." Tom stared out of the window of his room at Hugo and Maddy's house. The garden was still and dark. Shadows jumped and trees swayed in the wind. "He said he didn't want me to."

"I guess that's his right." Ashleigh was struggling to know what to say. She scratched her eye, scraping some dry skin off. It floated to the floor. She stepped forward and put her foot over it. She felt sick now.

"God, Ashleigh. It's just so fucking awful here, you have *no idea*. Outside the prison, there were these people... just chanting... They had banners and tee-shirts saying things like, I dunno, 'execution is justice; get the point?' There were two people even dressed in those things that the clan lot wear, you know the pointy hats and the white robes."

"Jesus! Really? The KKK? I thought they'd all gone these days." She coughed. "Tom? Can you come home now?" Her voice was so quiet Tom didn't hear her.

"What?" he said, "Ashleigh, what did you say?"

"I asked if you can come home now? Oh, Tom, don't stay there whilst they... it's too much. Come home. Please?"

Tom closed his eyes. "I have to, Ash," he told her, "I have to."

The execution was scheduled for six pm on April 15; two months shy of their 40th birthdays. Hugo, Tom, and Rob got ready in silence. None of them had dinner. Tom hadn't eaten all day. They drove to the prison at 4pm. No one spoke all the way there.

Hugo had, at Tom's insistence, explained what would happen to Tommy as the time of his execution approached. Two executioners would sit in an anti-room, just off the death suite. Tommy would be brought in and the warden would again read the charges. He would make sure to have it all official, that the inmate was, in fact, a 'volunteer' and that he had given up his rights to further appeals on his own volition.

Tommy had been offered a final meal, but he had refused it. He had also declined to have a spiritual advisor present. Once the warrant had been read, Tommy would be strapped to the gurney and the warden would ask if the prisoner wanted to make a statement. Once that was done, the warden would nod to the executioners in the next room who would begin the infusion.

He would be given a cocktail of three drugs, the first a sedative of sorts, to make him go to sleep. The second a drug which paralyses him, basically so they won't flop about in his death throes and make the spectacle uncomfortable for those watching. Finally, the third drug would stop his heart. Death, Brooks said, would follow between two – ten minutes later, if he was lucky.

Tom had excused himself at that point and had thrown up in the downstairs loo. "Will you be there?" he asked. Brooks nodded, his eyes searching Tom's for signs of weakness.

"Tom, you could just go home. No one would think..."

"No," said Tom, turning away. "I couldn't actually. I wish everyone would stop telling me that."

Rob shifted his weight; his backside was beginning to ache after sitting in the car for so long. Tom remained still, his gaze never leaving the big grey prison which loomed ahead of them like a nightmare. In silence, they watched the crowd as it grew. The closer the clock ticked around to six pm two definite factions were visible, those for and those against the death penalty. The latter group were clustered around, dressed sensibly against the elements, their chanting lilting and wafting around in the breeze.

Tom wondered how their candles were not blown out in the wind which buffeted the car, then he realised, they were fake flames. How fitting.

The group opposite them were chanting, competing with the melodic sounds of the passive group. Shouts and jeers as they counted down the minutes, cheering as someone announced each discrete stage in the death process.

Tom's jaw ached where he kept his teeth clamped together, it was the only way to stop them chattering. No one took any notice of their car; they were left to speculate between themselves what was happening.

"On *The Green Mile*, you know; that *Tom Hanks* film?" Tom spoke very quietly, "when a prisoner was executed, the lights would flash so those outside could tell it had been done."

"Did they flash the lights to tell them then?" Rob hadn't seen the film.

"No," Tom shook his head, still staring at the prison. "It was because of the power surge when they electrocuted the prisoner."

"Shit," Rob shuddered as he watched the spectators. "How can they stand there and wait like that? It's sick. It beggars belief." Tom shrugged. "I mean," Rob continued, "man, I've seen every sort of crazy in my job. Some of it tragic, some of it so fucking strange you can't do anything except laugh. But this..." He shuddered dramatically again, "This gives me the fucking creeps."

Tom twisted around to face him. "Thanks, Rob."

"Shit, I'm sorry. I didn't mean..."

"No, I know. I mean, thanks for coming with me. Hell, you deserve a medal man. I really appreciate it."

Rob shrugged and looked away. "You... you're like a son to me," he said, "where else would I be?"

Maddy was waiting for them when they got home. She had made sandwiches no one wanted. She had poured very strong drinks which everyone did. Hugo had hugged Tom and Tom had trouble stopping himself from crying. By silent agreement, no one mentioned the past six hours. Tomorrow was soon enough to do that.

Instead they all, Maddy included, proceeded to get absolutely drunk as skunks. The final act of the day was a toast to Tommy. "May he rest in peace," said Brooks.

"Aye," Tom clinked glasses with him as Rob and Maddy did the same. 'Rest in peace bro',' he whispered softly, 'it was real nice to meet you too.'

Brooks' words echoed in Tom's head all the way home. Through the flight, through the train journey to the car park, and even in the car, over and over he replayed the final conversations he'd had with his dead brother's lawyer.

"His was dignified and calm. He didn't make any real statement, his last words to me were, 'tell Tom I said bye'.

As they strapped him down, he turned his face away from the viewing window. I saw the warden nod to the guys in the medical room and they did their thing. Five minutes later he was dead. No sound. No words. No cough. Nothing. Tom, I... I'm so sorry..." His tone was measured and calm, but Tom could see the tension on his face.

"Thank you, Hugo." He stood and went across to the older man. "You are incredible. I wish... I wish my wife could have met you." Hugo smiled and shook his head. They shook hands.

"Keep in touch?" he asked.

Tom nodded. Both knew that, when things had gone back to normal, Brooks would be a reminder of all that had happened. Tom smiled anyway.

"Well," he laughed, "you know where we live. If you ever find yourself in the *original* Worcester, look us up?" Hugo laughed too, but it was unconvincing.

Tom stood at the side of the unmarked grave. A crude wooden stick marked the plot where Tommy's remains had been buried. At his request, no cross was allowed. No religious artefacts of any description. The weather, ironically, was calm and warm. There was a definite hint of spring in the air; Tom could see the tiniest of buds beginning to appear on the trees and hedges around the graveyard.

Rob stood back from the grave, his hands clasped as though in prayer. At last Tom moved away. He shook Hugo's hand one final time, hugged Maddy and walked away. He'd refused the offer of a lift back to the station; a taxi would be fine this time. At the edge of the path, the yellow taxi sat waiting; Tom turned back to see the plot one last time. Hugo stood watching him leave. The two said nothing more, they just nodded. Tom climbed into the car and they drove off.

Chapter Forty Two

Their days returned gradually to normal. Tom's 40th birthday was hard but he threw himself into it, for the sake of his wife and family. The only awkward moment arose when someone, Pauline probably, suggested that 'life began at 40!' and Tom replied, 'not for Tommy it doesn't.' Their gifts had been thoughtful and expensive and he worked hard to show how thrilled he was.

"Tom?" He turned at the sound of her voice and smiled brightly. She shook her head, "Nice try, love, but you're not fooling me!" His face told her she had hit the mark and he shrugged and turned back to face the garden.

"Are you ok?"

He nodded, but didn't turn around. She walked across and stood behind him, wrapping her arms around his waist. He turned and pulled her into his arms.

"It's just..."

Her smile was sad. "I know, babe."

He released her and banged his fist on the kitchen counter. She jumped in alarm.

"Sorry, Ash. I'm sorry. I can't stop thinking about it. About him. I have nothing of him, other than a fucking mug shot his death penalty lawyer gave me days before the United fucking States of America killed him."

"Oh, darling," she tried to pull him around to face her, but he turned away. She swallowed her hurt.

"I'm sorry," he repeated. "Did I tell you what Hugo said about his parents?" He barked a bitter laugh. "Parents! That's a fucking joke. Apparently, once he'd been given the date, his mother visited him. She told him that they wanted nothing further to do with him. That they regretted ever meeting him. Fucking bastards..."

"Jesus, how cruel..."

He sneered, "You think? Oh, I know I should give it time. I just wish... I wish I had something of him. You know?" Ashleigh nodded again. "Something to remind me of him. So I know it was all real. To know he was real."

In Tom's absence, Elliott had been suspended from the nursery for his fortunately unsuccessful attempt to stick a sharp pencil into the eye of one of the other little boys there. A child normally so placid, he had to be poked to make sure he was awake.

When asked why he did it, Elliott had replied, 'because he let me'. One of the teachers had managed to avert the disaster, but Elliott didn't seem to care. He shrugged and went up to his room to play with his cars.

Ashleigh had already made the appointment with their GP before Tom came home and nothing Tom could say would get her to change her mind.

Spring, when it finally came to the UK, was one of the wettest on record. Summer duly arrived and the children ventured outside, though they never managed to put the wellies away.

Two days after his return to the UK, Tom finally remembered the letter with the DNA results. They were negative. Bent was not his biological father. He breathed a sigh of relief. It was short-lived. If it wasn't Bent, who was it?

Chapter Forty Three

By the time Christmas rolled around again, Ashleigh was dreading it. Last year - God, this time last year was a nightmare, no question, but still, some faint sense of unease made her guts clench and her breath catch whenever she thought about it. She could not shake the sense that it was not quite over yet.

Halleluiah, the sodding tree had been up without incident now for almost a week. It was something of a record these days. All the delicate crystal baubles had been replaced. Cheap plastic trinkets adorned the artificial tree, new for this year. It came ready decorated from Argos. Less to break. Even the lights were already on, secured to the branches by cable ties. On the hand-made decorations the kids had made over the years were added on. Ashleigh hated it, but with Elliott around, it was easier.

They spent the day before Christmas Eve shopping. Meg was with Maggie and Elliott was with Ash's dad. He had taken him to a huge garden centre in nearby Bromsgrove, to see the reindeer and meet Father Christmas.

Lugging the bags in, Tom and Ashleigh silently unpacked and put away all the shopping. This year, Christmas was their turn and their tiny house was due to burst at the seams; Ashleigh's parents, Rose, Pauline and Rob and flying visits from Helen, Peter and their respective families.

"Where do you want the turkey?" Tom held it up, waiting for Ashleigh to get her head out of the cupboard.

"Where do you think?" she replied sarcastically.

"I mean," Tom aimed for patience, "which fridge?"

"Oh, God, sorry. Ummm... put it in the garage." She paused, thinking. "Actually, put in on the table for a while, there'll be other stuff we can put out there until Christmas Day."

He dumped the massive bird onto the table. It thudded, making the table wobble. "That's only the day after tomorrow babe!" he said.

"Yes. Thank you. I know that. Careful," she snapped, turning away and pulling open the fridge. Silently they worked to store everything, hiding sweets and chocolates which they would bring out in careful rations. Their first thing the GP had said was to limit Elliott's sugar intake, Christmas notwithstanding.

Ashleigh was rifling through bags piled everywhere. "Where's the cranberry sauce?"

"I don't know," he looked around at the still full kitchen counters. "I've not seen it."

Ashleigh sighed and slammed a cupboard door shut. "It's not here," she said, "I know we got some. Dad loves it. He won't eat turkey without it."

"Maybe it fell out in the car?"

She hesitated. "Oh no, don't worry," she said sarcastically, stepping over cartons of drinks littering the floor. "I'll go look!" He heard her stomp outside and moments later, heard the car door slam. He turned back to his task of putting everything away. The phone rang, but he ignored it. Moments later he turned. Ashleigh was poised in the door way, her face pale.

"What is it?" he asked.

"Brooks," she replied simply. Tom frowned. "Brooks?" he repeated.

"On the phone." Her voice held dread and he felt his heart jump. He checked his watch. It was early afternoon which meant it was still night-time in Connecticut. Putting down the tin foil, he hurried through to the lounge and picked up the receiver of the landline phone.

"Hi, Hugo!"

"Hi, Tom. How are you? You all ok?"

"Yeah, thanks," he laughed weakly. "Shouldn't you still be in bed?"

Hugo laughed too and Tom took a sigh of relief. "Is this just a social call?" he asked, sitting on the sofa.

There was silence on the end of the phone. "Hugo?"

"What's going on?" whispered Ashleigh. Tom shrugged again.

"Tom," Hugo's voice came faintly through the phone, yet Tom could clearly hear something in his tone.

"What's wrong Hugo? Something up?"

"Yeah. You could say that. Tom, I don't know exactly how to say this..."

"What?" Tom felt his heart hammering in his chest. His breath caught in his throat. "What? *Hugo*?"

Ashleigh whispered to him, "Put it on speaker phone!" Tom stared blankly at her, at first not comprehending what she'd said. Then, with shaking hands, he fumbled for the button so Ashleigh could hear what was being said.

"Tommy's... the man Tommy killed?" Hugo didn't wait for a reply. "It was his daughter that Tommy was accused of raping... Turned out to be more complicated than that actually, but that's not the point..."

Tom waiting, saying nothing.

"She had his babies Tom. Twins." There was a stunned silence. Ashleigh and Tom stared at each other, speechless. Hugo continued, "One of them died, his name was Sam. A freak accident apparently, I don't know much about it. Anyway, she... their mom, she's dying now. Cervical cancer. She's only twenty four... There's no hope for her. It's terminal. She's got just weeks to live."

Tom and Ashleigh stared at each other, eyes wide with shock. "Oh my God," Ash exclaimed. "That poor kid!"

Tom nodded then turned his attention back to the phone. "What's going to happen, Hugo? To the boy?"

"Well," again Hugo paused, "that's the thing. That's why I'm calling... She's heard about you... Tom, she wants you to take the boy in. When she's gone. She wants him to come to live with you and your family."

Chapter Forty Four

Hugo lugged the bags out of the car; both Maddy and Ellis were fast asleep on the back seat. Tom came out of the house and raced over to help usher them inside.

It was five o'clock in the morning and Meg and Elliott were both still fast asleep. The sky was a hazy pink colour, the early summer light which artists love to paint. Hugo carried a sleepy Ellis into the house and shuffled through into the lounge. He laid him gently on the sofa. Ashleigh stepped forward, dressed already, covering him with a blanket.

Hugo stood up and rubbed his back. "Damn, he's heavy!" he whispered. Tom and Ashleigh smiled. Ash gestured towards the kitchen and all four trooped wearily out of the room, leaving Ellis snoring softly on his makeshift bed. He looked totally angelic and Ash felt her heart contract. She hadn't really wanted him here; she felt that it was going to make things harder for Elliott. In the end, there was no alternative. Tom could not face the idea of the child going into care in the American system.

Introductions properly made, Ashleigh did what all good English wives do in such situations; she made tea. They sat around the glass table and talked about the journey that Hugo and Maddy had made across the ocean with a small, grief-stricken child with them. Poor kid had only met Hugo once before that. He must have been terrified.

Hugo yawned widely and Tom grinned. "It's good to see you!" he said.

Hugo smiled back. "You too, you too. And you, Ashleigh, we heard a lot about you!" He gazed around the small house, debris from the children everywhere. In the back garden, even in the semi-darkness, the trampoline was showing its age and a boy's bike was leaning up against the fence. "From the absence of a press welcoming party, I gather the media interest has died down. That's good news, for you and the children." He glanced at the sleeping child, "It's great that you agreed to take him." He shook his head, "So much tragedy in one family." He rubbed his eyes.

Ash cleared her throat and looked at Tom. He knew she had more questions. "So..." she asked, "this little boy, his mom died when?"

"Umm... a month ago today, actually." Hugo glanced at Maddy for confirmation and she nodded.

"And his... his grandfather, he was the one killed by..." Ashleigh glanced at her husband.

"By Tommy," Tom finished. Hugo nodded.

"What about his grandmother? Surely she wouldn't want the child to go to a relative of the man who killed her husband?"

Brooks looked at Tom with a frank gaze. "Probably not but she died of breast cancer when the boy was... oh about two or three, I think." He reached around, trying to scratch an itch on his back. Maddy reached across and scratched it for him. He grinned at her. Turning back to Tom he continued, "He was a twin; I told you that, didn't I?"

Both Tom and Ashleigh nodded. "What happened to him? The other one I mean." Ashleigh asked, glancing at her husband.

Outside, the darkness bled slowly out of the sky and the sun rose, chasing away shadows from the garden. They heard the sound of their neighbour and she got herself ready to go to work on the early shift. Her front door slammed and the sound of her car revving filtered in from the front of the house. They waited as she drove off.

Maddy stifled a yawn and Tom stood and opened the patio doors slightly, trying to keep them all awake. Maddy smiled her thanks.

Hugo looked down at the table. "The other twin died not long after the grandmother actually. A tragic accident. I'm not really sure of the details. Mary, his mom, she didn't go into it really. The two boys were together, playing around. Sam fell down a ravine. Ellis was the only one who saw it happen. That's all I know."

Ash and Maddy exchanged a look.

"Was the grandmother called Meghan?" Tom's voice was unnaturally high and Brooks frowned.

"Yes," he replied, "I believe so." He frowned. "How did you know that?"

Tom shrugged. "I... I saw it..." He gave a self-conscious laugh. "That's how all this started. I told you... I had, I don't know, visions or something? I have no idea why. I don't *now*, of course. Now that he's..." He gazed around the table.

"It's ok," he said, patting Ashleigh's hand to tell her it was a joke, "My wife thought I was going mad too. I think at one point, she considered having me committed!"

"What sort of things did you see?" Maddy's voice held none of the scepticism he was used to hearing when this subject came up.

He cleared his throat. "Err... well, the first time, I saw... I think I saw Tommy with Mary. She... she was telling him no." He swallowed. "I saw, shit, I saw something in a pub." He wiped his mouth and thought of Bent. He shuddered. "He hit a man who was going to rob him. He and his daughter were there. Tommy... he went crazy. It was like, I kept seeing myself in places I sort of knew, but where I had no idea how I got there. Places in England. Worcester. Glastonbury. Bristol." He saw Hugo exchange glances with Maddy and he laughed. "Yeah, I know; its mad."

"Oh, Tom," Maddy reached out and patted his hand across the table. "It's not mad, it's fascinating. I mean, maybe it was a twin thing? You hear about that, don't you?"

"Yes. No. I don't know." Tom rubbed his hand across his tired eyes. "Tommy said..."

"What?" Both Maddy and Ash leaned forwards.

"He said something about a tattoo. His 'war wound'."

"Yes," Brooks nodded. "He'd had it done sometime before he killed the police officer. It got infected. Probably something to do with being on the run maybe? Anyway, it was pretty bad for a while. They said he had septicaemia. It could have been fatal."

"It was Yogi Bear!" Tom spoke so quietly that those around the table strained forwards to hear him.

"What?" Ashleigh looked stunned. "Oh my God!"

Brooks was confused. "So? Anyway, how did you know that?"

"He told me. He said the name Yogi kept coming to him, he didn't know why."

"I'm not sure I understand..." Maddy looked at Tom, he head on the side.

Tom looked at Ashleigh who shook her head, amazed.

"Yogi is my nickname. Right back when I started school. 'cos my surname's Bearing."

"Oh!" Maddy sat back. "Oh my goodness. And he knew?"

"I don't know. He just said he felt the name Yogi meant something so he got it on a tattoo. I don't think he... I don't think he had the same experiences as me otherwise though. The twin cities thing, I mean. See," he gave a wry grin. "I told you it was nuts!"

"No," Brooks was serious. "This is stuff we are only just learning. It's incredible. Did Tommy say anything to you, when you met?"

"No. We didn't talk about his crime, about the case at all. We didn't say that much really. It all passed so fast."

"Anything else, Tom?" Maddy was leaning forward, rapt with attention and wide awake now.

He nodded slowly. "I saw him in the chapel. With Mary, when her dad was killed. And I heard a referee at our daughter's judo competition say something, like he was reading out the charges again Tommy. I knew then, Tommy – I think I still thought of him as Sam then – he'd been given the death sentence. And..." he swallowed, "I think I knew about the twins."

"Where are his papers darling?" Maddy asked, rifling through her enormous bag.

"In the car. We've got his passport and his birth certificate. Oh, and the papers approving his emigration here, of course."

"When's his birthday?" Ashleigh kept a calendar with all relevant dates marked. She was so organised. Tom grinned.

"Ummm... May first, that's right, isn't it Hugo?" He nodded. Tom and Ashleigh turned to face each other, mouths gaping in astonishment.

"What?" asked Hugo, turning from one to the other.

"That's the same day as Elliott!" Ashleigh's voice was breathless with surprise. Hugo raised his eyebrows and Maddy gave a surprised laugh.

"Oh my goodness," she said, "How strange is that?"

"What year?" asked Tom.

"2004," Hugo said.

"Same," said Ash and Tom at the same time. For some reason, the coincidence made them all uncomfortable.

Tom broke the silence with a snort. "Looks like I was seeing stuff that was real, eh? Maybe Ash was right when she said I was going mad!"

Ashleigh tutted. "I never!" She looked at Brooks. "I never said it like that! I never really thought he'd gone mad. Well... I mean, it was all very strange. *He* was very strange." She gave a strangled sort of laugh.

"God," she said, wiping her eyes, "so much has happened since then. It's incredible. We had two kids, now we have three. One of them the offspring of a convicted... Oh!"

As one they turned to the door. Ellis was standing there, wide awake, staring at them all with an intensity on his face that took them aback. Tom and Hugo gaped at him. "You look just like your dad," Tom told him.

Ellis eyed him balefully. His dark eyes were fathomless. His glance flitted from one to the other. "Can I go play on the trampoline?" he asked.

Ashleigh jumped up. "Of course, sweetie." She rushed over to him, one arm snaking around his shoulders. He pulled away. "Oh. Umm... our children will be up soon. You'll have someone to play with. That'll be good, eh?"

"Hugo said." The child was unnaturally still. "Will they let me play on the trampoline?"

"Yeah, sure." Tom twisted in his seat, moving to face the child. "It'll be like having a brother and sister."

Ellis nodded and walked towards the patio doors. He paused, his hand on the door handle. "I had a brother," he told them, "he died."

"Yes, sweetie," Ash bent down so her face was level with his. "We're so sorry..."

"He wouldn't let me use his stuff, so he died. I got it all then." He gave a weird little smile, turned away and stepped outside. Slowly, Ashleigh sat back at the table. No one had a response to that.

Chapter Forty Four

The dry, cracked earth was an irrelevance. The kids were running around, screaming with joy. The occasional howl punctured the party feel, as some child felt slighted, left out or wanted their turn on the swings.

The sandpit was barely visible for all the children packed into it. A massive line signalled the location of the ice cream van and moms sat around the edges of the play ground, something like fifty plus prams dotted around beside them. There was even the occasional sighting of a uniformed-Norland Nanny. It was, after all, still a part of London where people with money lived.

Greenwich Park had so many personalities. The playground, the Observatory, the deer park. Screams of joy wafted across on the fragrant summer breeze. Only one child, a little girl around five years old, sat on one of the ornate, wrought iron benches with a face like a slapped arse. Everyone else was having a ball.

"Tilly," called her mother patiently, "Come on. Don't be daft. It isn't just your swing!" Tilly stuck her lip out further and tucked her chin into her chest. Her mother sighed.

"Sweetie, come on. Shall we go play with Adam?" She checked the sandpit, clocking that her four year old was still there. He was, digging intently as he was when she left. He was trying to get to Australia.

Tilly stuck her nose in the air and her mother sighed with exasperation.

"Oh for heaven's sake. Well, I'm going to go and play with Adam and then we are going to have ice creams!" She turned to leave, fully expecting this to have had the desired effect. But Tilly was resolute - aka stubborn and awkward - and her mom pursed her lips and stood up straight.

"Well, darling," she peered across the park, shielding her eyes from the sun, watching with a smile at her industrious who son who carried on digging. She turned back to Tilly. "Ok, you win. You stay here all alone whilst your brother and I have lots of fun. Do not wander off, do you hear me?"

Tilly nodded once, still cross. Her mom walked away, calling out to her son, 'Adam, be careful darling, don't flick the sand at other children." She speeded up. "Adam, that's naughty, *stop it*!"

By the time she looked back, Tilly was gone. The screams of delight took on a different timber and a shiver raced down her body. Goosebumps broke out on her bare arms and her knees felt shaky. "Tilly?" she shouted, "*Tilly?*"

Several of the moms, none of the kids, looked up at the alarm in her voice. Craning their necks briefly for a stray child, their gazes snapped, like their eyes were on an invisible elastic band, to locate their own offspring, making sure they were still safe.

Dragging Adam with her, his little feet kicking up dust and sand, the mother raced over to the bench where Tilly had been sitting. Adam was bawling, snot and tears running down his face. He licked his lips. All the children in the sand pit and on the swings turned back and carried on playing.

From behind a huge Yew tree about five feet from the bench, Tilly stepped out.

Her mother almost sobbed with relief. Letting go of Adam's arm she raced across and threw her arms around her daughter. Adam watched them with curiosity.

"Oh my God," she held her tight, "Matilda Grace Gordon, where did you go? I was so worried." She pushed the child away and held her at arm's length. "Tilly," she admonished, "I told you not to move!"

Tilly, hands deep in her pockets, shoulders hunched, said nothing. Her eyes gleamed brightly and her mom assumed they were tears of fright.

"Come on you two. I've had enough today. Let's go home." Adam's tears began again, but Tilly followed like a good little girl. In her hand, clutched tightly, was her new-found treasure. Golden treasure – well, covered with mud and grime – but treasure none the less. When she got home, Tilly waited until her mom went to start lunch and took the dirty yellow ring out. She spat on it and cleaned it with the corner of her quilt.

The words inside were too small for her to read. She gave a secret little giggle of happiness and hid the ring carefully in the bottom of one of the many glittery bags, her favourite one, with Dora the Explorer embroidered on the front, hanging from her wardrobe door. It was her secret. Her treasure. She wasn't going to be made to share this.

Meghan was thrilled to see him. She danced around Ellis, dragging him from one room to another, showing him everything of importance and lots besides. He was solemnly introduced to the neighbours and their kids and although he seemed happy enough, his face had a bemused expression for days.

He and Elliott had shifted into Meghan's room and she decanted, quite willingly, in the small room that Elliott previously occupied. Already, extensive plans to redecorate the two rooms were underway, though Meg seemed to be doing most of the designing. Elliott and Ellis remained quiet, just nodding at appropriate times and smiling a lot.

Tom was reminded, as he stood, plate in hand, of the party at his mom's when he had started to learn about Tommy. He spotted Ellis standing on his own in the corner. As he watched, Meg came bounding over. She bent down in front of him as though she were an adult. He saw Ellis look up, a gleam of interest in his eyes. Tom scanned the room for Elliott but couldn't see him. He couldn't see Ash for that matter either. He sighed. Not a good sign. When he looked back, Rob was on his hands and knees on the carpet and Meg was gesturing to Ellis to climb on. Obligingly Rob threw his head back and neighed. Tom laughed.

He wandered into the kitchen. His mom was standing, hands deep in a sink full of soapy water.

"Want a hand?" He picked up a tea towel and wandered over. She turned to him with a smile.

"Hullo, love!" Putting a cup on the draining board she took the tea towel from him and wiped her hands. "No, I was just..."

"It's a great party," he said carefully. "It was good of you to throw it to welcome Ellis." She nodded. Through the open door they could see Rob galloping around the floor, a different child on his back now. Helen sat to the side, deep in conversation with Katie, Peter's wife. Peter was outside, no doubt showing off his new car, again.

"Where's Aunty Pauline?" Tom realised he hadn't seen her and his mom shrugged.

"Out in the garden I think." Her eyes suggested there was more too it and Tom flashed her a question with his eyes.

She leaned forwards, whispering conspiratorially. "They've had a big row."

"Really? Rob and Pauline?" he whispered back. She nodded, lips pursed. "What about?"

She spread her hands wide. "Not really sure. She's pretty mad at him though."

Tom regarded his mom thoughtfully. He brought his hand to his mouth, indicating taking a drink. "Is she... has she been?" The look she returned suggested that it was a bit of a ridiculous question and he shrugged one shoulder in acknowledgement.

Tom kissed his mom and turned, intending to go find his wife and son. As he left the room and turned the corner into the hall, he walked smack into Pauline. They bumped heads.

"Oofff," she rubbed her brow, "Goodness me, Thomas, you're like a bull in a china shop!" He smiled and apologised.

She waggled her glass at her sister in law. "Rosie, darling, we need more wine!" Rose threw a grim smile at Tom and turned to pick a bottle off the side.

Rob wandered in, rubbing his back. "God," he wheezed, I'm really getting too old for that!" Ignoring his wife, he went across to Rose, giving her a big squeeze around the waist.

"Ok to put the kettle on, Rosie?" Without waiting for a reply he flicked the switch down. He eyed his wife with distaste, "You going to have a coffee, Pauline? Might be a good idea!"

"No," her response was brusque. Rob sighed and shot Tom a complicit smile. Tom felt a bit caught in the middle and he turned to leave. "Anyone know where Ash and the boys are?" His family shook their heads, no. He wandered off. They heard him calling up the stairs.

In the kitchen, Rob made his coffee and stood with his back to the counter drinking it. Rose resumed her washing up and Pauline, her drinking. The silence between them was palpable and Rose rolled her eyes as the two bickered, sniping at each other again behind her.

"Don't you think you've had enough, love?" Rob's tone was harsh, contrary to his words and Rose grimaced.

She put down the plates she had just dried and looked over at the two brightly, "well," her laugh was forced and high, "I'd better go and do the rounds..." Both ignored her. She shook her head, put down the towel and hurried out.

"No!" said Pauline, taking a healthy swig. "And don't you tell me what to do. God, you must think I'm an idiot! Don't you think I have every right to ask what you are doing with *my* money?"

He gave an exasperated sigh. "We've been through this. I wanted to help Tom, I explained that..."

"Oh don't give me that. I know you went out of the country weeks before you went with Tom. The time you said you were in Scotland."

She slugged her wine. "Scotland, my arse! I saw the credit card statement; tickets to America and a hotel in Hartford. Even I know that's in Connecticut. I still don't understand how you ended up going there before Tom even knew about his brother, let alone why you would lie about it."

Rob stood twisting his wedding ring, staring at his wife. She watched him through narrowed eyes. "Want to take it off?" she asked in a deceptively mild tone, nodding at the ring. He smiled at her, but his eyes stayed hard and cold.

"No," he paused, "of course not... Anyway, it's better than wearing a ball and chain, isn't it? Lighter!"

She huffed and turned away, grabbing for the wine bottle again. "Well," she said, gesturing at his shiny gold wedding band, "let's see if you manage to keep hold of this one, eh?"

Rob sighed. "Pauline," he said, patience dripping sarcastically from every word, "I don't know where I lost it. I didn't mean to lose it, and it may still turn up. I told you that." He twisted the ring again on his finger. It left a mark on his skin. "Anyway, this one is just as nice. Even the inscription inside is exactly the same. Let it go, ok? Jesus! You're like a dog with a fucking bone!"

"Don't you bloody swear at me! I'm your wife!" Pauline spat wine as she hissed at him.

With forced patience, Rob eyed his wife. "Yes, dear. I know that!" He waited.

"Well..."

"Well, what?"

"Well, you shouldn't keep secrets..."

Rob sighed dramatically. "Pauline, I have no idea..."

Pauline turned away. She grabbed at an unopened bottle at the rear of the counter, knocking over two empty ones. Rob grabbed them before they fell to the floor.

Someone hovered at the door, but on hearing the furious voices coming from the room, clearly thought better of it and hurried away.

Rob hesitated. "Don't you think you...?"

She whirled back round to face him. "I don't believe a word you say anymore, Robert. You tell me bugger all about anything, work for instance. Like that doctor mate of yours who was arrested for having sex with patients. What happened to him? It was in the paper that they'd let him go. So who was it?"

"Who was what? Where the hell did this come from?"

"Who interfered with those patients, if it wasn't that doctor?"

Rob looked at her through hooded, narrowed eyes. "What are you getting at, exactly?" His voice was low, menacing.

She swallowed a slug of wine. "I just think... I think there is something odd about... about you and Tom. It was you who sorted the adoption, so you must have known about his brother. Oh, don't bother; I know you denied that already. It's just too much of a coincidence..." She drained the glass, refilled it.

Rob looked pained. "Pauline, love... look, you are getting a bit carried away..."

"It's like; you act like he's yours." She looked Rob in the eyes, glass halfway to her lips. Rob said nothing. "Well?" she asked. Still he remained silent. "Oh sod off then, Robert! Keep your stupid secrets. Like I give a crap anyway." She stomped out of the room, leaving Rob alone. He could not have gone after her if he had wanted. He was afraid to move in case his legs wouldn't carry him.

Two months after Ellis arrived, Hugo called. Having been nominated as executor of Mary's estate, which sort of included the child, he had taken to calling weekly.

After the usual pleasantries, Hugo cleared his throat. Tom grinned, he recognised the tic now; it was Hugo's prelude to an announcement of sorts. Jesus, what now?

"Well, Tom," Hugo was all business. "What I was obliged to withhold from you, as part of the will, was the financial arrangements concerning the child."

"What financial arrangements?" Tom was only half listening. He could hear Ashleigh telling the boys off in the garden and it sounded heavy. He closed his eyes, frustrated. Hugo said something else, but Tom missed it. "Sorry Hugo, can you say that again, I was distracted..."

"No problem! I said," his tone was patient and kind, "Mary, Ellis's mom, her estate was quite considerable. As the only offspring, Mary inherited the lot, the house, the land and the cash. It's a considerable sum."

"Right," said Tom, "So what, that'll transfer's to Ellis when he's older?"

"Yes. Well," Hugo paused, "She stipulated that half the estate be put in trust for the boy for when he's eighteen. The other half, she left to you and your family, to cover the costs of raising the child."

Tom sat heavily.

"Tom? You still there?" Hugo's voice was tinny through the receiver.

"Uh... yeah," Tom rubbed his forehead. Ashleigh appeared at the door, and without prompting, he switched the phone to speaker mode so she could listen in. He watched her face, she was looking a bit upset, but he turned back to his conversation.

"I was barred from telling you until he had been with you for two months," Hugo explained, "I think it was her way of making sure you wanted the child, not his money."

Ashleigh flashed a 'what's-he-on-about-' look to Tom. Into the phone, Tom said, "Hold on a sec, Hugo, Ashleigh has just come in, let me just explain it to her."

"Hey, no problem. Say, would you like me to call back in a few minutes or so? Give you some time to talk?" Ashleigh nodded. Tom agreed, said goodbye and disconnected the call.

"What are we going to do?" Ashleigh's sat beside Tom on the sofa.

"What about?" Tom spread his arms wide. "We might be able to move. This place is too small. It was before Ellis came."

She nodded. "Tom..." A thought dawned on him. "Shit, I didn't think to ask how much... is that what?"

223

"...No," she interrupted, "I'm not sure that..."

Tom looked at her in shock. "What? Ashleigh, please tell me you're not saying you don't want him to stay with us?" He jumped up, running a hand through his hair. "Ash, I know it's hard work, but I can't..."

She stood too. "No, love," she exhaled loudly. "I... they're outside. Between them they've just..."

"What?"

"They've been playing with a mouse they found." She carried on, ignoring his 'so-what-face'. "They were trying to pull it apart with their bare hands." Tom rolled his eyes. "Tom," her eyes glinted with unshed tears. "I'm worried. I don't care about the money. What if..."

He remained silent, looking at her. "What if, what?" he snapped.

"What if... Shit, they're just so alike." She released a shaky sigh that seemed to come from the depths of her soul.

He fought to soften his tone, "They're just little boys, Ash," he told her. "Just kids. They'll be fine. They'll grow out of it. You'll see."

"But what if they don't? Elliott already killed the hamster. Now, together, they're doing it again... And... Meg said that Ellis told her he killed a cat."

Tom rolled his eyes at the doom in her tone. "He killed a cat? Jesus Christ woman, have you heard yourself?"

Ashleigh snapped at him. "Don't look at me like that! Look, Elliott was already... troubled before this. You know he was. God, you heard what Ellis said about his twin... I think..." She rubbed at her face.

"I don't believe this!" Tom was resentful and angry. "I know what you're trying to say, Ashleigh. I'm not totally fucking stupid!"

"Please don't swear at me. I never said you were stupid, and I'm not *trying* to say anything..."

"Yes you are. You're saying Ellis... that he's going to take after his father. What, he's going to 'turn' our little boy too? Make him in a murderer like my brother was?"

"Oh for God's sake, Tom. Don't be such an arse! Look, we should talk..."

"I don't want to talk. I just want to get on with it." He stalked out, heading through the kitchen and out the patio door.

Ashleigh said something under her breath, but Tom didn't hear. He was already out in the garden, chasing after the boys, trying to get them to play chase.

224

She watched the boys, as with one accord they stopped, standing as still as traffic on the M5, saying nothing, clearly resenting the intrusion. They watched him with dark, hooded eyes. Tom tried again. Ash could hear him cajoling them. There was no response. Only when he backed off did they look away and begin to play again.

Ashleigh could hear the boys chattering in their sing-song voices they'd both adopted when talking to each other. Tom stood and watched them, determined not to peek to see if Ashleigh had seen the boys reaction.

She turned away, not wanting to embarrass him. "Oh, sweetheart. You said you wanted something of your brother's." Her voice was a whisper in the empty kitchen. She gave a strangled laugh, manically wiping down the cooker. "Be careful what you wish for eh, Tom? You may just get it."

The End.

Printed in Great Britain
by Amazon.co.uk, Ltd.,
Marston Gate.